THE HONING

Mel,
Best Wishes !
David Dumas
Great working with you !

A Novel by

David Dumas

Stone Valley Publishing

First Paperback Edition

February 2013

Stone Valley Publishing
5 Wallingford Court
Gansevoort, New York 12831, USA

The Honing

ISBN 13: 978-0615758862
ISBN 10: 061575886X

To contact the author: dumas5215@gmail.com

Cover design by Chris Dumas

Author website: daviddumas.org

DEDICATION

This novel came about in a rather unorthodox manner, but much of my life could be deemed unorthodox. As many a writer has done, I'd day dreamed of putting my sometimes wild and more often untamed imagination on paper. One hot summer day fate came crashing down like thunder as I wrenched my back playing with my children in the pool. I know some would say I'm too macho to be a writer but evidently that's not true. Idle all of three or four days I was driving my significant other crazy in the house. So she told me to buy a laptop and do what I'd always wanted to do. Unable to figure out the inner workings of email, I instead decided to delve into my twisted mind, be creative, and write my novel. A short three years later I find myself writing these acknowledgments.

My creative juices began flowing whilst in my first Creative Writing course in my senior year of High School. Through the following years those juices remained canned, on a shelf, stored neatly in the back of my mind. Many ideas, and as many failed attempts craned their collective necks over the peas and carrots from that dusty old shelf in an attempt to make it as far as the fourth chapter. The Honing is testament to not giving up.

I'd like to dedicate this novel firstly to my mother who absolutely lives for books and although she's not hip on the thought of her son publishing an eBook, I'm sure she'll learn to live with it. Secondly I feel much of the result of this work can honestly be dedicated to my other half. Jamie can be summed up by the very word dedication. She is driven like no other person I've met. Some of that must have rubbed off on me. She tolerated the late nights listening to the tapping of my keyboard, learning to sleep with the light on, and mostly learning to sleep next to a man who spent his nights penning the tortuous deaths of many. She is my driving force in life, the mother to our children, and yes, she's my best friend. This novel would have remained shelved if it were not for her influence in my life.

PROLOGUE

A disheveled woman sat, impatiently strumming her fingers on the cold, hard table. Seconds seemed like hours as the non-descript clock above the door slowly ticked away. She anxiously waited for the man across from her to offer an answer to the looming question. Dr. Miles Duvall, a renowned Psychiatrist, squared his massive frame on Patricia.

"Frankly, I don't know how long you'll have to stay in the hospital my dear."

These words hung in the air as Patricia Fordam drew the sharp blade across her wrist. Slowly, the memory faded as her life was coming to an end. She would never leave the hospital that had become her prison.

On the redeye back to Europe and his unloving father a well-worn diary lay in the seat beside Brad. His hand rested on the cover as he wept in his sleep for the untimely loss of his mother. Knowing that his future was laid out before him, something silently brewed within. It would be years before he would act on these feelings and his mother's wishes. A time would come when the darkness would seep from within and consume all in its path.

But life went on for young Brad. He excelled at university while distancing himself from his callous father. On his own he flourished, quickly rising to fame as a top Linguistics professor at Yale while also building a loving family. Paralleling his father's career path, the darkness slowly crept in from the recesses of his mind. Brad realized he would have to finish what was silently promised to his mother, so many years ago.

The Honing

PART I

CHAPTER 1

Darkness enveloped him as he lay on the cold, damp floor. An overwhelming feeling of disparity gripped him. Although blinded by darkness, Wesley's other senses thrived. His hearing remained intact, as well as touch, and smell, but without the ability to tell time he was losing his ability to remain in contact with reality. Wesley James Fordam lay shivering in the fetal position unaware of what was to come.

By his estimation, Wesley had been in this *cell* what he considered two days, cut off from everything he knew. Isolated, hungry and stiff he feared for his future. He awoke groggy from what he knew was an injected sedative. He could feel the crusty residue of blood at the injection site.

He'd walked the perimeter of his cell always finding the same things, cold, uneven stone walls. There were no windows, light fixtures, power outlets, or light switches. Nothing, except the damp walls and a forbidding steel door, void of any hardware. If his captors, or captor, he didn't know how many of them there were, were pushing for complete isolation they'd accomplished their goal with high marks. He'd been stripped of his shoes, his watch, his tie and his belt. Anything, Wesley thought, that he could use to inflict self-injury.

Thoughts of a lecture he had given on Tuesday evening flitted through his mind but everything after leaving the lecture hall was a blank. Wesley tried thinking of faces that seemed out of place during the event, maybe one. There was one familiar face. His mind raced as he attempted to inject logic into his situation. "Who would have done this? Why?" There were no answers, only more questions. He backed into a corner cradling his legs, searching for answers.

CHAPTER 2

On day two, as far as Wesley could tell, the loneliness of isolation evaporated. Blinding lights seared his eyes as wailing sirens invaded his mind. Wesley cowered in a corner, hunching toward the walls, unable to cover both his eyes and ears at the same time. The assault lasted minutes – an eternity. Anger grew deep inside Wesley giving him renewed strength. He found his footing and stood to assess the intruder, but there was none. Just as suddenly as the invasion began, it ended. Wesley stumbled backward, leaning against the damp wall.

"Thank God," he whispered to the dark room. Minutes passed and Wesley took a seat where he found the wall. His sight spotted with bright white dots that slowly faded. More minutes passed and when he thought his vision was once again complete darkness there was another barrage of blinding lights and that God damned siren. This time however, it made a warbling sound and the lights went on and off like strobe lights. Between brief periods of darkness Wesley saw the room remained empty. In a single breath he feared the possibility of facing his captor and quietly thanked fate for not introducing the two. As he canvassed the room the sirens became increasingly louder until he had to cover his ears for protection. Wesley tried to scream to his captors but was hardly able to hear himself over the invading noise. This went on for what seemed to be an hour but was actually closer to fifteen minutes, until it stopped. The sirens faded, making their final reverberations off the walls. The lights were turned off, throwing him back into the oblivion he'd been. Not knowing which was worse, system overload or the bleakness of total isolation and sensory deprivation, Wesley began to scream.

"What the fuck do you want you coward?" he yelled with the most intimidating voice he could muster. He ran to the door pounding it with his closed fist, yet there was nothing except the dull thud of the thick door. "What do you want from me?" he repeated. This lasted only a short time as Wesley found himself losing his voice as he succumbed to pain and fear. After what had been a short reprieve he had been thrown back into total darkness once again, "only for how long this time," he thought.

His feet damp and his fists bruised, Wesley returned to his spot in the far corner of the room. His back against the wall and crouched in a sitting position, Wesley did the only thing he could. He waited for whatever was next to come. He knew whoever was behind this was playing a game with him. A single question consumed his conscious, "How long will this go on?"

On what felt like day three, and after countless run-ins with the sirens and lights, each time a new variation of sequence, Wesley was startled by a scrapping noise of metal on metal coming from the steel door, the lock! Still blinded by total darkness he scrambled to his feet assuming a defensive position, ready to face his captor. He instinctively raised his shaking hands to shadow the blinding light as the door burst open. Wincing, he saw the outline of a lone figure standing in the brilliant light, a shadow created by the intense light from behind. As he lunged at the entity, he was overcome by a new, *alien* sensation. His body became rigid as he collapsed to the hard floor below. His breathing came in short, gasping bursts as half a million volts of electricity ripped through him from the stun gun. Wesley watched in frozen horror as his captor moved toward his still seizing body. He was unable to fight and soon felt the sting of another injection. Soon the light faded to a blur as he felt his muscles relax. It was too late to respond as the sedative took hold and snuffed out what consciousness remained. Once again Wesley was shrouded in darkness.

The Honing

PART II
THE BEGINNING

CHAPTER 3

"You should always keep a diary honey." Alice told her only daughter, Patricia.

"Did you have one when you were a little girl, mommy?"

"Yes sweetie, so did my sister and all of my friends. It's where we kept all our secrets. Things we didn't want anyone else to see." replied Patricia's mother.

"What if someone looked in your diary? Then they wouldn't be secrets anymore,"

"Well, you have to do your best to keep it hidden well. So no one finds it."

"Can you keep *two* diaries mother?" asked the little Patricia, quizzically.

"Why on earth would you want to keep two diaries honey?" Alice smiled at her daughter's naivety.

"Well, that way if someone finds your diary, they don't find *all* of your secrets," grinned little Patricia, practically patting herself on the back in triumph.

"You're one smart cookie Patricia Alice Redding!" Patricia smiled at the response, hugging her mother's leg.

"Then it's settled Mama, I'll keep two diaries, just in case!" announced Patricia.

Patricia Alice Redding was born into a gifted life. Born the daughter of Alice and Robert J. Redding of Bridgeport, Connecticut, she had little to worry about other than if her hat matched her dress as the family prepared themselves for church on Sunday morning. Her father, Robert was a successful broker on Wall Street, so money was never an issue during her childhood.

This afforded her the opportunity of having a stay at home mother and she found that being the younger of two children was not at all a bad thing. Her brother, Charlie was older by two years and was destined for greatness, according to her father. Patricia and Alice were able to pretty well do as they pleased during Patricia's earlier years, and in fact had spent a large part of it helping those in need. Alice had always preached that giving is better than receiving and will not only help you sleep at night but will assure you a spot in heaven as well. Patricia learned much from her mother in those early years, traits that would remain vigilant throughout her lifetime.

Robert Redding was a good man who provided well for his family. He worked in New York, so many nights he would stay at a small apartment he maintained in the city as a way of reducing commuting during his busy work week. More often than not Robert was a weekend Dad. He would, however make time for the important occasions such as birthday's, Patricia's First Communion, and the many nights Patricia was on stage either in a leading role in the school play, or when she played the clarinet in the school's band. These times were as important to father as they were to daughter.

She attended a public school as her father was a firm believer in the power of government creating a better America. Not that public school in Bridgeport, Connecticut was close to what the average public school system had to offer. She still however, received education of life as well. Patricia's mother took her everywhere if she was not in school and because of this they had developed a very close relationship. She preferred the weekdays as opposed to the weekends when her father was home. He was a good father, but Robert and Alice had a different agenda on the weekend. His attendance at school functions was more of a show than anything at the time. There were social events to attend and little Patricia often was left behind with the Charlie to watch over her.

There was also the fighting that Patricia had to endure when her father was home. During the week her mother had run the household but when her father was home, things changed. There were different rules to live up to and her parents often fought over how to raise the children. Robert was more conservative than Alice and was raised to believe that a woman's place was to 'mind her man'. For the most part that is

9

exactly what transpired in the Redding household but there were incidents that led to some disturbing memories of her parents' fighting. Back then a fight constituted her mother *getting out of hand* and her father putting her back in her place. This happened rarely and for the most part Patricia was able to put these out of her mind, to store them in a back compartment of her memory. Not the healthiest way to deal with an issue, but it seemed to work at the time. One thing Patricia's mother neglected to teach her, unfortunately were healthy coping skills. This would haunt young Patricia for the rest of her life.

As Patricia grew older she had fewer and fewer incidents to store away, and as childhood grew into adolescence; with it came more good memories. Her parents fought less and less it seemed. Patricia had a good life and she knew it too. Every weekend, she would volunteer at the local food bank and would occasionally help her mom with a children's literacy program Alice had started some years before. Robert and Alice were raising a good-hearted, self-minded child that they believed would do well in life.

High school was a memorable time for Patricia. She became involved in the Drama Club, cheerleading, and also took more of an interest in boys. She breezed through schoolwork with little difficulty and tutored some other kids as well, carrying on the traits her mother had instilled in her to help those in need. She also continued to volunteer with her mother at various places around town. Her parents were very proud of the child they'd raised.

In her junior year, Patricia had indicated to her loving parents that she wanted to attend a college that would allow her to obtain a degree in Social Services. Something Patricia told her mother interested her very much. She'd liked helping people. Patricia never discriminated against those less fortunate than her and when she looked at someone she saw the person as a whole, not a person broken into pieces. She had Alice's heart and with that heart she would heal others.

Skidmore College, located in Saratoga Springs, New York was happy to accept her into their upcoming freshman class. She not only had the grades and volunteer work to get in, but also came from *good stock*. A family with money. Although Skidmore was a progressive school for the times, it helped to come from money. Soon she would be off to start undergraduate work in a field Patricia embraced. She would be away for the first time in her life, with the exception of summer camp, which she usually refused to attend. Life was feeling like a new adventure, her wings would no longer clipped and she was free to go where the wind took her, within reason. This new feeling of freedom bode well with her. Patricia left for Skidmore with a promise to her father to do well and a promise to her mother to stay in touch frequently.

CHAPTER 4

Wesley James Fordam awoke with a smile. He and a few buddies were about to embark on a journey to unfamiliar lands. Cadet Fordam was in his senior year at the United States Military Academy, West point New York and currently ranked top in his class. The year was 1962. He was virtually a shoe in at attaining Valedictorian. His classmates nicknamed him "The General", expecting great achievements during his career. His drive was becoming legendary.

Wesley, along with three other cadets were granted a three-day pass which they decided to use for entertainment and educational purposes. They were traveling to a place rich in military history. They were about to leave for Saratoga Springs to spend a weekend "playing the horses" at the harness track which remained a year-round event since 1941. Unfortunately it was too late in the year to enjoy the Saratoga Meet which ended Labor Day weekend.

The cadets also agreed to visit the Saratoga Battlefield, which is actually a combination of a number of sites of historic value. One battle has been touted as a major turning point in the American Revolutionary war against the British.

The Saratoga Battlefield has been visited by such guests as George Washington, John Quincy Adams, Thomas Jefferson, and James Madison. In 1938, sites were recognized by the

United States Congress as the Saratoga National Historical Park. Theodore Roosevelt played a major role while he was Governor of New York State and then as President of the United States. To the four cadets, this was as close to heaven as you could get.

Cadet Nathan Moore hailed from Jacksonville, Florida and was the youngest of the four being in his third year at the Academy. Cadet Kurt Lewis was from Des Moines, Iowa and Cadet Joshua Tanner, Wesley's best friend, was from Alamogordo, New Mexico. Joshua was ranked a distant second at The Point behind Wesley. The four had decided a weekend at the races would be a good idea and get them out of the area for a couple of days.

It was early fall and the thought of a long New York winter was looming on the horizon. A trip to Saratoga Springs was what the doctor had ordered. They left on a Friday morning by bus and arrived about five hours later in Saratoga. Saratoga Springs was located just south of the Adirondack Mountains, along the Hudson River. Although small in size, the "Queen of the Spas" over-flowed with culture, entertainment, and history.

Because of abundant mineral springs, the area witnessed an influx of wealth and socialites, and with that came horse racing. The streets of Saratoga Springs saw the likes of Vanderbilt's, Whitney's, and Rockefellers. Saratoga survived two world wars and the Great depression with prohibition of gambling, to travel restrictions during wartime. The neighborhoods instilled a feeling of its' great the past while the area flourished, becoming "modern" in an effort to entertain business.

They'd wanted to get to the track but had no idea where it was, so they grabbed their weekend bags and walked downtown. Wesley, being the 'Alpha Male' of the group, approached a group of young ladies to ask for directions. When Cadet Fordam returned to his friends with four girls on his arms, all Skidmore students, his rank of General rose to that of hero, their weekend adventure had begun. By the end of the weekend and nearly time for the young cadets to return to West Point two couples had been formed. Joshua Tanner had made promises to see a young lady by the name of Miss Kimberly Johnson and Wesley had made arrangements to see young Patricia Alice Redding in the very near future.

"I'll call you as soon as I can. I promise" said the young cadet.

"You had better, mister. I'm looking forward to that call already!" Patricia retorted.

"We'll come back after the semester. I'm sure we can get another weekend pass. We can spend some time together before you go home."

"I'm not going home for break. Kimmy and I have an internship with the county." Patricia said. She leaned in to kiss Wesley on the cheek, whispering in his ear as she withdrew.

14

"Besides, nothing exciting ever happens in Connecticut."

Wesley's cheeks took on a red hue as his mind reeled.

As he began to speak, Patricia laid a soft finger across his lips.

"You work on getting back here as soon as you can."

She said smiling.

The cadets boarded the Greyhound for their return trip. Patricia and Kimberly waved and blew kisses in the air as the men stared out their windows, excitement etched on their faces.

Patricia had travelled home for winter and summer break the first two years of her college career and felt like she'd wasted time doing nothing important. The girls hailed a cab, returning to the Skidmore campus. They recalled their time with the boys and spoke of how much they anticipated their return.

CHAPTER 5

Patricia and Kimberly had taken a small apartment off-campus for the summer. The apartment was in Ballston Spa on West High Street, a short walk to their places of work. Ballston Spa was only ten or so miles from Saratoga Springs. There was not much of a night life there but it could easily be found in Saratoga. The two had decided that it would be easier if they had stayed in Ballston Spa. When the boys visited they would meet them in Saratoga at the train station. Their arrival was greatly anticipated by both ladies.

"I missed you more than you can imagine Patricia" Wesley had divulged. And he had. He spoke highly and quite often of his young new girlfriend when he went back to West Point. He greatly anticipated his return also. Although his friend and comrade Joshua had mentioned seeing young Kimberly only a handful of times, he did say that he liked her and wanted to see her again but felt that it was going to take "a lot of work" to bed her. This bothered cadet Fordam, but as he was so smitten with Patricia he hardly listened to Joshua's babblings. The two traveled by rail for their latest trip and found it much more enjoyable, arriving promptly on time and finding two beautiful girls awaiting them.

They had two full days to spend together and no plans were made as of yet. The foursome started their weekend off with a nice walk through Saratoga Springs and ended near the stables of the race track. They had decided to have dinner in Ballston Spa at the apartment. The girls planned a small yet inviting meal for the boys who surely had enough of cafeteria food for a couple of days. They welcomed the meal and gratefully thanked their lovely hostesses.

Wesley and Patricia planned to take a walk after dinner and left Kimberly in the capable hands of young Cadet Tanner.

"I thought we'd walk for a while and then maybe go to the racetrack afterwards." stated Patricia. Young Wesley was very in tune with this plan hoping to gamble some of his pittance of earnings away. This left Wesley in a very good mood as they began their walk. "Joshua seems like a nice guy, don't you think?"

"Yeah, he is, though he can be a little moody at times but who can't at The Point. Things can get a little rough there sometimes, but enough about that. We've got a whole weekend to enjoy together." Patricia smiled at that and her eyes widened a bit.

"I have no idea what the weekend has in store but I'm sure it will be unforgettable!" She practically shouted.

Before they knew it they were at the racetrack placing bets on horses they'd never heard of. They were having a great time and enjoying each other's company. The night seemed to fly by and before they knew it, they were heading back to

Patricia's apartment after having a couple of drinks at a local bar. What they found when they walked into the apartment would trouble them forever.

CHAPTER 6

Wesley accepted the keys Patricia offered as the two approached her apartment door. As the lock clicked open Wesley turned the knob and pushed the heavy wood door open. Patricia gasped as the door swung open. The apartment was trashed. Practically everything was out of place. Lamps were on the floor, one shattered into small pieces. Tables and chairs were thrown about in a fashion that made them to believe a scuffle took place. The couple entered slowly at first, taking in the unbelievable sight. Wesley pushed past Patricia searching with his sharp blue eyes for any danger. The apartment was silent and darkened, the only light coming from a standing lamp by the couch. A look of horror flitted across Patricia`s soft features as she strode toward a half closed door to the right.

"Kimberly." She whispered.

Patricia`s voice was soft and crackly. Her trembling hands moved to cover her mouth.

"Patricia, wait!" Wesley snapped as she pushed by his rigid frame.

The bedroom was dark with only a sliver of light shining through the window from a street lamp.

"Oh my God! Oh my God! What has he done?" she said, referring to Joshua. Wesley scanned the room quickly not finding Joshua Tanner anywhere in sight.

"What in the hell happened here?" Wesley yelled, "Josh! Where the fuck are you?"

He quickly ran to the bedside. To Kimberly. She had been left uncovered, her young body glistening in the dim light. Wesley could not help noticing Kimberly's beautifully sculpted body tied to the bedposts. She was soaking wet with fresh sweat, her nipples erect. He looked at Patricia, his eyes saying "Something's not right here." She moved closer to see what he was seeing. At that moment Kimberly's eyes opened slowly and seemed to focus on Patricia.

"She's awake, Wes! Her eyes are open!" Wesley looked up and noticed that Kimberly was indeed waking up.

"We need to untie this," he said as he gently removed a red bandana that had been rolled to gag her mouth.

Wesley's fingers stumbled as he released the girls right wrist from her restraints. Her wrists were cherry red against her otherwise pale skin. Instead of reeling from her restraint, Wesley noticed that Kimberly's hand remained on the bed. Patricia worked feverishly at untying her right ankle. Wesley stopped short of reaching over the girl's nude body to release her other wrist.

"Wait."

Patricia looked up at Wesley.

"What?" She asked, still shaking.

"Just wait. Something's not right here."

Kimberly's eyelids seemed heavy as she fought to keep them open.

"What do you mean?" Patricia asked, not stopping.

"I'm not sure yet." Wesley said as he looked to the front of the bed and Patricia. Just then a shadow appeared at the bedroom door. It was Joshua.

Standing in the doorway dressed only in his white boxers, Joshua Tanners voice boomed.

"What the hell is going on?" Joshua demanded as he stepped into the room, having come from the bathroom. In his left hand he held a glass of water, in the other he gripped a clear plastic bag, moisture pooling at its base.

Wesley stood quickly and approached the surprised cadet.

"What in the fuck is going on here Josh?" he yelled. Wesley and Joshua were quickly face to face, it was clear that Cadet Fordam was on the offensive. Joshua backed up a couple of steps and held his hands out in front of him at chest level. Wesley took this act as a sign of aggression and pushed Joshua back with enough force to slam him into the bedroom wall, shattering the glass against the door jam. Regaining his balance, Joshua tried to get control of the situation.

"Hey, this is not what you think!" he barked. "She asked me to do this to her! This was completely *her* idea."

As the two Cadets faced off, Patricia began untying her friends' remaining restraints. They were all similar in fashion to the gag that had been used. Patricia even noticed that two of the restraints used were from her own dresser drawer.

Kimberly was almost fully awake by the time Patricia freed her.

"Kimberly," Patricia said calmly," you need to tell me what happened here tonight." Joshua started for the bed but was thrown back into the wall by a red faced Wesley. "You stay put asshole!"

Kimberly looked up at her friend with a sheepish smile, her voice a little shaky.

"This was just for fun, you know?"

"What do you mean, Kimmy? You let him do this to you on purpose?" She spat.

"Well…" Kimberly paused, "Yes! Don't tell me you've never heard of this. It's like…roll playing. It's the greatest feeling in the world, Patty!" Kimberly countered rubbing her wrists as she sat up. "It's perfectly safe. It's all planned out in advance" she continued as she wrapped her sweat drenched body with a crumpled sheet.

Joshua started laughing from the corner where he was ordered to stay put.

"I'm sorry you had to see this, guys. I know what it must look like!"

The muscles in Wesley's torso loosened slightly but he refused to lower his guard.

"You mean to tell me you two planned this? What the fuck Josh? Just when you think you fucking know somebody!"

Wesley dropped to one knee, his body released from its remaining tension.

"What's so funny Wes?" shouted Patricia. "Kimberly could have been hurt!"

"I don't think any of this is funny. I almost killed you Josh, you stupid shit!" Wesley said smiling. "Come on Patricia, let's get out of here for a while. These two need to get cleaned up. Show me around the sprawling city of Ballston Spa." Patricia shot Kimberly one last concerned look as her friend's gaze turned downward in embarrassment. As she bit her lower lip, a habit she'd had since childhood as a response to stress, Patricia repeated Wesley's last words.

"Get cleaned up Kimmy. We'll see you later."

With that, Patricia and Wesley left together.

"How can you make light of what happened in there?" She asked, exasperated as they left.

"Look, Josh and I have known each other for three years now. This is news to me too, but you saw it for yourself. They were in it together! She was playing the game just as much as he was. Yeah, it's way out but it's something they were both okay with. You can't argue that!"

Patricia frowned and let out a little laugh.

"I just can't believe you saw her naked!"

"Well, I wasn't really looking at that point" Wesley answered, smiling. Patricia punched him in the arm and he let out a small groan to let her know that he understood where she was coming from. "Look, if that's what they're into so be it, as long as no one gets hurt."

"How can you still be friends with him after tonight?"

"I'm just going to act like it never happened. It was something that we were not supposed to see and it's *their* thing. Are you still going to be friends with Kimberly?" he asked.

"I don't know. I haven't really put much thought into it. She seemed like such a nice girl!"

"She still is a nice girl...just with some weird tastes!" This got a good laugh out of Patricia and Wesley could feel the tension leave the conversation. Stopping, she spun on her heel holding a hand to Wesley's chest, her face suddenly serious.

"You're not into that stuff are you, Wes?" She asked pointedly.

"Of course not, I'm a good Catholic boy!" he countered.

They walked for over an hour holding hands the whole way. When they returned to the apartment everything was in order, with the exception of the broken lamp that had been placed near the garbage can. Kimberly and Joshua were dressed and acting as if nothing strange happened.

"I want to apologize for what you both saw, we kinda got out of control there for a while. You know how it can get" Joshua stated.

"No, I don't." stated Patricia through gritted teeth. "But we accept your apology. Just don't do it here anymore!" she finished, fighting to produce a smile.

The four remained silent about the incident for the rest of the weekend. The boys left Sunday afternoon on the train out of Saratoga Springs.

"Is that the first time you've done that?" Wesley asked his friend as the train passed through a small village south of Hudson.

"No, actually it was the second time. There was this one other girl. It's kind of funny how it happened, though. Kim and I were asking each other about the wildest things we ever did. We both admitted it and one thing led to another. Before I knew it, she was asking me to tie her up and gag her. She has such a great body...I couldn't resist. Plus the fact that I've been showering with you freakin' guys at The Point for the past *three years*! There was no way I'd have said no." Wesley looked at his friend with cold, hard eyes. He'd been raised pretty strictly by parents who never spoke of sex. Joshua sat back in his seat,

25

noting for the first time since they'd met at school, how cold and passionless Wesley`s eyes were. A shiver went through him.

"I just want you to know I still think you`re an asshole!"

Joshua shifted the conversation back to Kimberly.

"She said she'll come down in a couple of weeks and we can hook up at a motel somewhere near post. Just thinking about her gets me going. There are some other

things she said she wants to try. We'll see!" He gloated.

Wesley lifted his face from his hands.

"What do you get out of it? I mean, what is the rush all about? I just don't get it. Maybe I'm just too old fashioned.

Wesley`s gaze was pulled to the window as the train shot past a clearing in the wooded area revealing a towering cliff rising from across the Hudson River. When he spoke his voice was flat, seemingly disconnected from any emotion.

I like Patricia and she's pretty cool. I think we could have something great, but I couldn't think of doing the things I saw you two doing. Sex is supposed to be different than that."

There was an awkward silence that was interrupted by the conductor yelling, "Yonkers! Next stop."

Joshua joined Wesley, staring through the dirty window. He unconsciously turned and looked at Wesley as the trees overtook the scene.

"I don't know. Sex to me is like…candy, I guess. You like certain things, but there's always something tastier that

26

comes along. Look man, we had fun and no one got hurt. You make up a safety word or something like that. Kim wanted to be gagged so she told me before, if she smacks the bedpost with her hand to stop and untie her. There's a safety net, so it makes it fun, sort of an adventure." Joshua shrugged.

The two kept quiet most of the way back to West Point. There was some small talk of upcoming tests and drills but for the most part there was quiet. Joshua enduring distant stares from his best friend as Wesley replayed everything in his mind with disgust.

Patricia and Kimberly spoke little of what had happened and spent a quiet night home reading. There was work in the morning and not much to say. Patricia had a very hard time accepting that a woman would willingly want that done to herself, to lose total control over a situation. To be controlled by someone else. She reflected on her own values and vowed never to be placed in such a precarious situation.

Over the next week Wesley called Patricia frequently. Neither mentioned that night, both wanting to see each other again soon. Wesley mentioned that Kimberly was planning a trip to West Point for the upcoming weekend and that it would be great if she could come as well. Patricia regretfully declined the offer. Her parents were coming to Saratoga Springs for the weekend as they did two or three times a year. Patricia was upset that the timeframe of the visit caused a conflict, but she missed her parents. Wesley assured her that it was alright and they would see each other soon enough. He would be busy at The Point with summer drills coming up and preparing for a two week stint in the field. Their next visit was left up in the air.

CHAPTER 7

It was dark when Wesley heard a loud knocking on his dorm room door. "What the hell is it?" he bellowed, half asleep.

"There's a call for you Fordam. You don't need to be an asshole ya know!" replied the faceless voice from the lighted side of the door. Wesley readjusted his boxer shorts and walked to the phone in the hallway, the only phone available for use by cadets in the dorm.

"This if Cadet Fordam." he stated simply, but directly.

"I need you to get over here, right now Wes!" Joshua whispered, his voice trembling on the other end of the phone.

"Josh? Is that you? Where the hell are you?" The feeling of anger dissipated, making way for one of concern.

Wesley arrived at the darkened motel after rousing another friend to borrow the keys to his car. The drive took fifteen minutes from post as the roads were wet from a late night shower. It was 3:45 in the morning. A breeze whipped through his shortly cropped hair as he exited the car. Cadet Fordam walked to room 106 as instructed and knocked lightly on the door.

"Josh, you in there?" he whispered.

The walkway was poorly lit with every other bulb removed along the first floor terrace. Old leaves from last autumn blew around like lost souls in the wind. After what seemed like minutes the lock unlatched and Wesley heard the soft scratching of the chain being drawn along its holder. Wesley backed away a couple of steps tentatively as the door slowly swung inward. At first no one appeared. The room was dark, only a sliver of light coming from the lone fixture outside the room. The night held an eerie calm and Wesley heard nothing for a few seconds. Suddenly an arm came from inside the room grabbing him with great strength pulling him toward the darkness. Wesley instinctively pulled back but entered the room on his own accordance after seeing his friend, pale and shaking.

"What the fuck is going on here Josh!"

Joshua mumbled more to the darkness than to Wesley as he walked to the corner to the right of the door and cowered. Joshua started rocking on his heals with his arms wrapped around his knees, slamming his back against the plastered wall, causing a cheap version of Vangough's *Scream* to sway on its single nail.

"I didn't mean to do it. It was an accident." Joshua pleaded.

Wesley quickly took notice of the layout of the room; he could see that everything was pretty much in order. The only light coming from a candle burning in what he assumed was the bathroom.

"Stay there Joshua!" Wesley barked as if speaking to a dog as he crossed the room. He noted some clothes folded neatly on a chair near the bed. When he pushed through the partially closed door to the bathroom his shoe squeaked from water spilled on the linoleum floor. He abruptly stopped after noticing the water and heard a faint sobbing coming from Joshua. Wesley turned to the right and found the light switch lifting it with a quick snap. The room flooded with light and overloaded Wesley's sense of sight momentarily. After a few seconds Wesley was able to stop squinting and absorbed the horrible sight in the room. Kimberly lay on the floor next to the filled bathtub, naked. She was clearly dead. Wesley moved toward her taking in the sight when the sobbing in the other room changed crying.

"I didn't mean it. It was an accident."

Wesley bent onto one knee to get a closer look at Kimberly Johnson. The color of her skin was that of a dark cloudy day, dusky with a ruddy purple quickly enshrouding her lifeless form. He looked at her body starting from her feet working upward. He saw no signs of a struggle. There were no marks on her skin. No cuts, no bruises, no bleeding. Then he looked at her face. Wesley held his breath for a few seconds before letting out a long deep gasp. Kimberly was dead, her face frozen in a state of shock. Her mouth lay agape, her eyes frozen open in fear. She died fighting for air.

As Wesley knelt by the girl's body he heard Joshua enter the room, still sobbing as his bare feet slapped against the wet floor.

"It was an accident Wes. It was an accident." he repeated.

Wesley stood to face Joshua. His pant leg was wet from the water on the floor.

"What the hell happened here?" No answer followed. "I asked you what in the hell happened in here Cadet Tanner!" There was a sudden authority in Wesley's voice that seemed to snap Joshua out of his trance causing him to reflexively straightening his stance. His voice trembled.

"We were having some fun. You know Wes. Like what you saw that night, just playing. Sex stuff, you know?" He replied. "It was an accident Wes. I...I liked her, a lot!" Joshua started to cry again.

"I don't doubt you, Josh. This is just..." Wesley searched for the words. "It's just really fucked up! What are you going to do?"

The question stymied Joshua. He hadn't thought of that. He was still in shock. So much had happened. He didn't have time to do anything yet.

"I... I don't know. All I could think was to call you!" he replied.

"Have you done anything else yet? Called anyone?
What else have you done?" Wesley questioned. Interrogated.

"No. Nobody else knows. Just you, me, and Kim". He
started crying again.

"Josh, this is going to end your career. You'll go to jail
for this" Wesley stated bluntly. That snapped Joshua back to
reality.

"Oh my God! I can't go to jail Wes. Oh my God! What
in the hell can I do?" he begged."

"I don't know Josh. This is beyond me. It's bad."

A long silence followed. Only the faint, slow dripping
from the tub filled the air. Wesley turned back to Kimberly who
still lay on the floor in the same spot she was found. He leaned
over her dead body.

"Don't touch her!" Joshua snapped. Wesley grabbed a
clear plastic bag that half floated in the warm water. He stood
and looked directly at Joshua.

"What's this Josh? Is this how she died? You fucking
idiot!"

Josh took a step back and held his hands in front of him
as if saying *"Wait one damn minute!"*

"I saw you holding a bag that night in Ballston Spa,
Josh. What were you doing?" he yelled. "Did you use this that
night too?" Wesley pushed the bag at Joshua's chest forcing
him to take it.

"No. We didn't get that far. You guys came in just after she told me to get it out from under the kitchen sink." As Josh spoke, Wesley looked at the bag, really looked at the bag for the first time. It was a clear garbage bag.

"I'm telling you the truth Wes!" This was Kim's idea. She wanted to try it. It was her idea!" Wesley looked down again at Kimberly's naked body. It was mostly dry now.

"You fucked up bad Josh. I don't know how to fix this. Jesus Christ! What were you two thinking?" He seemed to ask Kimberly.

"You're sure nobody else knows anything? Who answered the phone at the barracks?" asked Wesley trying to put a face to the voice that woke him so abruptly.

"It was Roberts. Cadet Roberts." Joshua stated. "I don't think I said anything to him. I just asked him to go get you."

Cadet Roberts' room was almost directly across from the hallway phone. It was logical that he'd be the one to answer the phone. It was the worst room in the barracks Wesley thought to himself.

"You're sure you didn't tell him anything?"

"Yeah, I'm sure. I probably sounded bad though. I was scared! I'm still scarred!" Joshua proclaimed. "All he said was that it was late and to hold on. The phone was quiet until you picked it up. I'm sure of that, Wes. What are we going to do?" asked Joshua, shaking violently.

"We? *We?* What in the hell does this have to do with *me*, Joshua?" Wesley asked as he sat on the toilet seat holding his face in his hands, the veins on his forehead protruding.

"You have to help me with this, Wes. It was an accident!" Josh seemed to yell the word accident as if trying to prove a point.

The two Cadets sat quietly for what seemed to be five minutes or so while Wesley collected his thoughts.

"You're sure you didn't say anything to Roberts? Did you give him your name?" questioned Wesley. He seemed to be gathering his strength. Gaining hold of his faculties "Whose name is the room under?" he asked. Joshua gave him a questioning look that Wesley could only interpret as confusion. "Was the room under your name, Josh?"

"No. No, it was under Kim's name. She came down here Friday morning. I wasn't expecting her to get here until sometime in the afternoon but she said she took an earlier train. She'd had Friday off and wanted to surprise me. I'd told her what motel we were going to stay at but I hadn't made a reservation yet. She got the room when she got here, under her own name."

With his revelation Joshua seemed to lighten a bit. He even smiled, although meekly.

Seeing this Wesley stood grabbing Cadet Tanner with one hand. With force he shoved Joshua into the wall beside the door, driving his open hand around his friend's throat.

"Listen you little fuck! You just killed Kimberly! You think this is funny? You're fucked and you don't even know it." Wesley`s cold eyes boring through Joshua.

"Listen man, I know what's going on here. I know I'm fucked. But maybe something can be done here." Wesley gave his friend a perplexed look.

"What in the hell are you saying Josh? Are you telling me this isn't your doing?" anger welled in Wesley's voice. "We are all responsible for our actions, Joshua."

"Calm down Wes. All I'm saying is that there may be a way out of this." Joshua rebutted.

"You killed her you asshole. You think you can change that? What are you saying?"

"All I'm saying is that nobody knows I'm here, only you Wes. No one else knows!" With this, Wesley left the bathroom and sat on the chair next to the bed. He'd had to move the clothes that had been placed there, neatly folded clothes. Kimberly's clothes. Wesley sat there for quite a while, looking down at the clothes in his hands. Joshua sat on the toilet allowing his best friend to gather his thoughts. There was only that damned dripping from the bathtub, which seemed to grow louder and louder with every passing drop.

"Get the rest of your clothes on asshole" Wesley ordered. Josh, startled from the break in the quiet went to gather his clothes that had been dropped next to the bed on the bathroom side floor. He dressed quietly. He had to remove his boxer shorts that were now cold and wet from pulling Kimberly out of her watery grave. After dressing, he shoved his damp shorts into the front pocket of his trousers. He then sat silently on the edge of the bed. The whole time Wesley sat in silence, holding Kimberly's clothes neatly folded in his hands. Unsure of what consequences his next statement may hold.

"Wait in the car, Josh. I'll be out in a few minutes."

Joshua gave him a perplexed look.

"Just do it!" ordered Wesley, his nostrils flaring. Cadet Tanner followed his instructions. Once Wesley was alone in the room he slowly stood and replaced Kimberly's clothes just the way he'd found them on the bedside chair. He took a few deep breaths then went back into the bathroom.

Thirty minutes later Cadet Wesley James Fordam joined his best friend of three years in the car outside room 106. He turned the key in the ignition and pulled out of the motel parking lot as if nothing had happened. It was still dark with only the slightest sign of the upcoming sunrise. The two drove to the barracks in total silence.

CHAPTER 8

Wesley pulled into the barracks parking lot at close to 0645 hours. The sun was beginning to show. The mood in the vehicle was somber. He turned the car off and sat for about a minute rubbing the car keys between his right thumb and forefinger. Joshua said nothing. He just looked out the front windshield, watching the sunrise.

"Did you have sex with Kim? Tonight, I mean. Did you two have sex yet?" Wesley asked as if trying to work through a problem in his head.

"No, we didn't get that far." Joshua said soberly. "Kim liked a lot of foreplay before sex"

"Why the plastic bag over her head? I don't understand. You need to tell me exactly what happened and in its exact order. There's only one way this can happen." Wesley finished. Joshua paused for a minute, tears welling in his eyes as he began to speak.

"She called me before she left the Saratoga train station. It was about 0730. She called me at the barracks saying that she couldn't wait for her later train and was leaving on the 0800 train. We had planned on her coming in later. I can't remember the time of the train but it was around dinner." Joshua started sobbing quietly again.

"Josh you have to hold it together. This is important."

38

"She told me that she would get a room at the motel I'd told her about and I could meet her there as soon as I could break free." he continued. "My last class got out at 1300 hours so I high tailed it to my room to gather my rucksack and change out of my uniform. I took a cab to the motel and checked what room she was in with the front desk."

Wesley gave him a stern look. "How many people saw you in the front desk? Where did the cab pick you up? These are all things you have to remember." Joshua lowered his head in contemplation then resumed.

"I had the cab pick me up off post at the bank. I needed to get some cash out first. Then at the motel there was only one person there, an older woman." Joshua said as his eyes opened a little wider as if he remembered something important. "The old lady mentioned that Kimberly had told her she was here to meet with her family. That had struck me as odd at first but then it made sense to me. She probably felt a little strange meeting a man. She'd lied to cover that!" Joshua exclaimed.

"So far we have a cabbie that picked you up at the bank off post and an old woman that saw your face but was told you were family." Wesley stopped himself, unsure. "We have no idea but I'd bet my paycheck that she didn't believe Kimberly, especially when a young military guy showed up." Wesley's eyes shifted as if in mid thought. "She might be our biggest problem. Did anyone else see you go there? Did you tell anyone that you were meeting her this weekend?"

"No. No. I don't think I told anyone else. I was too busy this week. You know. It was a busy week with classes and tests." Cadet Fordam nodded at that in appreciation. Joshua continued, "I didn't see anyone else as I went to the room. It was desolate. Mid- afternoon, you know? Most people don't hang out at a motel during the day." He paused then continued, "She did use her own name. I just asked and got the room number. I didn't have to sign anything and she didn't give me my own key or anything." he finished. For the first time Wesley could see an immaturity in Joshua that he never before noticed.

"I got to the room and we hung out for a while. We watched some TV, ordered some food...pizza from somewhere close by. They delivered it to the room."

"Who answered the door? Who paid the delivery guy?" Wesley was shouting out questions as he thought out loud.

"Well, I was in the shower and I told Kim that there was cash in my wallet on the table. She answered the door and paid with my cash." Joshua concluded.

Wesley sat in silence. This wasn't him. He didn't think like this. He didn't have the mind for this. He was raised to be honest. Joshua tried to interrupt the silence but Wesley waved him off as if to say "Hold on...I'm thinking". Wesley was scared. He wasn't sure how this would turn out. He started to doubt his course of action. He started to doubt whether or not what he did in the room would hold water. He started thinking that *he* may go to jail as well as his friend. Wesley realized that tonight`s actions would change him forever. "What about Patricia?" He looked at his friend.

"I don't know for sure. I think Kim was going to tell her she was going home for the weekend, but I'm not sure." Joshua said honestly.

"Go get some sleep. Or try to. I'll come around in a couple of hours and we'll talk some more." he hesitated. "Try to act normal." He concluded, shaking his head in thought *"We're so fucked."*

CHAPTER 9

"Hello? Can you please get Cadet Fordam for me?"

"Yes ma'am, hold one minute." replied Cadet Roberts.
It took about three minutes for Wesley to get to the phone.

"This is Cadet Fordam."

"Oh Wes, thank God! I've missed you."

"I've missed you too, Patricia." Wesley replied.

"I don't know what to do, Wes, Kim hasn't come home
yet. She was supposed to be home two days ago. She was
supposed to be at work, too!"

"Where did she go again?" asked Wesley as if forgetting
what he'd been told only a few days ago.

"Her parent's house in South Hampton" replied Patricia
matter-of-factly. "She was supposed to get back here Sunday
evening. I went to meet her at the Rail Station but she never
showed. It was the last train for the day so I went home
thinking she'd missed her train or something. I thought she'd
show up to work late on Monday. I had to be at work so I
couldn't meet her at the station. I think the first train due in was
around 11 am. But she never showed." Wesley could sense the
fear in Patricia's voice.

"Did you call her parents' house? Was she still there?"
asked Wesley finding it easy to sound sincere. He'd dreaded
this moment for three days now. Thinking and rethinking how

he should let it play out. He was covering for his friend. He was covering up a murder. Wesley's head still spun when he thought of it. Which, it seemed was all the time.

"Yes, of course I did." She rebutted. Wesley could sense the tension in her voice escalating. "They told me they knew nothing of her visiting them for the weekend. They're on their way up here as we speak." Patricia stated almost in tears.

"Try to stay calm Patricia." Wesley responded. "There has to be a mistake, a misunderstanding?" he was finding it easier than he thought it would be to lie to the girl he loved.

"Misunderstanding? Wes, what are you saying? That I heard her wrong?" replied Patricia with a growing anger in her voice.

"Calm down." Wesley countered. "What I mean is that there has to be a simple answer. "She told me that since my parents were coming up this weekend, she wanted to give us time to visit. She said that she'd call her parents to see if they were going to be home so she could spend a couple of days in the Hamptons." There was a short pause then she started back in on her oration. "She said that they didn't answer but that she'd take the train home anyhow. Catch up with some old friends." another pause "or something like that. Oh, I'm not sure right now! I didn't think much of it at the time, Wesley. My parents were getting here that the next morning and I was cleaning the apartment and stuff like that. I didn't pay much

43

attention. I'm sorry, Wes. It's not like she was acting strange or anything. She'd taken the train lots of times to her parents'. I didn't think twice about it." She started to sob, softly; as if she knew somewhere deep down that she was somehow at fault.

"It'll be okay Patricia. We'll all be laughing about this in a couple of days. You said her

parents were on their way up?" he asked.

"Yes they said they would arrive around dinner time. They're driving up." Patricia

replied.

"Good. They'll know who to call, maybe her old friends. Relax. She'll turn up." Wesley said consolingly.

"I'm so worried Wes." Her sobbing growing louder. "Can you ask Joshua if he has spoken to her lately? Maybe he knows something."

"I will. He's in class right now but I'll meet him at his classroom. I'll call you back in an hour or so. Okay?" Patricia sighed at that.

"Okay, I hope she's alright. Wes, what if something bad happened to her?" She said, crying now.

"It'll be okay Patricia, I promise." He lied. "They're looking for her." Wesley started. He'd summoned Cadet Tanner to a coffee shop off-post later that afternoon. Wesley had called Patricia back and informed her that Joshua knew nothing. He said Josh told him that he last talked with Kim Thursday night and that she had mentioned going to her parents' house but that was all.

"Did Patricia suspect anything?" Joshua asked nervously.

"No. I don't think they'll trace her back to you directly. You'll probably be questioned by the police, just play dumb. You should be able to handle that easily enough." Wesley snickered. They'll find her body soon and they'll wonder what the hell she was doing here. That will lead them to you I'm sure of it. Patricia will tell them about you." Wesley paused for a moment. "The time-frame all this took place will make it seem like you had no part in her death." Wesley concluded.

"What about fingerprints. Stuff like that? It's all over the room. It will lead them right to me!" exclaimed Joshua sounding hopeless.

"Don't worry Joshua. I cleaned the room when you were in the car. I wiped down anything you could have touched; looked for anything that might lead back to you. As far as you're concerned you were never in that room." Wesley said with a smile. It was a futile attempt at calming his friend.

"What about her body? They'll know there was foul play. We left her on the floor." He argued sobbing once again.

"I took care of it Joshua. They'll think she drowned in the tub." Wesley continued calmly.

"There was no water in her lungs asshole!" Joshua said, raising his voice. The only other patrons in the coffee shop looked up from their booth but showed no inclination of becoming involved. There was nothing out of the ordinary, just a couple of cadets arguing over coffee.

Wesley waited a few long seconds while the redness left his friends face before he answered the question.

"Joshua." he said leaning in closer so he could lower his voice. "I put her back in the tub. I put my mouth on hers and sucked any air that was in them out while I pushed on her chest." With a rush the events of that dreadful night came back to Wesley. The taste of stale air from her lungs overtook him and hung on his taste-buds. It was then that he realized how this would forever haunt him. "Then I held her head under and let her lungs fill with the bath water. I wasn't sure if it would work but she stayed under water afterward. I closed her eyes as best I could. All I had to do was wipe up the water off the floor and re-hang the towels. Everything else looked as it should. There was only one piece of pizza gone so it didn't seem out of place to me. You had already taken your stuff so I wiped the room down with my handkerchief." He paused once again. "The room is clean Joshua. Don't worry about that. You need to worry whether you can pull off talking to the police if and when they come."

CHAPTER 10

Patricia sat on a bench waiting anxiously for Wesley's train to arrive. It was already ten minutes late she thought to herself. There were only two or three others awaiting the arrival of their loved ones or friends. This made her look more closely at the others. Who were they waiting for: a wife, a husband, a lover? This last thought put a smile on her face. She had been through such a difficult time these last four days, she felt a twinge of guilt when the thought of Wesley overwhelmed her mind. He was the first man she'd really felt something for. "You've only kissed him you fool. How much do you really know about him? How much do you feel for him?" her inner voice echoed. Patricia shook her head at that thought. There were other feelings that had to be dealt with at this moment, the loss of a good friend.

The police had been summoned to the remote motel by the day manager two days after Kimberley's death. There had been a "Do Not Disturb" sign on the door the day before so the maid skipped the cleaning, but found it very rare to have the sign hanging two days in a row. After a futile attempt at summoning the guest she used her master key to gain entry to the room. She found the body exactly how Wesley had left it in the bathtub. Kimberly's eyes had opened and stared peacefully at the dirty ceiling, seemingly awaiting her call from above.

She'd turned an ashen ghost-like color and bloated during her two days of watery solitude. The maid ran to the front desk, frantically screaming for help. Finding a body of such a young girl dead in a bath tub immediately initiated a possible homicide file and the local cops found her identification with her clothes. The room seemed undisturbed and there was no indication of a struggle. Nothing was taken from the room, nothing obvious.

Wesley's train slowed to a halt. To Patricia it seemed to take eons for the metal monstrosity to stop. She stood when she saw the first coachman step onto the platform motioning for the trains' occupants to exit. She felt her heart beat faster with every agonizing minute she had to wait. Finally he materialized. His dark brown hair cropped tightly to his head. His chiseled physic under his West Point uniform caused her face to blush as his eyes met hers. They embraced on the platform. Neither spoke. Wesley knew enough to wait.

"I'm so sorry" The simple statement meant *everything* to her. He had to be strong for her, had to be there for her. He was everything she needed. Patricia sobbed heavily on his chest holding him tightly. He waited again, allowing her to let it all out. She couldn't ask for more at that moment. That was the moment she knew she had fallen in love with Wesley James Fordam.

Wesley had lied to the girl of his dreams without distress. He'd lied to Patricia about her friend's death. Kimberly's murder. He found it too easy.

Wesley remembered what his father used to say to him as a child.

"Wes don't ever let anyone stand in your way. Men like us have got to fight for everything we got, nothing is *given* to us. People will get hurt but no one is looking out for you, you need to remember this, son, you can't be the man you want to be without looking out for number one first."

Wesley's cold eyes stared blankly at the station as the two lovers held each other. He felt different after lying to Patricia. Not guilty so much as powerful. It was the first time he'd lied to gain something for himself and it was an intoxicating.

PART III

CHAPTER 11

The warmth of the day was a gentle reminder summer was quickly approaching. A slight haze hung in the air as the graduating class of 1963 stood to receive their diplomas from the Commandant of The United States Military Academy, better known as West Point, or simply, The Point. It seemed to everyone involved the past four years went by too fast. The country was mired in turmoil over a war on foreign soil fighting an enemy no one really knew. The expectant jubilation was overshadowed by a tone of disparity. Many of these fine young men would soon die, in a war like no other; warriors falling for a cause questioned by an entire country. However, none of that mattered to these brave young soldiers. They chose to fight anything that threatened the fabric of democracy in America and around the world. They chose to extend a tradition dating far beyond their own memory.

"You did it!" exclaimed Patricia. Her arms wrapped around Wesley. "You did it. I'm so proud of you!" she said, smiling. "I told your Mom and Dad that we'd meet them back at your barracks. Where's Joshua?" her eyes darted throughout the crowd. "Oh, I mean Lieutenant Tanner!" she giggled. "I'm so proud of both of you!" Wesley pulled Patricia closer and kissed her gently on the right cheek.

"Thank you Patricia, for everything." He said smiling. Wesley scanned the crowd for his best friend to no avail. There were too many people milling around to pick out anyone familiar. "Let's walk back to the barracks. I'm sure he'll catch up with us there. Today is important. I need him with me," Wesley stated cryptically.

The walk across post to the barracks felt different to Wesley. He had graduated West Point Military School. He was a Commissioned Officer in the United States Army. He was a changed man. That quickly, from one moment to the next with a firm handshake and a smart salute, his path was being paved in front of him. Wesley Fordam came from a long line of Army men but he was the first to be commissioned an officer. This was as important to his family as it was to him. Only one thing could make this day better. "All in due time" he thought smiling.

"You look happy Wes. It fits you nicely. I like it." Patricia said, pausing, "I love you Wesley Fordam. I think I always have." She pulled him closer as they walked hand in hand.

The barracks were as desolate as an old town in a western movie. They were the first to arrive. Wesley pulled Patricia into a corner in the lobby and kissed her hard, passionately. He loved her too. Patricia would make the perfect wife of a military officer. She was gracious, polite, and beautiful and she would help him reach for the stars he so craved.

"Hey there!" a deep voice boomed from across the hall. "Public displays of affection are not permitted!" The man said smiling.

"Father, Mother! There you are! We just got here ourselves." Wesley said trying to change the subject.

"Um hmm, looks that way. Looks like you two got lost in each other!" Wesley's mother prodded. "We're so proud of you son. You have no idea!" she continued.

Wesley turned to his father, a retired Sergeant Major. "Does this mean I have to salute you son?" he said grabbing hold of Wesley's arm, pulling him into a hug. "Damn boy. You did it. You're the brightest star in our family!" he snapped proudly.

"I couldn't have done it without such a good role model father. You're the one who we should be congratulating." Wesley whispered to his father hugging even harder than before. The hug broke quickly but not without Wesley's dad wiping a tear from his cheek.

Without missing a beat Wesley's mother side-stepped to Patricia and hugged her with a soft, endearing kiss to the forehead. "You're such a fine young lady. We have missed you." Patricia kissed her cheek in return, smiling. After receiving a warm hug from Wesley's father, Patricia asked if they had seen Josh. As if on cue Joshua snapped a loud Hue Ra from across the lobby, walking briskly toward the party in the corner. Wesley stepped toward the young man and snapped his first official salute to his best friend and newest colleague. Lieutenant Tanner returned the salute and countered with a bear hug of his own lifting Wesley off the floor.

"We did it you son-of-a..." Joshua trailed off realizing their being in the presence of ladies. The Fordam's embraced Joshua like he was family as tears flowed from more than one of the group. Joshua was raised by his grandmother who had passed away during his freshman year, both parents having died in a car accident when he was young. The Fordam family had basically 'adopted' him during his stint at West Point. "Let's celebrate!" proclaimed Joshua.

The night was perfect starting with a fine meal...off post, and finishing at a nice club with live jazz being played from somewhere in the back of the bar which had been separated into three smaller rooms. Everyone smiled and laughed together as if they were one big family. After two hours of small talk and a late lunch Wesley disappeared to ask their waitress to deliver a good bottle of Champaign and glasses for five. Five minutes later Wesley stood holding a glass of Champaign in front of his chest at arm's length.

"Call to order!" he proclaimed "I have a toast I'd like to make. Sit down Lieutenant Tanner" he said smiling. "This toast is to those of you who helped us get to where we are today. To those of you who taught us well and to those of you whom we are forever in debt. To you mother. A woman with the strength and resolve of any man I've met. To my father he said turning to his left. A man who made it his life defending this fine country we call home. To a man who taught me to have inner strength and the intestinal fortitude to overcome any barrier I may encounter, to a man who I owe *my* own manhood." Wesley paused for effect. "And finally to you my dear Patricia, a woman who brought me out of my youthful shell" he said with a wink. "To a woman that possesses strengths she has yet to discover. And to a woman" he continued as he knelt on his left knee taking her hand in his "that I want to make my wife. Patricia Alice Redding" another pause leaving everyone at the table breathless, "Will you marry me?" Wesley concluded, his eyes never leaving hers.

It was as if the entire place had come to a halt, everyone in the dimly lit room aware of what was transpiring in front of them. All eyes it seemed were on Patricia, anxiously awaiting her response. The music continuing from the back room was all that could be heard. That and the one answer Wesley had been hoping would follow.

"Of course I'll marry you Wesley! Yes, I'd be honored to be your wife." The room exploded with clapping and whistles. All of that unnoticed by Wesley as he stood along with his new fiancé embracing her passionately.

CHAPTER 12

The following week for Wesley was filled dealing with administrative stuff. Leaving the school he'd learned to love over the past four years was sad, but he was looking forward to his next challenge. Another trait bestowed upon him by his father. "Always be one step ahead of yourself". Lieutenant Fordam had requested to attend training at The Defense Language Institute Foreign Language Center located in Monterrey California. The Presidio. He'd done well on his initial aptitude tests which gave him the option to choose which language *he* wished to learn. Being no fool he chose Russian. He had already watched as some of his friends and schoolmates left for combat training in advance of deploying to Vietnam. Wesley loved his country but did not wish to die in a conflict with no meaning. He understood very well the implications of an ever growing Communist threat, but thought Vietnam to be of little importance if lost. Wesley was a realist. He knew the presence of communism throughout Europe was the real threat to The United States and to democracy itself. He prided himself on being ahead of the curve. He therefore opted to learn the language of the *true* enemy, believing that when the conflict in Vietnam ended there would be no lasting ramifications on the world. Reign over that region was insignificant compared to Europe and the impact of losing it would have on the world.

The real battle lines existed between Russia and its satellite countries and the democratic rule of its neighbors. Mastering the Russian language would virtually assure Wesley that he'd be stationed in Europe. His father took his family to Germany on assignment shortly after returning home from the Korean War. Since the end of WWII there had been an increasing American presence in the Federal Republic of Germany, West Germany. Donald Fordam brought with him vast knowledge and experience from his deployment to the Korean Theater.

In 1961 the rift and political and ideological differences between East and West had escalated brining a more overt separation. Until then, people from East Germany and those of West Germany could travel with relative ease between the two entities.

Wesley took advantage of the situation, crossing into the East on evenings to witness firsthand what life was like in a state-run environment. These 'field trips' with his friends inspired Wesley's beliefs in the advantages of Democratic rule and a free society. They fueled his passion to fight for democracy.

From his time spent there as a child while his own father was stationed in Germany, Wesley knew there would be an immeasurable amount of history and culture he and his family would be exposed to.

While Wesley was preparing for his first assignment after graduation, Patricia was at home in Connecticut with her parents.

"Mom, I've got some news to tell you and dad. I don't know how he'll react so I'm dropping the bomb on you first" trepidation taking hold of her waning confidence. "Wesley has asked me to marry him." She cringed at the response surely to come. Alice Redding sat across the table from Patricia, who had been watching her mother prepare dinner.

"You're sure about this honey?" Smiling awkwardly, Alice tried to hide her angst. "I like Wesley. He's a good boy, but marriage? We knew you were involved romantically but this is an entirely different thing. This is for life Patty."

Patricia had been expecting much worse from her parents. She knew they liked Wesley but they also looked at him as if he were less of a person. They had money. He didn't. She wasn't a fool. She understood the economics of life.

None of that mattered to Patricia. She was in love with a good man, and was going to travel the world with him. Let him follow his dreams. The money never had anything to do with it. Not to her. She anxiously awaited the arrival of her father, due back from the city in less than an hour. With each passing moment her heart raced a little faster, her breathing came more rapidly. She was not looking forward to this conversation. She'd postponed it as long as she could but the time was now.

The funny thing is that she already knew what reaction her father would have. At first he'd explode with fury. He would have nothing to do with her daughter marrying a man of no substance. Robert Redding judged people on their financial status and little else, especially when it came to his little girl. He was very protective of his angel. There was an underlying 'economic' logic Robert Redding used when quantifying Patricia's relationship with her beau. She was attending school at Skidmore College in Saratoga Springs and he was training for a life in the military. He was sure that's as far as it would go, nothing more. She would have her fling then come to her senses when it was time for him to move on. He liked the young man enough but there were economic considerations. Wesley would surely move on after graduation. After all he was a year older than his little princess. She would remain at Skidmore for her senior year and she would become a fond memory. Robert also felt assured that his only daughter would come to her senses and not want to follow Wesley after her own graduation. He felt sorry, but this was how it was at their caste. You did not allow your child to do such a thing.

As the cab pulled up the drive to their upscale home Patricia straightened herself where she sat on the edge of the top marble step that indicated the entrance to their well-established home. Her father caught the train out of Penn Station then hailed a cab at the rail station in Bridgeport. He took care of the formality of paying the cabbie then smiled as he stood from the cab seeing his little girl waiting for him. He briskly walked the twenty feet or so to the bottom step and held out his arms after dropping his briefcase. The two had repeated this ritual for years and as the years passed Patricia would embrace her loving father from lower steps as she grew into the woman she now was. She still had to stand on the first step seeing her father pushed six feet in height. They hugged and kissed each other on the cheek. One kiss for her and one for him. Tradition.

"I missed you Daddy!" she proclaimed refusing to let go yet.

"I missed you too Princess" Robert replied also not wanting to release from the hug so soon. They saw each other far too little these days. "One of the shortcomings of growing old" he thought. They reluctantly released from their hug and walked up the five steps to their beautiful house. Hand in hand. Alice remained in the kitchen waiting for all hell to break loose.

"Absolutely not!" roared Patricia's father, fuming. "I'll hear nothing of this rubbish." There is a vast difference between seeing the boy and marrying him Patty. You know that." And she did.

"Daddy, look at this from my point of view. We're in love. We have been for over a year!" she exclaimed. "We want to spend the rest of our lives together" she stopped, interrupted by her father

60

"We've not raised our little girl to live the life of a" he searched for the proper word. Something Robert Redding rarely did. Usually in command of every situation he suddenly found himself speechless. "The life of a military wife." he concluded, red in the face. You know where you come from. *What* you come from. Your breeding dammit!" he rambled. "We have not raised you to live a life in poverty." He ended, storming across the living room to the bar. He poured himself a double shot of brandy drinking it briskly then slammed the expensive crystal on the bar top. Hunched over the bar, the hulking man mumbled to no one in particular, "God dammit!" Patricia watched her father's chest heave with anger and anxiety. With each labored breath his suspenders stretched then relaxed over his tailored shirt. She knew when to back off and did so leaving him alone to stew in his anger. Anything she said at this point was a waste. She'd let him cool off then try again later.

"I'm going to help mother with dinner". And she left.

CHAPTER 13

"He wanted nothing of it, Wesley! He eventually refused to talk about it." Patricia cried frantically.

Half asleep, Wesley was awakened by banging at the door informing him of a call. He wiped sleep from his eyes as he prepared to calm her down.

"Patricia, this is difficult for him. You're his little girl. He's not going to give you up that easily. Not without a fight. You're his *Princess*, right?" He said referring to Mr. Redding's nickname for his daughter. But you are a grown woman now and you have to get that through to him. He needs to understand *that* more than he needs to understand our love for each other."

"I don't even think it's that Wesley." She wept. "He thinks" she paused unsure how to explain this next part to him. "That you are below us. That you're not good enough for me!" She started crying loudly. Wesley let her cry for a minute before trying to talk. Then he broke in softly.

"Patricia, you come from money. I don't. It's logical to him. It's how his mind is wired. He won't take this easily. You must have anticipated this would happen at least to some degree." He paused letting her take it in, then continued. "We just have to make him see us for what we are, two adults completely in love. That's it."

62

"I don't know honey. I want my Dad's blessing. I want him to walk me down the aisle of the church. I want him to give me away. I know it sounds cheesy, but it's what all girls dream of."

"We'll do it together. This weekend. I have a few days off before I have to ship out to California. I'll come out there and we'll talk to him together. How does that sound Patricia?"

Changing the subject Patricia interjected, "Why don't you ever call me Patty?"

"That's your fathers' pet name for you, Patricia. I'm not your father."

"We can try Wes. I can't promise anything though. He's in a rage right now."

"Look, Patricia you still have a whole year at Skidmore left. If we can show him that we are ready for marriage after being apart for so long he'll see what *we* see. We belong together Patricia. Get some sleep please. I have a long day ahead of me. Promise me you'll keep the peace there. I'll call you tomorrow night and we'll make arrangements for me to visit." Wesley stated simply as if this were just a bump in the road.

"Okay honey. I'm sorry I woke you this late but I needed to talk to you. I promise to keep the peace." She said smiling, a little more hopeful. The two young lovers said their goodbyes and hung up the phone. Wesley returned to his bunk and fell asleep without any further thought on the subject. Patricia however sat curled in her favorite chair in her bedroom cuddling her favorite teddy bear. She could not stop thinking about the whole situation. Were she and Wesley right or was her dad the one with the logic? Both sides had valid arguments. This war was not over by a long shot. She had decided to call her brother Charles in the morning. Charlie, as he was known only to Patricia, would come to her defense. He'd met Wesley a couple of times and they seemed to hit it off.

Charles Redding worked at his father's Brokerage firm in Manhattan as an associate broker. Receiving his undergraduate degree from Yale just two years ago, he was planning on returning to his Alma Mater for his Master's degree in the upcoming fall, more as a way of avoiding the draft than any other reason. He was a prime candidate to be drafted. Charles Redding was a young man with a very bright future in business. Not war. His father saw this not as dodging an upcoming draft but as a way of preserving lineage. Robert Redding felt no angst toward his son's decision to further his education. He believed there were persons better equipped to fight a war than his son.

Patricia called Charlie early at his apartment on the Upper East Side before he left for the office. She did not want her father getting wind of this.

"Hey Charlie how's the big city treating you?" she jibbed.

"Hello Sis. What trouble are you up to now?" he asked, smiling. This was how they began all their phone conversations.

"Me?" she questioned, I'm innocent I tell ya!" This broadened her brother's smile. She readied herself for the upcoming speech she'd rehearsed in her head a dozen times. What she didn't know was that their father had already spoken to him about this issue. Patricia braced herself as she readied to speak only to be interrupted by her big brother.

"Sis," Charlie paused collecting his thoughts. "Before you start lobbying for your cause I need to tell you that I'm siding with Dad on this one." There was a long silence broken only by Patricia's sobbing. "I know how much Wesley means to you, Sis. I really do. But there are things that have to be considered. You and I," another pause, "we come from a different world than Wesley. Our world..." he trailed off searching his mind for the right words, "our people are different than most. We are the privileged, the rich; whatever you want to call it. But *we* are not *them*." He stressed. Before Patricia could offer a rebuttal he continued. "Patricia, he can't offer you the things that you need, the things that you're used to. He's in the Army Sis. They make pennies. They have to go wherever they're told to go. They are not the privileged. They are not...*us*", he concluded.

Words came slowly for Patricia. She felt betrayed by her brother. They meant so much to each other. They always had. When he left for Yale she was devastated. It took her a while to get used to not having him around all the time. She stammered the only words she could.

"You bastard." She was trembling, almost dropping the phone. "I can't believe that you of all people believe that crap Charlie! That's not *you* talking. That's Dad! I can't believe he's brainwashed you into thinking this shit! Charlie, you know Wesley. You know he's a good man! You know what we mean to each other." She stopped cold. Realizing for the first time what was occurring. Her face reddened as she screamed.

"What did he threaten you with Charlie? What is he holding over your head?" After what seemed to be a full minute came the answer she was dreading.

"He won't pay for my school in the fall. He won't give me a dime if I side with you." Charles could practically hear the veins throbbing on her forehead. He felt ashamed. He knew he was a better man than this, but he also knew that without Yale he would be drafted to Vietnam. That was unacceptable to Charles Redding. He knew he was a good man but he also knew he was no warrior. The phone line went dead without another word spoken. Charles sat in a chair holding his face between his manicured hands, crying. He knew he'd lost his sister.

PART IV

LENNY

CHAPTER 14

The night was warm, humid for June and a soft breeze left Brad's hair tasseled as he strolled across a bridge spanning a branch of the Raquette River in a small college town in northern New York. Potsdam was known in the region for its colleges and also its bars. Voted in the 1970's in some obscure magazine as the number one 'college party town' in America, it took no great effort to find yourself sitting in a dimly lit bar with a cold beer in hand. Brad was in search of one such patron. A man he'd had a difficult time finding. "Hiding in plain sight", he thought.

Brad Fordam found it easy to blend in with the local population. He was able to slide into a summer teaching job at Potsdam State University, one of the town's two colleges. Potsdam State, as it is referred to is part of a much larger establishment known as SUNY or State University of New York, one of the many marvels of the Empire State. He was quickly accepted as an instructor for the college that pulled in students from all over the globe as it was known for its' renowned Crane School of Music. He was replacing a tenured professor that had decided to take a sabbatical and travel Europe. The job was on a temporary basis and he would be teaching American Literature to students of European countries.

Summer in this part of America, to put it simply, was quite beautiful, although much shorter than most seasons. The area was defined by its location. Close to the Canadian border with a crossing in Massena a mere 19 miles from the Township of Potsdam. With the border between The United Stated and Canada being the Saint Lawrence River itself there was bountiful fishing, boating and tourism with the Thousand Islands just to the west starting near Ogdensburg, New York, extending to the opening of Lake Ontario near Watertown, New York, home of an Army post called Fort Drum. Brad found humor in the irony, after travelling throughout Europe as a child and then teenager as an army brat, that he found himself in the 'Sister City' to Potsdam, Germany.

Brad visited a number of drinking establishments tonight searching for one person in particular. A monster named in his mother's diary simply as Lenny. He'd been an orderly at the Saint Lawrence Psychiatric Center while his mother had been interned there. Lenny found it easy to fall off the grid in Potsdam, blending with many of its' *locals*. Through a private detective, Brad had discovered that Lenny was in fact Lawrence Anthony Mattison. He was able to get a brief background on *Lenny*, although there truly was not much to report. He had been employed as an orderly at the St. Lawrence Psychiatric Center in Ogdensburg for a number of years after leaving the Army with an Honorable Discharge, having done his four years shortly after the Vietnam War had ended. Lenny was a cook who found army life not to his taste. Declining re-enlistment, he went in search of employment in the area. Having only one skill to offer he'd had a difficult time finding a job at first but he'd persisted not wanting to go home to Allentown, Pennsylvania.

He originally applied for a kitchen job at the Center but was told of an orderly position that was available immediately requiring no prior training. That and his honorable discharge from the Army were sufficient to land the job. He began his time at the center about eighteen months prior to the arrival of Brad's mother, Patricia. His employment record was sketchy at best, having been reported for a couple of minor indiscretions throughout his nearly ten years at the Center. But near the end of his stay there had been complaints of physical abuse and one report of a possible rape which had been investigated by the local police. The report was refuted as heresy due to the nature of the circumstance, and lack of a *credible* witness. Lenny had been accused by a female patient of rape and sodomy while she was in an isolation room, restrained. The police found the alleged victim had been in a state of acute psychosis and was an unreliable witness, and thus no charges could be filed. Lenny however had been released from employment shortly afterward due to his indiscretions involving some of the female patients. The Center understood that keeping Lenny employed would be a liability and wanted no further police inquiries. He was asked to leave and did so under his own will, creating no trail of his *indiscretions*. Within two weeks of leaving the center he was hired as a cook's assistant at Potsdam State where he remained an employee all these years. He had worked up to kitchen manager and made a meager living.

"Hey there", Brad called out to a couple crossing the bridge in the opposite direction, "Can you tell me where the Rusty Nail is?" referring to the next bar on his list to visit.

"Yeah," the girl answered with a slur to her voice. "Keep going straight. It's on the island over there," she said pointing to the other bank of the river. "Up on the right; can't miss it. We just left there. It's starting to die down too much. too many locals there," she said as she held her boyfriend's arm and stumbled across the bridge.

"Thanks" Brad simply answered. He didn't move however. Instead he turned to lean on the concrete railing of the bridge watching the fast running water pass by, blackened by the dark night. The water was shallow here but quick with rapids ahead he could hear well enough but could not see. It was dark on the bridge with only a few street lamps lit, a couple of them flickering in and out of consciousness. He stood quietly for about ten minutes taking in the calming sounds of the river, surrounded by its quaint village made mostly of pink sandstone buildings. The backs of the buildings faced the river; each with three stories apiece, all had black wrought iron stairs descending to the floor below and an occasional balcony that was most likely connected to an apartment. Walking in town during the day, the street sides of these buildings were littered with apartments on the second and third floors. Most of the first floors fronted a local specialty store, gift shop, and a drug store. There were also a couple of small pizza places. But what had overtaken this small village were the numerous bars catering to the largest component of the local populace, college students.

Potsdam was the sister town of Potsdam Germany, and was originally settled by the Clarkson Family. There now stood an engineering school by the same name just up Route 11 across the island he was about to enter. Brads mind wandered to Europe and his youth there.   He'd had many opportunities to travel and sightsee, and to use the local libraries of course. But tonight was not a night for reminiscing. No, tonight Brad was scouting his prey, his first victim. He arrived at the bar in just a few minutes, the girl being correct that it was just beyond the bridge. She was also right about the crowd in the establishment. There were a few small groups of college age kids; one playing pool, another throwing darts stumbling themselves, and another sitting in a booth playing what looked like a drinking game of some sort. All quite inebriated. None aware of his entrance. There were a handful of locals on hand as well, all sitting in what looked to be bar stools permanently embedded with their ass prints. Brad took a seat at the 'L' shaped bar. From his vantage point he could see everyone at the bar easily. Ordering a beer from the tap he settled in for the hunt.

He had been to two other bars tonight, having a drink or two at each. Slowly sipping on a beverage, waiting. Searching for the face faxed to him by the private investigator that did the background check on Lenny. This was his second night scouring the bar scene looking for his quarry, trying to pick him out from the crowd. Brad knew where he lived, knew where he worked and he knew what vehicle he drove. All pretty easy stuff for an experienced private detective to uncover. The one thing he didn't know was where he hung out. To find that out his associate would have had to have been here watching Lenny, following him. He'd offered, but Brad said that he'd not really needed any more information, secretly thinking to himself that he would be doing *this* bit of investigatory work himself.

As manager of Dinning Services for the college Lenny had pretty much made up his own schedule making it difficult to track him from work. So he left the hunt up to the one last piece of information which he'd received, Lenny liked to drink. "Now…if I could just find his lair" Brad thought. It was just a matter of time. Lenny was not what you would call brilliant.

He spent four years in the military in the late '70's, yet had done nothing out of the ordinary while in the service. His DD214, the military's equivalent of a final report card showed minor achievements and a soldier that met the minimum requirements to get an Honorable Discharge. His life before the military was even less tantalizing to the reader. Below average grades in high school, and no real extracurricular activities with the exception of being on the wrestling team four years in a row.

Brad stood watch from his stout bar stool for more than twenty minutes before he saw him. Tall and lanky in stature, Lenny stood at the far corner of the bar, near the waitress station. He had in his hands two beers, Genesee, Brad thought, and a basket of greasy french fries. He'd been waiting there all this time for his order. Brad looked at that man, really looked at him. He was at least six feet and weighed around 175 pounds. Seemed to be pretty well built but not overbearing by any means. His face was pale and scruffy with long red hair pulled up under a worn John Deere hat. His face was thinned by something he could not make out at this time. He'd rounded the corner and sat an uncomfortable three seats to Brad's right. Brad did however notice that the two beers and fries were for Lenny himself. He sat drinking and chewing the greasy fries, talking to no one else, but caught him glancing at the waitress station as if in anticipation of seeing someone there. *"His* prey, perhaps?" Brad thought to himself smiling. *Hunting the hunter.*

Brad sat for over two hours watching Lenny, learning. This was all new to him. He was smart but had never done anything remotely similar to this before. Nothing he'd read in a book could take into account the sheer rush of locating your prey, nor did it account for any of the number variables Brad had learned since his tracking came to a close. What if Lenny noticed he was being watched? He would have no reason to feel paranoia but may sense something was wrong. Brad realized he had to blend in better with the normal events of this establishment. This being clearly more of a local's establishment than that of a college bar. There were no dance floors and no DJ's here. No lights mixing with the drinks, just a plank floor, an old maple bar and the stench of cheap, stale beer.

Brad took notice of a posting above the bar for a dart league starting up soon. He summoned the bartender for another beer and to put his name on the rooster. This could be fun. Lenny's name was just above his own. Guaranteeing one night a week that he would know where Lenny would be. Brad had already decided to take him from the bar. Not from work, nor the house Lenny rented, too many variables. A bar had variables, but far fewer. More standards, like a certain closing time. They were usually darkened so fewer patrons would really *see* Brad. And finally, bars were full of the worst witnesses, drunk people.

CHAPTER 15

February 3, 1980

I had another bad night. I feel terrible regret for leaving my only son, Bradley. He deserves to have a mother. I should be there for him. This was not his doing and I thank God every day for his innocence. I however am not. I vowed to get out of this hell hole as soon as possible showing the doctors and nurses here that I am sane, that I was placed here under false pretenses. Today after talking in group about my concerns, I became angry at Wesley. At many I guess. I found it difficult to restrain my feelings which turned to rage. I threw chairs and upset a lot of the other patients. My 'behavior' was rewarded with a shot of Thorazine and being placed in four point restraints in a holding cell, just overnight. Just until I came to my senses and realized that I'd had a small break from reality. The Thorazine which they so aptly jammed into by left butt cheek stung and reacted with my body quickly and I don't remember much after that. At least not until the orderly Lenny had been asked to check on me. The check basically comprised of "is she breathing and is there a pulse, and are the restraints still in place", this Lenny had checked with ease. Then he said he was checking my cheek where the nurse had given me the shot. His words were garbled in my head and I showed no interest in his doings. I fell back into a drugged sleep quickly, the room went black and my mind slipped back into the abyss. I awoke later to a thrusting of my entire body. At first I thought I was vomiting but soon realized it wasn't me making these motions. The jerking brought me out of my stupor and I moaned. It seemed to be all I could get out at the time. As my senses came into focus, I realized Lenny had removed my pajama pants to my ankles and was sodomizing me. Something felt wrong though. I felt more than just "him" in me, there was another pushing.

As I awoke Lenny sped up his pace and came in me. His breathing was heavy and labored. He dripped beads of sweat onto my lower back, moaning in return to my own. Something was still wrong. I felt something else violating me. I was sickened by what I was learning coming out of my stupor and vomited on the bed. My face was turned to the left and with each dry wretch I felt a twinge of pain in my neck telling me that I'd been in that position for some time. I could feel Lenny withdrawing himself trying to compose himself and return his breathing to normal, all the while still feeling something else in me. Lenny slid on his pants zipping them quickly and buckled his belt with shaky hands. All I could seem to do was lay there in the prone position but on my knees. I fought the restrains to no avail and quickly ceased through exhaustion having fought most of the night already.

Lenny walked to the front of the restraint bed, smiling at me. "Thanks Patty but I'll need that back". He walked to my side slapping my bare left butt then sharply pulled his night stick out of my rectum. He returned to within my sights holding the night stick to my face saying "Well I don't think I'll be needing this" as he smeared fecal matter and blood across my face. The smell overwhelmed my dulled senses. The sight of my own blood tore at my insides.

All I could do was cry, it was my only defense. I sobbed while he cleaned my private areas and finally wiped my face clean. "Can't let anyone know what went on in here, ya know sweetie? You've been here five years and I've wanted to fuck you from day one; just never had the chance, 'til tonight. I hope you enjoyed it as much as me darling."

I lost something dear to me last night that will haunt me forever. Having been with only one man my whole life I'd lost that innocence forever. It was taken from me as a toy is taken from a child, with ease. It left me defenseless. If it could happen like that, there were no barriers this monster could not overcome. I hate myself for thinking this but I hope he moves on to his next opportunity. Dearest diary, tonight I died a little. And I am deeply, deeply ashamed of myself.

CHAPTER 16

"Good morning. My name is Brad Fordam. Not Mr. Fordam, not Professor Fordam." Brad started with a smile. He next removed his sport coat, draping it over a chair. "But please just call me Brad." The twenty or so students in his class collectively sighed. He had them, already. "This class will enable you to not only speak the English language well but will also allow you the opportunity get your message across, whatever that may be, without sounding like a bloody idiot", his smile broadened. But with you, you'll take a deeper appreciation of one of the most widely accepted languages in history and a much greater appreciation of the masters of American Literature. "I am only here for the summer and expect very little from you. With that said, let's get started."

Brad was hired to teach two classes, five days a week. His time otherwise was his. The classes themselves were primitive to what he'd been preparing himself for all these years. When being interviewed for the temporary position he'd even been labeled as being overqualified. He had responded to this with an explanation that he wanted to spend his summer in Potsdam while he decided where he would like to start his career in teaching. They hired him after one interview knowing they had received the better end of the deal. The job after all did not pay that well, but this left Brad with quite a bit of time to toy with his prey, like a cat would with a new toy as he decided exactly what to do with him.

During the summers in Potsdam, a town with roughly seven thousand year round residents, the student populace was far fewer than during the school year. The streets were quiet at night and there was a broad range of housing to choose from. Brad decided to rent a small house about five miles from the college, situated on five acres and set back from the small two lane highway. It was nestled in a stand of pine trees about five hundred feet beyond the edge of the road. The nights were dark and Brad found this to be a peaceful respite. The house came with a shed that was about three hundred square feet and filled with some equipment the owner had stored and was left unlocked. The owner felt Brad seemed to be a nice guy and hadn't felt an urgency to protect his property from his new tenant. Brad had wandered out to the shed that was thirty feet or so from the back porch. The building was filled with all sorts of antique farming equipment that the property owner had inherited from his own father many years prior. The equipment seemed in pretty good repair having been kept out of the elements. The stash had ranged from old hand hoes to an old John Deere tractor and pretty much everything in between. The walls were riddled with sickles, rakes, shovels, and everything else you would expect to find loitering around an old farm. There was power run out there with two single light bulbs hanging from the rafters and one electrical outlet tacked to a wall. Brad had thought, smiling "this would never pass code."

The owner, a man that went by the name Bud was an old, and not well aged 64 years. He worked as a meat cutter for one of the local markets and told Brad that he'd been raised on a farm and even had a small plot of land close by that he used to grow vegetables for his family but that real farming had passed with his father. He'd just never had the heart to sell any of the old equipment his dad acquired throughout the years. Brad had spent an afternoon with the old guy and learned quite a bit about the local area. He'd even learned of a few good fishing spots.

Brad paid for the house up front with cash for the three month lease he'd agreed to with a firm handshake. He told the owner that he'd inherited some money from his mother's death and it really was no longer a factor in his life. He was teaching because that was what he'd wanted to do. That's who he was. Brad had even offered to mow the lawn for the summer after noting a push mower in the shed. The old man gladly accepted these terms and ensured that he would have a peaceful summer and if Brad needed anything to just call, letting him know that he almost never used the shed for anything but storing his dad's crap and the mower. Now that he was off the hook from mowing he'd not have to come by at all unless Brad summoned him. Brad reassured Bud the house would be in good repair after the summer and that he would be a quiet tenant.

Potsdam, as it turned out was a nice place to spend a summer. The weather was much like that in Europe and the people were pleasant. Brad could drive into town, park his Honda and walk the quaint streets admiring the beautiful sandstone structures that were the heart of the village. He walked the mile or so between the school grounds and the village, almost daily passing by students that were busily strolling between the two. He would stroll the grounds of Clarkson University, a rapidly growing engineering school that had a large endowment and plans to broaden their educational base. But at the time the two schools in Potsdam could not be any more different. Clarkson was comprised of highly intelligent individuals that would move on to be leaders in industry and research. Potsdam State's student body was comprised of budding teachers and musical prodigies. It was actually quite comical watching the two student bodies mingle and intertwine when thrust together in the many local bars.

CHAPTER 17

Brad spotted Lenny at his usual seat. It was close to eight and by the look of it Lenny had already tipped back a few too many. He was louder than normal tonight, seemed a little jovial to be more precise. Definitely not his normally obtrusive self. Brad took a seat in a booth where he had a direct line of view to Lenny. Watch and wait. That was the mode he was in at this time. He was learning his foes patterns, watching for areas of opportunities that could be exploited, then pounced upon. Brad's heart raced at the thought of what he was about to undertake. He was preparing to repay a debt in his mother's name. His 'first kill' he thought to himself, unsure if he was even up to the task.

Ever since first reading his mother's diary for the first time Brad had constantly questioned if he'd have the fortitude to undertake such a task. He let his mind drift to the flight back to England after his mother had killed herself. Thinking that she had been robbed of her life and that someone had to pay for her pain. Then, turning the page in her diary he registered the final passage she'd written.

February 24, 1981
Dear Diary,

This is my last entry. I can no longer bear what has been thrust upon me by God. Somewhere in his divine knowledge He'd forgotten me, leaving me to wander this path of disparity and hopelessness. I cannot go on any longer. My will has been broken. I feel I am transformed into what Wesley believed I had already become, a lost soul.

I have left this journal for you my dear Bradley. It was you that had kept me going all these years. The thought of you saving me from this hell gave me what little hope there was to grasp. I have given up on hope Bradley. Please do not think I am angry with you. I know what your father is and how he manipulates people. I am sure he has made you feel that I left you long ago. Ages it seems. But that is a lie. You are my child and I have always loved you deeply.

I regret that I was not there for you all these years while you were learning to despise me. I now know that I was in no state to be your mother. At least not a good mother. I let you down. I deprived you of a basic need in life. To be loved.

As I write these last words I beg your forgiveness and ask you to understand that I have always loved you. I was deceived into coming here and I now ask you Bradley to help me hurt those who stole me from you. They are the true reason I was not there for you. They are the reason you have felt abandoned all these years. They are the ones who have to pay.

You have now read my inner most thoughts. You have read what I have told no other. I now ask you to complete my journey to absolution and make those responsible pay the ultimate price.

I don't think you ever found out that I followed you on occasion when you were younger, full of hatred for your parents. I needed to know where you were going. What you were doing all those hours that you chose not to be home with me, and your father. I understand now that you were in search of solace and found it in the past. The ancient history of Europe and all its' splendor. I pried into your private life to find a son I never knew existed, one who loved learning more than anything. Absorbing all you could about ancient cultures. Learning how people were dealt with in those times. I now know what you are capable of and I am asking that you complete this journey for me. I can no longer fight. I am myself spent and have lost what was left of my soul.

You, my son are the greatest single thing in my life. I absolve you of any guilt you may have. You are not at fault my child. The pages in this diary will help you unlock the demons of my past. They will steer you on a course of retribution. These pages will be your guide to your future. In resolution you will find that I may once again reclaim my soul and find peace in death. I trust you will make the right decision. My love for you is endless. Mother.

Brad bowed his head in quiet remembrance of those final words. He understood what she had gone through, the pain she had endured, and he knew what was being asked of him. The journey back to England had been difficult, full of anger and regret, but he felt he owed his mother this last request. She had taken her own life because of another's doing. The *hell* she'd endured while being locked away was a taste of what was to come. He had read and re-read those pages countless times and knew who had to succumb to her wishes. "It all starts here", he thought. The first of many payments to help his mother reclaim her lost soul. It would all start with Lenny. He whispered.

"My love for you is endless."

CHAPTER 18

Summer came with a rush of warmer weather and lots of free time. Brad took up fishing for the first time in his life, having had no real father to show him how, and was beginning to rather enjoy himself. Being a loner he felt most at peace alone. The first half of the summer went by quickly but Brad knew that it was time to get to work. The *real* reason he was here. He was leading a split life, one during the day where he spent his time teaching and enjoying his new found recreational activity and the other, night's where he spent his time watching and learning. Composing his first act of retribution. Lenny was luckily a creature of habit. Most people like him usually were, living life from one day to the next without really having to think. "Autopilot", Brad thought, smirking.

His line of thought was interrupted by a young woman in the second row of his morning class. She'd asked her question twice now sensing that her instructor was someplace else. Brad had apologized to her for his rudeness and went into a long lecture answering her question and more.

"Mr. Fordam, I mean Brad?" the same young woman asked as she approached him after he released class for the afternoon.

"Yes? Linda, isn't it?" he replied stacking papers and gathering his things.

"Is everything alright? I mean, you seemed very distant in class the last few days." she continued. Brad noticed that she was French and smiled in response to her question.

"I'm fine, just busy lately. I hope I'm not intruding but I sense a dialect that tells be you are from southern France. Am I correct?" he continued, trying to change the subject.

"Well", a pause then a smile in return, "yes I am. I've been in the states for two years but have not seemed to lose much of my accent." She admitted.

"Quite the contrary! You're doing very well. Your English is well thought out and you have easily adapted to the *American* version of the language" he joked. "Would you like to have dinner with me tonight?" he asked surprised by his forwardness. "Please don't feel obligated. I just don't have many acquaintances here in Potsdam. I don't want you to feel any pressure to say yes." He paused then smiled "unless you don't want that A minus you have been earning in my class?" Brad blushed at how foolish he must have sounded, but Linda smirked, cradling her books in both arms as if she were a young school girl.

"Oui, I'd like that, Brad, sure."

The two decided on keeping it light and meet at a local pizza place at seven o'clock.

Brad felt lighthearted the remainder of the day. He was not generally a lonely person but found an excitement brewing about the upcoming date. To tell you the truth he had not really noticed Linda in class. He spoke to them mostly as a group and did not like to single out students from the rest unless provoked, and that rarely happened. Brad maintained complete control in his classroom. As the afternoon waned Brad's apprehensiveness grew as he second guessed his initial thoughts. He arrived at Sergei's Pizzeria at seven sharp deciding to keep it casual wearing jeans and a worn blue sport coat over a white shirt, unbuttoned at the neck, no tie. His eyes darted back and forth hoping not to find his date waiting for him, but she was. The room closed in, leaving only Linda in his narrowing sights silhouetted against the soft lights emanating from back wall. Brad felt his heart quicken making him pause before gaining strength to fully enter the restaurant. She was leaning casually against an old jukebox one hand on top of the aging machine, the other in her left front pocket exuding an innocence Brad thought sexy. The room was nearly empty as Sergei's was renowned for being open when the bars closed and the crowd would surely pick up as the night progressed. "Good" he thought. "Keep it light". As he walked in the restaurant his date turned finding his eyes meeting hers. She smiled. Brad noticed that she too went casual, dressed similarly in old faded jeans. The difference was the white V-neck tee shirt she wore showing curves that had gone unnoticed before. Grinning and knowing he would soon be with the prettiest girl in the joint Brad approached her.

"Stop right there *Professor*. We need to get something straight right now" she said with a genuine seriousness in her tone. Brad reeled, trying to regain the cool composure it seemed to take a lifetime to muster. Linda grasped the nape of Brad's neck and pulled him into a sensual kiss, taking him completely by surprise. "That is how we say hello where I'm from". Brad returned her kiss this time with one kiss to each cheek.

"No, *that* is how you say hello in your country". Linda gave him an inquisitive look then pulled him by his hands to the booth where she'd been waiting.

"Let's eat!" she exclaimed. I'm dying for a cold beer and some pizza. You Americans and your pizza! I already ordered a pitcher of beer".

They sat and ordered and talked. Brad spoke of being an Army brat which he had to explain in great detail to Linda and how he grew up traveling throughout Europe. She sat wide-eyed absorbing all of the stories he'd told her. She explained that her family was very poor but she had been blessed with a strong mind. And will. She was offered a scholarship to come to America and study engineering.

"Then why are you at Potsdam State this summer?" he asked.

"There is an agreement between Potsdam State and Clarkson that allows us to take one class a semester at the other institution. I could not afford to travel home this summer so I thought I'd sharpen my language skills".

"So you plan on staying in the U.S. when you graduate?" he prodded.

"I think so. This is a wonderful country and there are so many opportunities", she said, taking hold of Brad's hand.

Four hours and three and a half pitchers later the two were completely engrossed in conversation. They had learned so much about each other and felt a genuine connection budding. Brad had felt a pang of guilt about the whole teacher/student thing but was put in his place when he learned that he was only three years older than his date.

"So, you like the engineering program?" he asked.

"I don't think I'll stay with it. I've always wanted to take care of animals", she stammered "what you call a...Veterinarian?"

"Yes, a Vet, an animal doctor", he said plainly.

"Yes that's it, an animal doctor!" she exclaimed maybe a little too loudly.

Shifting gears Brad admitted, "Linda, I've had a wonderful time tonight. I want to thank you for breaking the rules and asking your professor out on a date", he laughed as he finished this last statement.

"You're welcome *Professor* Brad", she said the word slowly and with a broad smile.

"This class is over next week. Can we pick this up then? Can you try not to break any more rules?" he smiled at his own joke.

"I think I can wait that long. But you have to promise me that we will go out again. This was fun", she rebutted with a serious look on her face.

"I've enjoyed tonight as well, Linda." They kissed lightly once again upon their departure but this time held their lips together long enough to draw a breath. No 'good nights' were said, just a smile and a slow release from each other's embrace.

CHAPTER 19

Brad awoke with a start. Beads of sweat trickled down his forehead, tears streaming from his eyes. His breathing was labored and choppy as he slumped over the side of the bed regaining his bearings. He shuffled to the bathroom. These nightmares or night terrors, whatever they were took a toll on his physical being as well as his psyche. He closed his eyes momentarily after flicking the light switch and looked in the mirror. His face was ruddy and blotchy, he'd been crying in his sleep. Splashing cool water on his face woke him up and his nightmare came back with a rush. He'd not had one in several months and this one took him by surprise. Tendrils of his past reached out to pull him toward some unknown place. They had always been based on his mother's writings. Small parcels of her life reborn. Faces had been derived from her vivid descriptions of whom she wrote. Some of the faces he knew all too well, some he'd fabricated in his own mind to fit the story but once he'd accounted a face to a character it never wavered, at least not in his sleep. He'd started having these terrible nightmares after reading her diary in his senior year of high school. The graphic details she'd included in her writings had forever scarred his mind. He was just 18 years old. He'd learned too much, too fast and he had a difficult time dealing with the anger and regret he was feeling. These feelings, he surmised years later, had manifested themselves as demons that he'd need to rid himself of eventually. Demons he would eradicate one at a time in a very intimate, methodical manner. He had made a promise to his mother that she would be given her soul back so she may rest in peace.

... "Can't let anyone know what went on in here ya know sweetie?" You've been here five years and I've wanted to fuck you from day one, just never had the chance, 'til tonight. Hope you enjoyed it as much as me darling."

The words whirled in Brad's head. "How can you do that to someone?" he kept asking himself through the years. He would never find the answer, at least not until he faced the monster who perpetrated this act upon his mother. Not until he faced Lenny.

Sleep eluded Brad after his nightmare. He graded some papers that he needed to get back to his students. He cleaned the kitchen as the sun came up. Then he wandered out to the shed. The lawn needed to be mowed and he thought he'd knock it out before he had to leave for class, all the time the ugliness of that night so long ago clawing to be released. When he opened the door to the shed he reached around to the right to turn the two light bulbs on. One of the two flickered and popped. Brad stared up at the rafters, at the shoddy wiring, when it hit him like a train. He knew what he had to do and now finally he knew how he was going to accomplish it. Smiling, he grabbed the mower and went about his chore.

CHAPTER 20

Brad spent the next few days finishing up his class work and readying the grades his students earned. For the most part they all had done well, at least they all passed. He also looked forward to the beginning of the dart league he'd opted for earlier in the summer while looking for Lenny. Tonight was the first night of the league, preliminaries that led eventually to many of the league goers taking on one another for the hell of it. He'd been paired up with a guy by the name of Robert who had apparently been drinking since the start of the meeting. Needless to say Brad breezed through his match gaining some notoriety as folks gathered around to watch his blistering victory. Many of the players struck up conversations with Brad as to how he became so good and a few of them jokingly called him a hustler. Brad explained that he'd grown up in "Merry Old England" and had been taught by the best. He did however have to get used to the American version of the actual dart as it was longer and much lighter. Although this did not hamper his natural talent. He was soon being offered drinks and asked to play by the better of the throwers in the league. Lenny however had kept his distance. Brad watched him throw a few games and was slightly impressed with his accuracy. He did notice though that Lenny was also a big talker. Always using his "in your face" mannerisms to hinder his opponents' chances of winning. He decided to let Lenny come to *him* for the challenge. Unfortunately this opportunity had not come the first night. Brad would have to wait.

The second night of the tournament, Brad was set to play against Lenny after a couple of rounds. They introduced themselves and began a grueling showdown as this was the semifinal match. Lenny proved to be a worthy opponent but eventually succumbed to Brad's almost flawless game, who had to bite his lip as Lenny ranted afterward that his game was off and that he could have won the match. Brad stifled his opponent by buying him a beer and shot of whiskey. After mingling for a while he approached Lenny, striking up a conversation. Lenny toned down his attitude toward Brad and they had even talked of fishing together some time soon. Brad went on to win the tournament with ease and retired for the night with a strong buzz. He fell asleep on his couch still wearing the clothes he left wore for the night.

Brad awoke to the sound of the doorbell ringing in his ears. His head was heavy with drink and he reeked of smoke and alcohol when he opened the front door.

"Well good morning *Professor* Brad", Linda bellowed noticing the signs of a hangover immediately.

"Hey" Brad whispered, silently wishing he were dead. "What time is it?" Brad asked in a raspy voice.

"Eleven o'clock. Rough night?" she asked smiling.

"Uh, I think I died somewhere around 3am. I'm too old for this shit!" he whined.

"Well, go take a shower and I'll make you some eggs for breakfast. You do have eggs don't you?" She teased.

"Um, yeah I should but you don't have to…" he trailed off as Linda walked past him toward the kitchen. "Did we have plans today?" he questioned, wondering just why she was at his house.

"No, but class is officially over and you no longer have to hold your *position* over me; now we can get to know each other", she continued smiling. "You told me to stop by after class was out. Don't you remember?" she said poking fun at his expense.

"Yes, but I didn't think you would *actually* come see me". He trailed off as he walked back toward the shower knowing it was no use. He stepped into the steaming shower and felt the heaviness of the night wash away slowly. He was rinsing his hair when he felt a slight breeze and turned to see Linda stepping into the shower, her body more beautiful than he'd imagined.

"I couldn't stop thinking about you after we went out the other night Brad. I've wanted to be with you ever since then. I hope you don't mind." Brad was in shock. He had felt the same about her but never expected to find her like this, naked in his shower at eleven in the morning. He pulled her closer feeling her hard nipples press against his wet chest. They kissed hard and long before releasing each other. She washed his body admiring it at close range. Starting at his feet and working her way up. He was embarrassed at how easily he became aroused but felt that wash away as well as Linda slowly lathered his midsection. She took extra care washing that area and seemed to enjoy herself. Brad started to lather her as well spending more time than usual on her breasts which were firm and erect as well. They touched each other as if they had been lovers forever and made love until the water turned cold.

After eating a light breakfast Linda grabbed Brad's hand.

"It's Sunday. Spend the day with me please. I want to be with you Brad. And maybe if you play your cards right you'll get lucky tonight". This brought out a chuckle from both and they kissed at the thought.

"I certainly wasn't expecting this, nice surprise. What do you have planned for us today?" he mused.

The two lovers spent a brilliant day hiking. Linda packed a light lunch and had found a cooler of Brad's. After cleaning the fish smell she loaded it with sandwiches, a couple apples she'd found on the counter and some bottled water. Linda described an area up the road referred to by her fellow classmates as Stone Valley. It was about ten miles north of Potsdam that was used as a swimming hole by students and locals.

Comprised of natural waterfalls and rapids that were topped by stone smoothed throughout the ages by the fast running water; it had been a sunbathing haven for years that a friend of Linda's had shown her. The two had hiked about a mile down a well-worn path that included shimmying under a giant pale green water pipe that easily stood twenty feet above them. With ease they had found a dug out area that was the path marker for the students venturing here in the past. It was still less than two feet high and Brad found himself pushing the cooler ahead while he crawled and shimmied on all fours to cross the green monstrosity. After dusting himself off on the other side he'd noticed Linda crawl under with the deftness of a cat and had no debris to dust from her clothes. The trail ran along a steep hill that developed into a number of short switchbacks leading into a valley divided by a small stream, which the two easily navigated. The trail then wound up the other side of the valley. As they approached the top of the hill they could discern the growing sound of rushing water.

When they reached the top Brad saw that the river was only twenty feet to their front even from behind a patch of dense trees and undergrowth. Once out of the woods Brad and Linda welcomed the bright sun beating down on their faces with the warmth of the day at its peak. The rock here was smooth and dry. This was the top part of the falls and they leapt over *pot holes* worn smooth over thousands of years of erosion to the middle of the formation. Brad smiled showing his agreement as he took in the sight.

"I Thought you would like it" stated Linda. "I've been here a couple of times with friends. We usually get a box of wine and spend the day.

"It's beautiful" replied Brad. Looking back to Linda and smiling. "So are you."

They found a good spot and lay their towels out and basked in the sun. The rest of the afternoon was a blur to Brad. They had spent the better part of four hours there and took their time walking back to her car, picking berries along the way. By the time Linda had dropped him off at his house, he was ready to ask her out again. They parted promising that they would see each other very soon. Brad felt he was falling for Linda, and the thought of this worried him. It would take years to finish what he was about to start, at least five, maybe six. He told her quietly that he had something to share with her. Soon, but not yet. Something he thought he may live to regret.

CHAPTER 21

Lenny arrived at Brad's house at six in the morning. The sun was starting to shine through the dense tree line that surrounded three sides of Brad's property. Hearing the small truck Lenny drove crunch on the gravel driveway, Brad wandered to the side door off the kitchen and waved a friendly gesture toward the man. Lenny clearly consumed too much drink the night before, having a worn look about him. He'd not shaved for a couple of days at least and had been in the same clothes he usually wore. An old faded pair of jeans, a worn tee shirt covered by a red and black checkered flannel shirt, unbuttoned and of course, his John Deere hat.

Lenny seemed to Brad as the kind of guy that had plenty of drinking buddies but few, if any real friends. That was about to change as the two of them shared some coffee with eggs and bacon that Brad had cooked up.

"This'll help wake me up. Thanks for cooking breakfast. I barely had time to wake up and get dressed this morning." Lenny said.

"Rough night?" replied Brad with a crooked smile. "I was a good boy and stayed home. I had to get my final grades in the books for the class I'm teaching. They're late as it is. I spent a lot of time with Linda this week, too." He smiled even broader at that thought.

"Humph. No time for women right now, too busy." responded Lenny, impassively.

At that, Brad stood up and gathered the dishes on the table leaving them in the sink for later. Something he normally would not have done, but this show was for Lenny's benefit.

"Well what do ya say? Want to get fishing?" Brad asked, turning toward Lenny. "Let's get this show on the road." The two walked to Lenny's truck after gathering a cooler Brad put together. Lenny throwing him a condescending look as if saying "what are you bringing?" "Just some cold beers for the drive home" Brad said, all the while thinking, "Knowing your prey is very helpful".

"Sweet deal. You're not so bad."

Lenny's truck was covered from front to back with an old green canoe that had seen better days. They headed out a few short minutes later travelling north to the small town of South Colton. There were a few fishing spots Lenny had told Brad about a few nights prior at the Rusty Nail while they played a few games of darts.

"I was up here a few days ago. Pike were hittin' real good; got a few small mouths, too. See what we can do today" Lenny stated in a monotone voice as if speaking to no one in particular. Something Brad felt Lenny did quite often.

"Well, it's been a few years since I have been out fishing so I hope you don't expect too much from me today, buddy."

Brad stated plainly. "I've been too busy finishing up with school. Never had time to get out", he finished.

"Never too busy fer fishin'!" Lenny blurted as if wondering where his new friends priorities lay.

The sun was now fully over the trees and Brad knew it was going to be a warm day ahead of them. He opened the small cooler and grabbed two beers.

"One to get us going. What do ya say?" he asked. Lenny looked sternly at Brad and finally released a wide smile showing a mouth full of half rotted teeth as well as his approval of his new found friend. The two spent the day fishing and drinking, at one point pulling the canoe out of the water about a quarter mile from a small mom and pop store to replenish their rapidly emptying cooler. The fish came with ease and the two men ended the day promising to meet at the Rusty Nail later after getting cleaned up and grabbing a bite to eat.

Brad called Linda and broke a date he'd made with her to go to the movies saying that he needed to do something important and would let her in on the secret soon. He ended their call with a pause and then said, "Linda, I think I'm falling for you. I'll call you in the morning, promise." The line went silent making Brad think that the connection was lost at one point, and then heard Linda's soft voice.

"Now I will sleep with a smile tonight. You're not the only one falling. I'll talk to you in the morning. Goodnight." Against Brad's wishes the line went painfully dead.

CHAPTER 23

Brad awoke trembling once again. His forehead besieged with beads of sweat, his heart thumping in his chest. He sat on the side of his bed grasping the mattress firmly, his knuckles white, searching for reality to take hold. Trying to gain his composure, he wiped the sweat from his face with his hands then stumbled to the bathroom, splashing himself with cool water, which helped almost immediately. His eyes, reddened and watery looked back at him. He held his gaze, looking for answers. He found none.

"What the fuck?"

February 7, 1980

Lenny cornered me in the bathroom today. Putting his hands on me, like he'd done it before. I felt nauseous and violated. He smiled at me and said that we would have another go at it soon. I pushed him hard to the floor and ran as fast as I could to the nurse's station. He denied it happened and they told me to stop acting out. I went looking for Cindi to tell her about it. I couldn't think of him doing such a thing to me. Cindi was engaged in her own crisis so I couldn't talk to her. Her son had died in a motorcycle accident that morning. I felt so terribly sad for her. She found out only a couple of hours before my run-in with that asshole Lenny. I'd barged into her room looking for

105

help and found her on her bed lying in the fetal position crying. When she told me I couldn't think of my own problems any more. She needed me as a friend. So we held each other crying for hours.

They told her they could let her go to the funeral but that was it and that she would have to be accompanied and properly medicated. This world I was tossed into is absolute chaos. How can they treat people like this, like we're animals? I feel so utterly sad for Cindi. She is a good person. I know what it's like to lose a child. Her son's death brought back so many horrid memories that I had a breakdown. I actually asked for medication to get me through it. The nurses were more than happy to oblige.

Brad dreamed of his mother. He stood in that bathroom, beside her, facing Lenny all those years ago. He'd felt all her fear, and anger, and rage. He was inside her mind and he suddenly felt enraged. He felt his mother's hatred like it was his own. Brad silently renewed his vow to his mother as he stared at himself in the mirror. He knew what he had to do. His promise would be kept.

Brad remained sleepless the remainder of the night, so he sat in the kitchen penning a letter to Linda. It was his confession to her and not knowing how she would respond was burdensome. She deserved to know, as this was larger than just him, much larger. He wanted to have Linda in his life and wanted to share this with her. He couldn't do this without telling her everything.

My dearest Linda,

I have spent so much of my life utterly alone, with no one to share life with. It is time for this caterpillar to spread his wings and live life to the fullest. I cannot grasp the notion of not involving you. I have loved two women in my life. You are the beat to my heart. You course through my veins spreading your love and your life throughout me.

There are things in my childhood that I had repressed and pushed to the darkest regions in my mind. I have been driven toward a path that I cannot alter, and I must satisfy a covenant to the only other woman I have loved, my mother. I don't expect you to fully understand what I am about to undertake, although in time I pray you will. Tragedy had consumed her life when she was a young woman and she was robbed of her autonomy by people that walk freely today without recourse. My promise to her has become my destiny.

I ask you to love me no matter what you decide upon discovering my path. Love me for who I am, but please do not hate me for what I must do. There will be a time when this will be over and my pact fulfilled and that time will be for us. There will be a time for us. But for now, there must be justice repaid in her name. I owe her that, as I am partly responsible for her misfortunes and cannot move forward until her soul can rest peacefully.

By the time you read this I will have done what I have come here to do. I beg you to not judge me for my actions, but rather understand the guilt and pain I feel daily for having allowed atrocities to occur to my mother. In time you will know all the details, so all I ask of you now is that you try to understand what you will soon learn.

Love me for who I am. Love the person you know. The person you fell in love with. That is the real me. I have fallen in love with you Linda. You have opened my heart to a whole new world, one full of happiness and commitment. My heart is forever yours; I pray yours is also mine.

Forever, Bradley

CHAPTER 23

Brad held onto the letter for close to a week before mailing it to Linda. There had been preparations to be completed. He had to ready not only the shed, but also himself for what was to come. The terror and torture that would soon define the pinnacle of Lenny's existence, and ultimately his death.

Brad purchased some metal, steel; cutting it with care to follow the detailed blueprints he'd drawn up years before. He used the acetylene torch and arch welder found in the shed. Years of dust had settled on the equipment, but it still remained functional. He built the structure; a four sided pyramid atop a four legged stand, tack welding the two together for increased strength. The top was made of four separate, but identical pieces of metal welded precisely together to form a small pyramid. At its base the cold iron pyramid measured four square feet. Brad welded a fine bead and used a grinder to make the four sides look seemingly like one continuous structure. Solid. To the unknowing eye the contraption resembled an ancient pyramid, only on a smaller scale and made of metal. Benign in nature.

Brad purchased some simple supplies in town at the local hardware store. Pulleys, a stout hemp rope, and riveting materials. At the local tannery he found sturdy leather that would be used to fabricate handmade shackles. Brad spent nearly two days hiding the farm equipment in the woods and transforming the rugged shed into a makeshift chamber of horror and death. It was now time. His creation stood in the center of the dimly lit room.

Brad placed his letter to Linda in a mailbox on one of the street corners in town; then spent a couple of hours with her enjoying a nice lunch before parting ways.

"What are you doing later?" she asked coyly.

"I'm meeting Lenny for a couple of beers later. Then I'm going home for a good night's sleep. I've got to get up early tomorrow and do a few things at the college." He answered. Linda turned her face downward, clearly pouting.

"I see how you are" she said smiling, kicking at the dirt in the eateries parking lot.

"You're incorrigible." He leaned over and kissed her softly, holding his lips to hers longer than he had in the past. As if he didn't want the moment to pass.

"Is everything alright?" Linda asked quietly.

"Yeah, I've just got a lot on my mind today. I'll see you later." He turned and got into his car sighing as he turned over the ignition and drove off without looking back.

CHAPTER 24

"Hey Lenny, what's up?" asked Brad as he entered the bar and approached Lenny at his usual bar stool.

"Hey man! Where the hell have you been? I've already got a couple of beers in me! You're late. Sit your ass down and get caught up," he replied, slapping Brad on the back. "Jill," Lenny said looking down the bar toward the bartender. A young woman with dark hair and tan skin, wrinkles starting to appear at the edges of her eyes and mouth prematurely, a sure sign of a heavy smoker. "Gimmy a couple more for me and my friend." Lenny was slurring his words already, a given that he was far more than a couple ahead of him.

Brad arrived about an hour later than agreed in anticipation of this. Knowing Lenny would be in a drinking mood tonight, he was too weak not to start without Brad.

"Thanks Buddy. I need a cold one." Brad replied, "I'll get the next round." It was close to eight o'clock. In five hours the two of them left the bar together; Brad promising that he had a twenty-four pack in his fridge at home. They drove off together in Brad's car, leaving Lenny's truck in the parking lot.

At about three in the morning the two were quietly sitting on Brad's front porch drinking together as if they'd known each other for years. Brad's bottles of beer however were filled with tap water, the brown glass hiding the true contents well enough.

"I've got to take a piss", Lenny simply stated. "I think I'm drunk old buddy", he said enunciating each word slowly for Brad's benefit.

"Just go over by the shed", Brad slurred loudly, acting out the part of a drunken friend. "Nobody here to see that little worm in your pants", he continued, laughing and pushing Lenny in the direction of the shed.

"What the hell. I'll go bleed the lizard over there. No little worms here asshole!" he said as he stood and staggered off the porch nearly falling while trying to navigate the one step to the ground. After two sidesteps and an over-correction, Lenny was out of the dim light provided by the sole porch light. Bradley quietly followed Lenny, staying about ten feet behind walking slowly on the grass. Lenny never saw the crow bar that struck the back of his head with a dull thud; nor did he feel the flash of pain it should have delivered. He was unconscious before he hit the ground.

CHAPTER 25

The veil of darkness lifted with the shock of cold water that suddenly blanketed Lenny's body. Slowly he opened his eyes, blurred by the blow to his head along with the obscene amount of alcohol he'd consumed throughout the night. Crawling out of his unconscious state, Lenny unsuccessfully attempted to wipe his eyes clear of the film that developed and clouded his vision.

Again, this time more alert he failed in moving his hands more than a couple of inches. His stupor began to lift as his brain computed that something was dreadfully wrong. It was then that Lenny felt the burning soreness in his shoulders running in threads to his wrists. Trying to focus his vision only produced a cloudy, unfocused presence of being suspended. Attempts at pulling his arms toward his face produced only agonizing pain in his shoulders and a sharp stinging of his wrists.

Sluggishly, the room came into focus and Lenny was able to discern that he was inside a darkened, shadowy room. A dim light shone from somewhere behind him. He soon came to the frightening realization that he was floating in mid-air. The thought of this overwhelmed Lenny's mental reasoning and he began to struggle against his unseen bindings. As he fought, he realized that it was not only his wrists that were bound but his ankles as well. Lenny was unsure what denied him the ability to raise his head; he felt something like a strap around his neck, forcing him to look down. That's when he saw it.

"Good morning sunshine. It's about time you woke up", a voice sounded from behind. Lenny could tell it was Brad but there was something different about the tone. It sounded strange, almost foreign. Flat.

"What the fuck is going on here?" Lenny cried out, his voice grated with dryness. He pulled even harder at his restraints causing an insurmountable level of pain that shot through him like a freight train. Screaming, half in pain and half out of fear, he had no understanding of what was transpiring around him. "Help me get down from here Brad" he said after clearing his throat. What's going on? What are you doing?" Bradley circled the room to face his prey, looking up into Lenny's eyes. Realizing that this put him at a disadvantage, he brushed it off as being a necessity to achieve the outcome of the moment. Lenny looked down at Bradley catching his gaze immediately. There was something different in the way he looked. He was as calm as ever, composed even, but there was a look in his eyes that showed no mercy. A cold stare looking through Lenny's soul, and then he noticed Brad had closed his eyes as if drifting away to a far off place.

February 26, 1980

I was served divorce papers today by a man hired by Wesley. I cannot see ever going back to him. I lost him years ago. And yet, I don't think I ever had him. I miss my family.

I signed the papers without hesitation. I actually felt liberated for a while, and then I lost it. I attacked a nurse who brought me my evening medications. I hurt her and they rushed both of us to the infirmary, although they placed me in a meditation room. At least that's what they call it. It's actually a room with a poorly cushioned stretcher with an ante room just off it where they kept equipment locked up. I remember them giving me a shot in the leg then the lights went out.

I was brought back to my room after only two days of "treatment". At least that's what they call it. They check you out then sedate you to keep you in a coma like state. This time I played the game more smartly, acting like I was sedated more than I actually was. I knew they were watching me through the window so I had to constantly lay there "asleep". That night Lenny came in to see me. He relieved the night nurse so she could take a break. He came into the room and poked me to see if I was awake. I had to know. I just lay there while he groped me. His hands were sweaty and cold. His fingers entered me forcefully. I had to stop myself from screaming. He did notice that I was awake though. I was still in four- point leather restraints. There was nothing I could do short of screaming.

Then he shoved his underwear in my mouth. Crying, I tried to yell, tried to free myself. Then he was on top of me. He was hard and I could feel him pressing his cock against my belly. He pulled up my gown and rammed himself into me hard. It hurt so badly, yet my muffled screams went unheard. He then had anal sex with me. He was talking the whole time about how he wanted to "fuck me in the ass" ever since the first time he raped me. He used the words so freely, like he was proving that he had total control over me. I screamed louder but he only laughed. He knew how long he had before he had to finish. He came in me saying that at least I couldn't get pregnant this way and that I should be thankful. Then he wiped his penis on my cheek. I could smell everything so vividly; his semen, my feces, and my own blood from being violated so brutally. All of it mixing with my tears as they ran down my cheeks. He had taken so much from me. Something I'd never get back. How could this be happening to me? I was put in here to keep me from hurting myself. This man took what he wanted without any recourse. By the time the nurse had returned from her break I had been cleaned up and ungagged. I was screaming at the top of my lungs when she came into my room so she sedated me. I told her what Lenny did while she was gone. I begged her to help me. I was astonished when she started to cry for me and promised that he would never do anything to me again. God left me that night. He'd abandoned me. I would never be the same.

Bradley opened his eyes and immediately locked onto Lenny's. His face remained expressionless, spreading his arms as if offering to give Lenny a loving hug. He found a switch on the wall near the front door to the shed. Flipping the switch he showered the darkened room with light. Brad spread his arms open wide, as if inviting his captive into his home and stated, "Welcome to hell, Lenny."

CHAPTER 26

May 16, 1978

I have been given back the right to venture the grounds once again. It's spring and the trees are budding. There is a cool breeze coming off the St. Lawrence river and I thought about going back inside, however I decided to walk some more. I came across a small cemetery on the grounds. Most of the headstones worn, eroded by time and the harsh winter elements here in Ogdensburg. I sat wondering who these people were. What afflictions did they suffer? Will I be buried here, alone with no family? I wept alone for some time, if not for myself then for the others. To die alone is misery in its' purest form.

Her hands shaking while she cried, Linda replaced the diary on her coffee table. Wiping tears away, she could read no more for the moment, having gone through this same ritual three times already. The writings depicted a life of anguish and sorrow. Not real life. Not in Linda's world. Her heart went out to this woman she'd never met; to Brad's mother.

Linda spent the afternoon worrying about Brad. There was something different about him at lunch. He seemed distant, almost as if he were drifting to another place, sometimes in mid-sentence. He argued that it was nothing, he just needed some rest. He told her he was going to call it an early night. She didn't believe him. He was becoming part of her and *she* part of him. There was an unseen connection evolving between the two.

When she arrived at her apartment later in the day there had been a package wedged in the mail box. It was a manila envelope that held an aged book with a letter neatly folded between the front cover and the first page; the book clearly battered by time. Her heart sank as she quietly read the letter Brad had penned. His words touched her heart and at the same time sent a shiver down her spine. In the letter he had instructed her to read the diary in its entirety in one sitting. He pleaded his case hoping she would understand making her promise quietly in his absence that she would. There was nothing that she wouldn't do for Brad. She was in love with the man, however the boundaries of that love were about to be tested.

CHAPTER 27

"Brad" Lenny huffed, clearly not fully understanding his predicament. "What the fuck are you doing man?" Bradley's cold stare fell to the device located directly under Lenny's body, pulling the victims eyes with his. Lenny realized he was naked. Amid the confusion and shock when he came to he hadn't realized Bradley stripped him of his clothing. Taking notice of his shaking body, still wet from the bucket of water thrown at him, Lenny, with sudden acute clarity knew he was in trouble. He was hanging by all fours over a metal contraption. There were leather straps that connected a neck collar to his upper thighs, successfully preventing him from lifting his head fully, thus forcing him to watch the horrors that would soon follow. He thrashed at his bindings to no avail. Screaming at the top of his lungs he pleaded with Bradley to let him down, cold beads of sweat dripping from his terrified face.

"Relax. Isn't that what you told her?" Bradley asked. "She wrote that she had died that night. Died on the inside. You stole what little she had left." he continued, looking through Lenny as if he didn't exist. The transformation surprised Brad. He was unsure of himself until this moment. Unaware of exactly how he would react to the situation. He sensed a change in his inner being, a metamorphosis of his soul. Who and what he had been his whole life were now trivial, he was now about to become a killer, and it frightened him how easily it came.

Bradley's period of self-reflection was interrupted by Lenny groaning as he pulled and fought until exhaustion set in. With his head slung low, he hung in his restraints like a ragdoll, almost lifeless.

"Wake up my friend, we have work to do, debts to repay, and you have sins to repent." Lenny fought to lift his head, as much as the neck strap would allow, looking down at his one-time friend. He started to cry softly. Something Lenny was unaccustomed to. Noticing Bradley move toward the wall to his left, Lenny winced at the leather bindings on his wrists noticing for the first time that they were connected to a rope. The rope led through a pulley and back down to where Bradley was now standing. His ankles were similarly attached to the system. The straps on his thighs pulling on his neck made it seem that he was crouching, yet suspended in mid-air.

"Lenny, I'd like to know if you like my creation, or to be proper, re-creation? What do you think of it?" Bradley jabbed. "It's called The Judas Cradle. Old world stuff, you know?" he continued. "Of course you don't. You're an ignorant man, if you're a man at all." There was a pause before Bradley pushed on. "She was my mother you know. The woman you raped and sodomized. She was my mother." Bradley's head bowed as if in prayer or remembrance. "She wrote it all down in her diary.

Everything you did to her. *Everything*" he stressed. "How you fucked her. How you raped her of life." He lifted his head once again looking straight into Lenny's bewildered eyes. "That's why I picked you to be the first to pay, the first to die."

Hearing these last words launched Lenny into another bout of panic. He pulled and thrashed in his restraints until the two men heard a resounding pop. Having pulled so hard on his bindings Lenny dislocated his left shoulder. There was a strange silence before an agonizing scream. "Pure pain" thought Bradley, *just the beginning.* The time had come to start a journey that was long overdue.

"Oh! That had to hurt", Bradley bellowed humorously. He started to howl like a wolf, laughing hysterically. "Shit Lenny, don't get ahead of me!" he cackled. Lenny didn't hear a word though, as he screamed in agony. Bradley grabbed two ropes that trailed down the wall. One led to the two ropes restraining Lenny's wrists and the other to his ankles. He pulled on them releasing the weight of Lenny's body from the steal spike on the wall. Bradley thought that he would have to fight harder to hold Lenny's weight, but surprisingly he was easy to control. Lenny's body jerked upward about a foot from Bradley's extra effort making him groan and shriek with pain that struck him like a hammer. "Sorry about that buddy" he stated simply.

CHAPTER 28

Linda raced to her car when the realization of what Bradley wrote hit her. She had to get to him. She had to stop him. She couldn't lose him. Turning over the keys she revved the engine to its maximum rpm's and squealed the tires as she plowed out the driveway. The Toyota she drove was standard and she shifted from one gear to the next as if she were in a race. It was five forty five in the morning; the sun peering over the horizon, as she sped out of town toward Brad's house ignoring the speed limit. Her heart pounded as she closed the gap between herself and her lover, and what she hoped was needless hysteria.

Minutes before her departure she had finished reading the last entries in the diary. Brad's letter and the last passage in the book collided into what Linda knew was an inevitability. She now understood what Brad had meant in the letter and why "he had no choice". There was no imagining the horrors she was about to witness.

March 3, 1981
My Dearest Bradley;
These are my final words, my last thoughts. I have written this diary for you, my dear son. You needed to know that what I have endured all these years was not your doing but rather the

doings of the people I have written about. I feel I have been unjustly treated by these monsters. I ask only one thing of you, my child. Use my writings as a guide to rain justice upon those who are guilty. Redeem my good name and allow my soul to rest for it shall not until your work is done. I will someday be with you again, in Heaven. I have always loved you with all my heart Bradley. You are my blood. You are my legacy. Mother

The trees, their tops glimmering in the early morning sun, raced by as Linda neared her destination. Her throat was burning as she fought back her rising stomach. She gripped the wheel tighter as she rounded the final corner. The tires fought to grab hold of the gravel on the narrow shoulder.

CHAPTER 29

Lenny opened his eyes after the sudden upward jerk subsided, unsure what was about to happen to him, he prayed silently that it would be quick. He'd never felt pain like this and naturally feared what was to come.

"This is from my mother Lenny, for what you did to her."

Bradley closed his eyes as he dropped his head. He released his grip from the two ropes and waited as he held his breath. There was almost complete silence except Patricia Fordam's soft voice whispering "Bradley." The pyramid shaped device penetrated Lenny like a bullet. When he opened his eyes Bradley stared in awe of the horrific destruction the Judas Cradle had done to Lenny's body. His victim straddling the structure as it penetrated through his rectum. Lenny unleashed a blistering howl, physical damage overshadowed by the searing pain he suddenly felt. Blood ran down the Judas Cradled splattering across the floor as the metal point first ripped into his anus then speared through his bowels. His body slumped to a halt as the device penetrated so deeply that it could go no further. He was forced to witness the trauma that would soon end his life, just before slipping into unconsciousness. Lenny was perched atop the Judas Cradle, a crude and grotesque puppet, its strings gone slack before being jolted off its' point and propelled into suspension once again. The movement aroused Lenny from his stupor, but too weak to speak the men could only look in bewilderment at the damage from the trauma he had just endured. His eyes wandered to where Bradley was standing, ropes taut in hand he bore a cold expressionless face. The Puppeteer.

The room filled with a foul odor as Lenny's bowels dangled below his near lifeless body, the pungent smell began to make Bradley wretch. Garnet colored blood steadily flowed off the sides of The Judas Cradle like a hard rain running off a metal roof, before splashing to the concrete floor below.

Bradley jumped when the door suddenly flew open; Linda took in the incredulous scene. There were no words for what she witnessed. She remained frozen in place staring up at Lenny, his body damaged almost beyond recognition. His skin was faded into a pasty white, contrasting with the blood that now covered nearly every surface of the room. Lenny moaned quietly with what little life remained; life that literally drained out in front of Linda's eyes.

Face sagging, eyes open to slits, Lenny examined the horrific sight that was once his body. The Judas Cradle had split him to the umbilicus. His bowels began slowly falling under the weight of gravity to the floor below, coiling like an old garden hose. He looked once more into the unforgiving eyes of his soon to be killer. Their eyes locked briefly. A thin smile crossed Bradley's mouth as he released the ropes entirely from his grip in a final blow impaling Lenny, instantly snuffing out what little life remained.

Linda forced herself to look at Brad. His eyes locked onto her, snapping him out of his trance-like state. His face transformed from what Linda had thought as alien into the one she recognized. He walked over to her, tears streaming from his eyes. Linda pulled him into a loving embrace, knowing that instant they would forever together.

"I'm so sorry Brad." She repeated, "I'm so sorry." They held each other crying, "I understand." It was all he needed to hear. He knew he could get through this with her help. He had started down a path that would lead to redemption. He would walk that path with Linda at his side.

PART V

JOSHUA

CHAPTER 30

"You can run but you can't hide" thought Brad, smiling as he drove down the lonesome stretch of dirt road; a curl of dust whipping up behind his rented SUV. He had arrived in Albuquerque the night before having stayed at a Red Roof Inn near the airport, resting for the next segment of his journey. He knew what to do; he'd rehearsed it a hundred times. There were few variables that could hinder his success, but unfortunately, they were always there, things you can't possibly foresee. That was the difficulty in dealing with people, he was discovering. They could be unpredictable. Except in his eyes, these were not people. They were his prey; *creatures* that fathered their own destiny long ago, without even knowing it. He smiled again.

The road has been long, the journey even troublesome at times. He'd not planned this destiny. He was merely acting as an appendage of his mother's will, her drive, but mostly of her need for revenge. The day her diary was handed to him by that disheveled woman, his life had changed. His mother must have known it would lead him down this path. She must have known, right to the end that he loved her and that love was unquestioned; otherwise he would not be driving down this shitty road in the middle of nowhere. Brad's knuckles whitened as he gripped the steering wheel tighter; nearing his prey.

It was just before noon in mid-June and the temperature was already up in the 90's. "Why would you want to live here?" Finding retired Brigadier General Joshua Tanner was a difficult task indeed. Joshua, as Brad's father had referred to him, was involved in some 'mishap' while in command of a data collection and interpretation unit in while at the Pentagon.

General Tanner was Brad's father's best friend for years. They had graduated from West Point together and while Brad's father had gone on to become one of the top Russian and German Linguistics Officers in the military, Joshua Tanner followed a different calling doing two tours in Vietnam and making quite a name for himself. He was fast-tracked for promotions and was a very competent leader. That was the official take on General Joshua Tanner. What was left out of his official files was that while commanding a unit charged with intelligence interpretation during the cold war, he and a few others under his command misinterpreted pieces of vital information that lead to a sticky situation between the United States and a satellite country of the U.S.S.R. The whole thing apparently was 'swept under the carpet', as they say. Unfortunately the individuals involved were forced to take retirement. General Tanner stood up for the men under his charge and was subsequently chastised. He had twenty two years of faithful service in the United States Army. Forced to take his one star and leave quietly with his dignity intact. Brad shook his head at the thought of hunting down and killing a man with such an outstanding record. General tanner had made few mistakes during his career, but it was one in particular that put him in Brad's sights.

Brad pulled into the narrow driveway that was indicated by the *Lazy J* sign at the road. The SUV rumbled as Brad drove over the cattle guard smoothing quickly as he crossed onto General Tanners' property; close to half a mile from the highway. The land was peppered with Joshua Trees, leading Brad to smile as he pulled the rented Explorer to a stop next to a white three quarter ton Ford pickup truck at the end of the driveway.

The ranch style house was nice. Rustic would be a good word for it but was built in a way to blend into its environment. A small patch of grass grew in the front yard but for the most part the surroundings of the ranch consisted of scattered cactus gardens. Different cacti littered the landscape, some with flowers but most without; this being the dry season. Monsoon season was about a month away, then much of the yard would be in bloom. A collie with a red bandana tied around its neck ran toward Brad, more as a greeting party than a threat. Her tail wagged as she playfully barked. There was no collar but it was evident that this dog clearly belonged to the owner of the house. Brad stepped out of the Explorer and patted the dog, making her tail wag all the more. It was clear that the dog was receiving visitors willfully; He wondered if the same went for the owner. Joshua.

"Hello there!" boomed a husky voice down the front walkway. Turning as he stood, Brad was eye to eye with 'the man' himself. Brigadier General Joshua Tanner was a hefty man, pushing two hundred twenty pounds and standing about six feet even. He kept his hair short and it was grey and thinned on top; his features were jagged and his skin leathery; a sure sign of too much sun and hard work. Brad took a few steps toward him, with the collie matching him step for step, and gave the man a casual wave holding out his hand. General Tanner accepted it with the strength of a rancher. "Welcome to the *Lazy J*, how can I help you?"

"Good morning, you probably don't remember me, Sir." Brad started. "Name's Brad, Brad Fordam," he said smiling. With a confused look on his face Joshua responded.

"Fordam? Wes' boy?"

"Yes sir" Brad replied simply.

"Holy shit. What in the hell are you doing way the hell out here son?"

"Looking up an old friend of the family, Sir." Brad answered broadening his own smile. "Well, come in out of the heat son.

131

Let's get something cold to drink." The two walked inside the house after Brad was released from the man's monstrous grip. The moment felt surreal. Joshua Tanner actually was an old family friend. For a while at least; until he crossed the line.

The two sat down at a small kitchen table with two glasses of ice cold lemonade already sweating from the heat. Brad explained that it took some doing tracking him down. There was a block on his permanent address listed on his official paperwork. He further explained that he dug a little deeper and found that this property was purchased shortly after the Generals' retirement showing him as the co-owner; he and his wife, Marsha.

"It's amazing what can be done on the internet, isn't it, Sir?" Brad questioned.

"Wouldn't know. We're a little off the grid out here. Hell, the power company doesn't even supply power this far off the highway. Everything is either solar or fed by generator. I've got no complaints though; I like the peace and quiet. Marsha, well it took her some time to get used to it" he said, smiling. "But I got her hooked up to the world through satellite TV. How in the hell is your old man?" he continued.

"My father isn't doing so well." Brad stated. "He's okay for now but I'll be honest with you. It's terminal. My father is not the kind to see it that way so he's sort of in denial. He'll come to grips with it soon enough." Brad concluded, picking brush from the grooves of his boot, silently telling his new chum he was uncomfortable with the subject.

"Well that's not good news, is it Bradley?" Joshua stated, shaking his head. Brad raised his head leveling his gaze on Joshua's concerned eyes.

"Only my father calls me Bradley, sir. Please, call me Brad". Just as he finished that statement a Lincoln Town car came rambling down the driveway. Mrs. General Tanner, Brad presumed.

"Well let's go help Marsha with the groceries and I'll introduce the two of you." He said, standing. The two of them walked out to greet Mrs. Tanner.

A short while later they were all seated, introductions having been made.

"I remember your mom and dad," Marsha stated. "Your mother was a very lovely person".

"She was indeed," agreed Brad.

"How is she doing...?" Marsha trailed, her eyes leaving Brad's, going somewhere back in time. "What I mean is that she was so terribly depressed, so young and so beautiful. She didn't handle Army life well. Your father and I had a long discussion shortly after her..." She searched inward for the right words. "Commitment", she finished flatly. "He told me about all the horrible bouts of depression she'd had." Marsha shook her head. "The Army can be a difficult place for a wife. Especially if you're used to living…" another pause, "Better", she concluded. "Wesley told me she came from money; gave it all up for him. That's quite a statement. She must have loved him dearly."

Joshua interrupted, "Well it was a sad story but better forgotten if you ask me. She was a good person. I didn't know her that well but from what I gathered she was very much in love with Wesley, but needed help." Brad shifted in his seat a little.

"Now Wes, he and I had some great times together!" The General looked as if he'd lost twenty years. His face showed a toothy smile. "Your dad and I went to The Point together; graduated together. That bastard always got better grades. Never could beat him."

"It sounds like you two were pretty close, Sir."

"Hell yes! Your dad and I were best buddies back in the day. We used to run the roads together. Stir up all kinds of shit, too!"

"My father never really talked much about the old days. He was always looking to the future. Always looking for that next promotion."

"You want to know what we called your dad at The Point?" asked Joshua; enthusiasm clearly returning to his face. He continued before Brad could answer. "The General. We were sure he would get a star first. I guess I showed him." Brad noticed the smile had left the Generals face. The years flowed back as fast as they had left.

Marsha caught the slight change in tone in her husband's voice and cut in the conversation.

"How does some lunch sound boys?" Brad could sense tension in *her* voice as well. He wondered just how much she knew of her husband's past; one of the variables he couldn't gauge.

"Sounds good, Marsha. I'll help." Joshua stood and crossed the room walking around an island to get to the kitchen. "What do we have?" he asked as he opened the refrigerator and rummaged through. Marsha rolled her eyes as she turned to help her husband.

"Move over. You don't even know what you're looking for." She pushed Joshua out of the way. Brad thought that they made a cute couple: too bad. "What would you like Brad?"

Brad stood, "Anything is fine with me Mrs. Tanner." He turned and leaned on the opposite side of the island counter. When did you two meet?"

"Oh dear God," a smile appearing on her face, "We got married after Josh's first tour in Vietnam." She looked back at her husband who was now scouring through a cupboard for something. "We've been together ever since."

"Is that when you met?" Brad prodded.

"No, we dated some when he and your dad were at West Point. I just couldn't resist those uniforms!" She reached over and smacked her husband on the ass with the back of her hand. "The uniform still looks good at least." She giggled like a school girl.

"I don't hear you complaining old woman." Joshua countered as he pulled a bag of potato chips out of the cupboard.

"You knew each other at West Point? Did you know my mother?" Brad asked.

She was putting some turkey and swiss sandwiches together as she talked. "We met when the boys were seniors, I think. We didn't really get to know each other until years later." Her voice had grown a bit meek suddenly.

"Mrs. Tanner, I didn't know you knew my mother. My father never mentioned you." He stated flatly. "Were you stationed together in Germany before we got shipped back to the states?" he asked with enthusiasm. Marsha nodded indicating she had been stationed in Germany with his parents. "Hmm", murmured Brad. "This changes things a bit," he murmured. "Can you please excuse me for a moment? I need to get something from the car. I'll just be a minute", Brad said smiling as he turned for the front door, the dog at his heels. "You need to go out girl?" Her tail wagged at the words making Brad smile.

"You like our guard dog, son?" Joshua bellowed out as he laughed.

"She's great, Sir." He leaned down and patted the collie on her head. When he opened the door Brad felt a rush of hot air. The sun was high in the sky and the desert seemed to be on fire. He walked to the rental thinking "how can anyone get used to this heat?" He opened the rear hatch of the Explorer and grabbed a dark blue backpack, holding it firmly in his left hand. He reached up taking hold of the hatch and pulled it closed. Standing in the heat Brad stared out at the property; small beads of sweat formed on his forehead, and he held his right hand up over his brow squinting in the bright sun. As he lowered his hand his face had become as barren as the land surrounding him. All emotion had been wiped clear.

When Bradley entered the house the Tanners were just setting the sandwiches on the table. He walked to the kitchen table and set down the pack, opening its main zipper. He slid his hand in the bag keeping his eyes on them.

"You've been together a long time. That's nice." There was an eerie evenness to his voice.

"Twenty two years this August", Mrs. Tanner replied, smiling. She wrapped her arms around her husband's neck and kissed his cheek, never noticing the pistol Bradley had brandished from the backpack he'd retrieved; a Sig Sauer forty-five.

As a confused grimace crossed her mouth, Bradley silenced any forthcoming scream as he placed one well aimed shot in Marsha Tanners forehead. She died instantly, crumpling to the floor, a splay of blood exploding from the back of her head. General Tanner did not try to disarm Brad, but rather slumped over and held his dead wife in his arms, shock and confusion riddling his features. Tears welled in his eyes.

"Why?"

CHAPTER 31

Joshua Tanner awoke with a rush of confusion. He was sitting, his wrists restrained to a kitchen chair with gray duct tape. Bradley was perched on a bar stool across the room. He noticed the look of comprehension when the reality of the situation surged back into Joshua's mind.

"Why Brad? Why?" He started crying again craning his neck to find his dead wife.

"I put her in your bed, Sir" The sharpness in Bradley's voice indicated that it was said with respect.

"What the hell did she ever do to you? Why would you do that?" Joshua continued as tears ran down his face.

"I apologize for your loss, Sir. I honestly do. Your lovely wife was not intended to be involved in this. I didn't do my homework well enough, apparently; I didn't realize she knew my mother. She got caught in the cross-fire. Collateral damage isn't that what you call it in the military?" he mocked. "You however," he trailed before regaining his composure. "You know why I'm here. Don't you?" Bradley asked now squatting in front of the general, eye to eye.

"I don't know what you're saying boy!"

Bradley decided to push him a little.

"She didn't know the *real* you, did she?" He was stoking the fire a little, sensing the disparity. He was now in total control of Joshua. "My mother mentioned you in her diary a few times. She was confused of whom… or *what* I should say you really are" Bradley continued. "Good old dad called in a favor you owed him, didn't he, Sir? I'll bet good money Marsha," he said as he pointed the pistol toward the bedroom, "didn't know the real you. Did she?" Joshua shot him a disconcerted look as if saying *"you've got nothing on me."*

Bradley walked to the counter and opened his bag producing a single piece of paper. Walking back to Joshua he held it out at arm's length. "It's amazing what you can find when you're pointed in the right direction; as I was," he continued, "my mother had a difficult time pondering your reasoning. She knew you and my father were good friends but what you did was more than that. You exceeded your duty friendship requires, you crossed a line. The question that confounded my mother was 'why would you help him?' She was smart, though it took her some time to figure it out; to put all of the pieces of the puzzle together." Bradley took a couple of steps back and held the paper so the general could focus on it better. "Can you read this?" He snapped the paper away from the Generals face. "Don't bother Sir; let me read it for you. This is the official death certificate of a girl my mother once knew. A girl who took her own life, if you believe what you read. This is Kimberly Johnson's death certificate." Shock plagued Joshua's face once again. "Long time ago, huh General. Or should I call you Cadet? That's what you were when she died. Correct?" Bradley didn't wait for a response starting in so quickly the general hadn't a chance to reply. "This is the *chip* you owed my father", Bradley stated. "You killed her. My mother wrote all about what she saw that night she and my father walked in on the two of you; kinky for those times. I did a little research on this. Asphyxiphilia was just becoming vogue around that time in the United States. Oh sure, it'd been around for a long time but it was really a guy thing. Please stop me if I stray, Cadet Tanner." Bradley continued smiling. "But this was nearly unheard of at that time. A woman? I'm sure the authorities didn't even think of it when they ruled her death an accidental drowning." Bradley paced back and forth in front of Joshua with his hands firmly grasped behind his back. He stopped suddenly with his back to Joshua.

"You see, my mother's diary told of how you were my father's commander in Germany; when we *mysteriously* received orders to the states: shipped off to an Army Post that didn't have any need for linguistic specialists. Fort Drum, New York. The closest thing they would need is a French-Canadian interpreter, eh?" Bradley smiled. "No, my mother was right; you had something to do with Kimberly Johnson's death, something kinky and no less, perverted." He turned toward

Joshua tapping the now rolled paper on the man's diaphoretic forehead. "She also indicated that she silently questioned it as an accident. She felt my father had swept it under the carpet and covered it up for you. I obtained the files on the case. All I had to do was fill out a Freedom of Information Act form. The police contacted you afterward. Even took a statement from you. But you had a good alibi, plus there was nothing that pointed to foul play. My father took care of that; covered your tracks well. He was your best friend, right?" Bradley pushed. The general tried in vain to conceal any emotion. "What would dear Marsha think of you? You killed a young woman in the prime of her life. Mistake or not…it happened!" Bradley boomed as if preaching from a pulpit.

The tears had dried on the Generals face. He sat taking it all in with little emotion, stoic even. This was a man who'd commanded soldiers during the height of the cold war. His station was on the front lines, he was no push over.

"All this means nothing however General. I'm not here because of poor Kimberly, however improper your actions that night. Bradley squared his frame with that of his foe's, bending at the waist. I'm here because my mother asked me to kill you" Bradley said bluntly. At that, Joshua looked into Bradley's eyes for the first time since this interrogation started.

"Me? Why would she want you to kill me? I never touched her!" he replied.

"You played an integral part in my father's saga. You helped set her up; in essence you helped lock her away." Bradley paused to maintain his composure. "You were directly involved. You owed him in a big way; in a way that would have ended your career, could have sent you to jail. He gave you your life back. The only thing I haven't been able to conclude is what evidence he actually had on you. He must have had something that placed you at the scene, something that would incriminate you." Bradley trailed off in thought. He needed more information for the final showdown in this saga. He needed to get what he came here for, evidence.

Bradley walked to the front door, needing fresh air. He had to remain in control of the situation. "Do not let the General control the situation", he thought. Things had already not gone as planned today. Killing Marsha took him by surprise. "God damned variable!" he thought. Bradley stared out the door in quiet respite. It was still hot outside as the sun waned, falling westward. He decided he needed to pick up his pace; wanting to get back on the road by dusk. After a few moments he walked back to where General Tanner was being held captive.

"Don't go anywhere, Sir. I'll be back in a few minutes." He smiled, leaving Joshua to himself.

The dog came running up to Bradley as he crossed the distance to a flower bed he'd noticed as he was pulling up the drive. She playfully barked wanting to play with her new friend. He stopped and bent over petting her briskly behind the ears.

"You wanna play, girl?" He searched the area and found a small branch lying on the ground picking it up to wave in front of the dog. Smiling, he threw it as far as he could into the desert. She bolted after her prey with enthusiasm. Bradley continued along his original path while the collie fetched the branch. The two continued their game until Bradley arrived at the flower garden. He stood, staring at its centerpiece while the dog barked and nosed the branch toward his foot. Bradley squatted and rubbed her chin.

"Good girl, good girl. We'll play some more later, I promise." Bradley stood, stepping into the flower bed to fetch the item he'd come for.

General Tanner sat in the center of the kitchen where Bradley had secured him earlier. He'd tried to wriggle himself free but was also hesitant, not knowing when his captor would reappear. His ankles were securely duct taped to the legs of the chair. His wrists were secured as well with the grey restraint. The shirt sleeve on his left arm had been cut off above the elbow, exposing his tan skin. He looked around the house helplessly, not able to think of a way out of his situation. He noticed the shadows from the retreating sun were lengthening. Straining to look over his right shoulder, he noted it was six fifteen on the oven clock. He had heard his dog barking down the driveway, but also thought he heard what he took to be the back hatch of the Explorer slam shut; then silence, broken only by an occasional bark from his dog. It would be dark in a couple of hours, if he only knew the horrors to come.

Bradley stepped into the house wiping his feet out of habit. He looked at Joshua Tanner with a blank stare. He seemed different to the General, colder in some way. More focused, but withdrawn. Joshua noticed his heart beating faster suddenly, seeing Bradley concealing an object in his right hand, obscured by shadows. Walking over to his captive, Bradley held out his hand revealing a syringe with a needle attached. General Tanner looked up into Brad's eyes, man to man.

"You think you can get me to tell you whatever the hell it is you want with *that*?" he scoffed, hatred now in his eyes.

"No Sir. I wouldn't dare think that little of you. I know you won't tell me what it is I need to know; at least not with a drug. No, this is to put you to sleep for a while." Bradley concluded as he knelt; all the time holding the General's stare. This is going to help me get you from point A to point B." As he said this last statement he plunged the needle into a large vein protruding from Joshua's forearm. The general's curses vacillated between a bark, then a slur, then finally nothing. He slumped forward in the chair; chin drooping toward his chest. His breathing slowed a bit but this was wholly expected by Bradley. "Time to get some answers Joshua."

CHAPTER 32

Bradley carefully cut away the duct tape and the general slumped deeper into the chair. Cutting the bindings from his ankles Bradley held him in the chair with one hand; he then hoisted the General from the chair, carrying him in a fireman's hold. He walked out of the house and turned toward the barn, the dog at his heels, of course.

General Tanner was heavy for his size, solid for his age, Bradley thought. He hoped the dose of Versed, a powerful sedative, was going to be enough. He needed about fifteen minutes before the General awoke from his drug- induced slumber. He had retrieved all the essential material from the Explorer prior to injecting the General. Everything was laid out precisely just outside the front door of the barn.

Bradley laid the General down on his back with a small thud. "Too heavy to do it nicely," he thought, smiling. There was no response from Joshua. He gathered a pouch he'd placed earlier that held all the essential tools and equipment he'd need for the task at hand. Positioning the General with his arms and legs extended in a position like that of Leonardo Di Vinci's *Vitruvian Man,* Bradley pounded four metal stakes in the ground about two feet beyond each of the man's limbs. The stakes were hand made of thick, black steel and were constructed with a loop at one end and a sharp point at the other and measured eighteen inches in length. He pounded each into the caliche with a sledge hammer he'd fetched from the barn. After he assured each stake was properly embedded in the hard ground he fed a one inch leather strap through each loop. Each strap possessed a clasp on one end similar to a belt with holes punched at intervals of one inch and a shackle at the other with another clasp and sturdy Velcro fasteners.

Bradley placed the Generals wrists and ankles into the shackles then began pulling his extremities taut latching the clasp of each as he went, in a circle. The sun was fading quickly and he knew time was at a premium. He hastened his pace. Joshua awoke slowly, groggy from the drugs. He was no longer sitting in a chair but rather on his back looking up at the evening sky. It was still light but some of the brighter stars were beginning to shine through the cloudless sky. He tried to move but realized he was being held down by something.

"What the fuck?" The old man winced against the setting sun to get a better look of Bradley, who hastily tied off a rope through something that lay on the ground at his feet. He tried pulling at his restraints again, trying to free himself. No such luck.

"Don't waste your energy, Sir. You'll need it." Bradley responded.

"What are you going to do to me?"

Bradley finished tying off the knot in the stout rope then walked over to where the General was being held.

"Earlier I told you two things, Sir, do you remember? The first being, that I *will* get the information out of you that I need. The second, that you *are* going to die." he finished as he grabbed one of the restraints tethering the General to the ground.

"In mid-evil times this was a popular method used by the church for a couple of reasons; the first, and most important, to gain knowledge from the accused. Whatever knowledge it was they sought. The second, to show the people what the church was capable of doing, just how far they were willing to go to get what they needed. Mostly, the church wanted people to accept God, and this was a particularly effective method of winning that acceptance. Sometimes however, they would use this method to gain other information", he continued.

"Remember General, those were times the church had the last say on just about everything. They devised this method as a way of torturing their victim but, not to kill him, *or her*; whatever the case may have been. They named this method appropriately, '*The Wheel*'.

Joshua fought to absorb what Bradley said and began to panic. He looked around the immediate area, but there was nothing except the four shackles holding him down. He craned his neck pushing his worsening arthritis to its limit, seeing it at once. His heart pounded. His breathing became rapid. He screamed at Bradley.

"You little piss ant! What the hell are you going to do to me?"

Standing motionless, Bradley stoically gazed at his victim. He walked toward the barn leaving Joshua's line of sight. He returned carrying two small blocks of wood and a five pound sledge hammer. Bradley slid the two 4 X 4's under the General's right arm, placing one at the wrist and the other at the elbow. There was just enough slack to slide the block underneath the arm with the restraints in place.

"You see Sir, this method of torture, and torture is what it truly is, to cause terrible pain, all the while rendering non-lethal wounds. The difficult part is to weave the victims' extremities through the narrow spokes of the wheel. To do this they had to make the long bones more...", he paused looking for the correct word, *"pliable"*, he said as he raised the five pound sledge hammer above his head. Joshua's eyes widened as the reality of what was occurring flashed through his mind. As Joshua cursed Bradley swung down directly, striking between the two pieces of wood.

Joshua's curses exploded into screams as a deafening 'crack' shot through the air. Bradley moved the piece of wood from the wrist up securing it directly under the shoulder, all the while Joshua screamed in agony. The Generals face contorted in awkward angles as the horrific pain tore through is arm. His face turned a dusky red and veins on his forehead bulged as Joshua fought. Bradley repeated his actions creating two breaks in the arm; one below the elbow and one above. Each time there was an audible 'pop' as the bones broke in two. The legs were mangled in much the same way with breaks created between the shackled ankles and the knee and again mid-femur. Bradley miss-hit Joshua's right lower leg, grazing it, but tearing through the fleshy part. He had to take a second swing at the leg successfully snapping it in two. By this time Joshua was spewing frothy spittle from his mouth, blood trickling down his cheek from where he bit through his lower lip. Luckily neither femur break severed the femoral artery as this would have hastened the Generals death by exsanguination, bleeding to death.

General Tanner, floating somewhere between consciousness and unconsciousness, faintly heard Maggie barking somewhere in the distance. He occasionally cried out but for the most part was only able to muster the strength to watch as Bradley continued his work; one extremity at a time. Joshua's face was tight with pain, foam forming at the corners of his drying mouth. There was little blood; the skin tearing only from three of the breaks, which included Bradley's missed attempt. Having only read about this ingenious method of torture, Bradley found it quite simple, although highly effective.

The General lost consciousness a handful of times; but each time it was short lived.

"Tell me General, what did my father hold over your head to get your help? What evidence did he have that would incriminate you almost twenty years after you killed Miss Johnson." Joshua wept softly, tears and blood pooling in his ears. He felt little physical pain now; it was becoming a fleeting memory. He only felt his life fading into the coming night. "If you repent your sins, you may be able to save your soul", Bradley continued in a taunting manner.

General Tanner hadn't realized he was not shackled anymore. Feeling came and went like a tide. He heard Bradley dragging the wheel closer as the sunlight dipped behind the distant mountains displaying their familiar red and orange hues. Joshua muttered, almost inaudibly.

"The bag." A rattled and bloodied cough sent shards of pain through his body.

"Tell me… what bag, Sir?" Joshua faded out but roused quickly when he remotely felt his arm being interlaced between the spokes of the wheel.

"Tell me Cadet Tanner, what happened that night." Bradley said, more as a statement than a question. By the time he had completed his work Bradley had been given the inviolated story of the happenings of Kimberly Johnson's final night. At last Bradley knew how his father skillfully recruited

General Tanner to abet in his scheme to discard his mother. He dragged the wheel, now laden with General Tanners' nearly lifeless body closer to the barns red doors, now glowing in the brilliance of nothing less than what could be described as a majestic sunset.

Above, a gantry held the stout rope neatly fed through an old rusting pulley; both ends methodically coiled at Bradley's feet. Its normal use was to hoist bales of hay for storage, although tonight's use would differ. Bradley Fordam was setting a venue to show off his latest trophy. He pulled the wheel upward with some difficulty, inching toward the pulley. Joshua was conscious, but unaware of any happenings.

"The living dead", Bradley thought aloud, Joshua's mangled body lay intertwined within the wheels spokes. It was a horrific sight.

As he tied off the stout rope to a ring fastened to the barns outer wall Joshua swayed lazily in the gentle evening breeze, occasionally bumping into the barn. The soft creaking of the gantry was barely audible from Bradley's vantage point. He looked upward in fascination.

"It looks good General. Looks like the real thing."

Soon after, Brad opened the corral doors freeing the Tanners horses to escape then collected the dog from the barn where he had placed her earlier before breaking the *unbreakable* General. Nose to the ground and tail wagging she sniffed searching for her owner, but found nothing. The sight was grotesque for even the strongest person to witness. General tanner was unrecognizable as he hung in mid-air entwined in his spiral grave. Barely awake, he was able to mutter one sentence before cascading into unconsciousness.

"It was a mistake Wes." Then silence.

Brad looked up at the General perched ten feet above him and calmly replied, "I believe you Josh. " Brad retrieved everything he'd brought to the *Lazy J* ranch. He quickly cleaned the scene inside wiping down the pistol he'd used to murder Marsha Tanner, leaving it on the kitchen counter along with Kimberly Johnson's Death Certificate. The gun was untraceable and served no further use and the Death Certificate would have the authorities chasing their tails. He grabbed a half full plastic container of dog food and left the house just as he'd found it, the only difference being the final disposition of the owners. His duty for the time being, complete. He opened the back door of the Explorer and threw his belongings in, along with the hammer he'd used on the stakes, which he'd left in the ground. He walked around the driver's side door and opened it; calling the dog to come. She obeyed and the two left the property together; a man and his new best friend. Together they turned left onto the highway and headed for Albuquerque. By noon the next day Brad had acquired the proper passes for his new friend, he'd named Maggie, to travel home with him and they took off for the east coast. Roughly by the same time, the crows had found Joshua Tanner and had begun tearing him apart one bite at a time; his remaining life being torn with each bite.

PART VI

MAGGIE

CHAPTER 33

It began so innocently. "Isn't that what they all say?" she thought. She'd been waiting fifteen minutes before he showed, running into the pub dodging rain drops. He was in full dress uniform with a trench coat that he slipped off quickly as he walked to the bar where she sat.

"Sorry I'm late. Meetings went longer than expected." He simply stated. She took her eyes off him for a split second to find the straw in her drink and took a pull. He sensed something was amiss. "Is there something I'm not getting here, Maggie?" She hesitated looking up from her cocktail, then returned his gaze.

"No, everything is okay", she lied. "Let's get a table and have a bite to eat." She stood without waiting for a reaction from her suitor and walked to the back of the pub easily finding an empty table. They sat opposite each other.

The pub was small and isolated from the post and they'd frequently met over the last few months. These meetings usually ended with a few hours at a nearby motel. She stared at her companion.

"Wesley, I found out about your wife." Simple, to the point, and effective just as she had rehearsed.

Wesley had been dreading this moment. He'd drilled his canned response countless times in his mind but nevertheless felt a sting of what he thought might be pain, regret, or remorse? He wasn't sure. It was meaningless however, this scene was inevitable. He knew Maggie would eventually find out. They worked at the same post for close to a year now. He and Patricia were rarely seen together in public but it was eventually going to come out. He took a deep breath and grabbed her attention with his dazzling blue eyes. *'Dreamy'*, Maggie had once said.

"Maggie, I'm sorry I didn't tell you about her yet. I had to be sure about us, I'm sorry." With just a hint of a smile, Wesley's face transformed from one of repentance to one of relief. "At least I know about us now." he smiled again.

Major Margaret Drewer, MD hesitated before speaking. She was an intelligent person and she was moving along well in her career with the Army. She reached across the table taking his hand in hers, looking him straight in the eye; testing him. She searched for any sign of deceit; any wavering in his eyes, in his tone.

"I need to know something Wesley." She paused for effect "Are you in love with me? Will you leave her for me?" her face was stone; showing no emotion and calculating his response. Wesley had anticipated this moment. He'd known that this would be one of the toughest tests of his fortitude in this whole ordeal. He *had* to convince Maggie he was sincere, or the whole thing would unravel.

CHAPTER 34

Maggie worked at the Post Hospital on the Psychiatric unit. She was a staff Psychiatrist there for over a year now. She'd attained the rank of Major quickly while Wesley remained anchored to his Captain bars for too long now; he needed her help. He needed her to do something she would protest…unless she would benefit. Her role in the events ahead was vital. Wesley had already invested three months into this relationship; into this part of the plot. He needed to convince her, without doubt that he was sincere.

"Every time I look at you I'm more convinced this is right. Every time I look into your eyes I fall more in love with you." He paused looking at her hand in his. "You are the most incredible person I've met. I'm sorry I didn't tell you about her." he stopped, letting her respond. He knew she would become the aggressor now and he had to defend himself and his actions.

"Why would you do such a thing? Why would you knowingly not tell me you're married?" Maggie was having a difficult time controlling the level of her voice, but she controlled her tone well, showing she was distressed but not out of control. This is what she did for a living and Wesley knew it, but this was a test *he* had to pass.

"Look Maggie. It's been difficult for me to face this situation. My wife has not been herself for some time now. Patricia left this relationship a while ago. She keeps falling further into this depression and it has taken its toll on us. We keep circling down this path of destruction. And then I found you and saw there was still life to live. I used you to help myself" he stated bluntly hoping she took the bait. "I just happened to fall in love with you along the way." He ended looking down at their laced fingers.

"Look Wesley, I think I'm in love with you too but that doesn't change the way things are right now. Wesley, this is serious. Not only have you cheated on your wife, you deceived me! I don't want to know how many Army regulations we've broken. We could get into big trouble!" She emphasized.

She could overlook the deceit if she thought it truly was in earnest. She didn't know the details of Wesley's relationship with his wife yet; but she would. Maggie was a career Doctor. She did not want this affair to affect her standing in the Army. Unknowingly, she'd stumbled into the trap her suitor had so meticulously set. After Wesley ordered a beer and another Tom Collins for Maggie she let go of his hand.

"What's her name, your *wife*?" Wesley once again looked her in the eye and answered honestly.

"Patricia" he said lowering his head. Maggie took control of the conversation again; something Wesley knew she would do.

"Has she been diagnosed as depressive yet? Does she see anyone for this?" she pushed. "Just her regular doctor, I don't think she's been 'officially' diagnosed yet. She's also dealing with a drinking problem," Wesley said holding up his own beer for reference. She has been labeled as a binge drinker by her doctor. She goes to AA meetings a couple of times a week but that hasn't changed anything. I think with her, one thing feeds off the other." He looked into her eyes with resonant sadness.

"How long have you been married to her? Patricia? Do you have any children?" The questions came at him like bullets now. "Wesley, these are things you have to come clean on," she said sharply. "No more lies Wesley; no more deceit. You need to be completely honest with me right now."

Wesley smiled inwardly. This is where he wanted Maggie; feeling in control, taking command of the situation, helping a friend in need. He took the next half hour explaining everything to his lover. Where they'd met, about how her family ostracized her for marrying a military man, about their son Bradley who, it seemed, took no interest in his parents. He described in detail how Patricia started to change when they had moved overseas. At first it seemed to be an adventure but that feeling quickly dissolved into one of disparity. She longed to regain a dialog with her family. Wesley explained how they shunned her and refused to take calls soon after their marriage. How her Father was in control of the family and how she had grown up thinking of him as a great man; only to find out his pettiness actually ruled his thoughts and beliefs. Wesley told Maggie everything, most of it true, only having to cast a slightly different light on some issues, like how his wife started drinking because he was never home, how he placed his career above his family life. He put a spin on it to make it look like her drinking was what drove him away. How their son was avoiding home as much as possible. How he didn't know where his son went all the time, but he had the top grades in his class. Wesley explained to Maggie in detail everything that was happening at home.

"She needs professional help Wesley. Whether or not you and I stay together, you need to get her help." There was genuine concern in her words. "Her General Practitioner is not help, she needs to be evaluated by a Psychiatrist and steered toward healing, toward getting better." Maggie stopped; regaining her composure, unsure if she should continue with her next thought.

"Even if you do leave her Wesley, she needs help. You can't just leave her hanging. It almost sounds like she would benefit from being back in the states. It sounds like she didn't

know what she was getting herself into when she married you."
Wesley felt the plunge of the dagger of judgment with that last
statement. There was a part of him that knew he would be
hurting Patricia by following through with this plan. What he
didn't know was just how many people he would hurt by going
down this path.

Wesley and Maggie ended their night at the pub, not the
motel. He left promising her he would get Patricia in as soon as
possible at the outpatient clinic to be evaluated and get her the
right help. Maggie added that she would quietly pull some
strings and get her in right away. Wesley thought of the
exchange as a win, Maggie having accepted his apologies and
her offerings to get involved. He caught a Taxi back to the Post,
returning to the office; not wanting to return home to Patricia.
Why ruin his jovial mood?

CHAPTER 35

(Present Day)

It was a typical Monday morning for Maggie. She was running late for her first appointment of the day; which unfortunately meant no lunch. She frowned at the thought, as she entered her office through the side entrance, the one that her clients generally left through. Dr. Drewer had a full day ahead of her.

Her office was nicely appointed but in a simplistic manner. There were drapes on the windows but no blinds. The walls were a cream color but offset with dark paintings that seemed to explore the inner workings of the darker side of thought. Maggie's favorite painting was of a woman holding her head in her hands, long thin fingers pulling at her hair. She seemed to scream with her eyes. The office portrayed the hurt found inside each of us. She felt it was important to not sugar coat life but rather deal with it head on.

Sitting at her simple but modern desk she brought up her schedule on the computer and then checked her personal email out of habit. She had a simple rule; no email on the weekends. Finding nothing of great importance she looked at her schedule; three clients before lunch then a full afternoon. One thing did stand out on her schedule, however. One of her morning clients was new to her practice. She pulled out his thin file, reading through it quickly before meeting him face to face. "Always good to know your clients better than they do" she thought smiling.

She read aloud "Bradley Smyth", 'neat spelling she thought', "35 year old white male, dissociative disorder, abandonment by father at young age, exhibits rare but aggressive tendencies toward others." She replaced the folder and called in her first "regular", frowning when she realized it was Mrs. Carothers. Her heart went out to women who had been victims of spousal abuse. She peeked her head through the door into the waiting room and called her name.

"Ellen? Come in, will you?" And so began another typical Monday morning.

After navigating her way through her first two clients Maggie took five minutes to fetch cup of coffee from the Duncan Donut shop on the first floor of her building. She had recently retired from the Army as a full Colonel after twenty one years and had decided to move back to her hometown of Cleveland, Ohio. She opened a small office and started picking up patients from two colleagues that were readying for their own retirements, 'thinning their herds' as one of them put it. Dr. Margaret Drewer, MD was only 41 years old with a military pension and a good fifteen years of practice ahead of her before she would start to think about her own retirement. She savored her coffee as she stepped into the elevator with the only other person in the lobby. The man punched '3', and turned to her.

"Where are you headed?"

She looked at the board and noticed what floor he had punched. The man smiled and asked politely once again when there was no answer. Maggie smiled.

"You've got it. Three," she said smiling politely in return. The lobby was much cooler than her office and she rolled the coffee in her hands, embracing its' warmth.

The third floor of her building had four offices. One was Binder & Sheffield, LLC, a corporate law firm. Another was the main office of Sherman Cleaning Associates, headquarters of a commercial cleaning service. The other two were her office and one that had been vacant for close to six months. She surveyed the young man in the elevator and surmised that this was her eleven o'clock appointment: her new client.

"Are you Brad?" she asked, directly. The man turned to her and smiled.

"Actually, I am. And you must be Dr. Drewer?" She nodded in the affirmative and held out her right hand while seizing the coffee in her left. Brad returned the gesture, noticing the scribbling on her cup of coffee.

"French Vanilla, two sugars."

Maggie shot him a perplexed look before examining the cup. She had never really been able to decipher the lettering before. It had always amused her.

"Very good, I'm impressed. I've never been able to read this cryptic writing before today" she said smiling.

"Don't think too much of me yet. I worked for Duncan Donuts while I got my master's degree." Brad said, smiling.

Maggie thought she was going to like this young man as the doors opened to the third floor. She indicated for him to proceed before her and he did.

"The front door is the second on the right" she indicated with her cupped hand. "I've got to see to a couple of things before I call you in."

"Take as long as you need Doctor; enjoy your coffee first. I can wait a few extra minutes." Now Maggie knew she was going to like this guy.

"Thanks. I'll just be a few minutes" and with that she turned down the other corridor that led to her side door. Five minutes later Brad sat uncomfortably in front of her desk.

"So Bradley, what brings you here today?" Dr. Drewer started off. She noticed his stature had changed slightly since their meeting in the elevator. He seemed more rigid, fidgety, weaving his hands together. She smiled, "It's okay Bradley, I'm the same person you met in the elevator. It's safe to talk with me." She left it at that and waited to see if he would take over the conversation.

"Please, call me Brad. Only my parents called me Bradley." There was a short pause, then he started "Well, I've been having 'feelings' lately. It doesn't happen very often, but I find myself ... I don't know how you'd put it; "*acting out*" I guess. It's always been directed toward men; nothing violent, nothing like that. I think of myself as a nice guy. Real easy to get along with, but once in a while I go into a mental rage of sorts. It's happened three times so far. I didn't get the connection at first, but after the last incident, about three weeks ago I'd realized there seems to be a common thread to it all. Each person I "*blew up*" at all happened to be men. They were all about forty five to fifty years old, and they, in retrospect somehow remind me of my father."

The session lasted an hour and was a very productive first meeting, a little more in depth than the usual 'meet and greet' she was used to. Maggie was convinced that these tendencies Brad had exhibited seemed to be derived from the apparent abandonment by his father. Brad had told her that although he has not seen his father in over thirteen years, he still has a face created in his mind. All three victims of his recent outbursts looked relatively the same: how Brad pictured his father in his mind. Maggie felt she could help him through this problem; always a feeling of victory in a field rarely privy to such advances.

Psychiatry can be a very difficult field to practice. You generally have to distance yourself from your patients as to not bring home *their* baggage; but every once in a while you feel like you can make a difference, a *real* difference in someone's life. This always puts a little pep in one's step. They ended the session having made an appointment for the following Monday. Brad asked for the slot before this first meeting, ten o'clock next Monday citing a conflict with a prior appointment.

CHAPTER 36

Brad decided he liked his newest adversary, Dr.
Margaret Drewer. Maggie. He'd read all about the torrid
relationship she shared with his father. It lasted close to a year
before it was abruptly ended by Brad's father just after "Dr.
Maggie" was coerced into committing his mother into St.
Lawrence Psychiatric Center in Northern New York, Brad was
eleven years old. His mother's diary did not have much in the
way of particulars delineating why Dr. Drewer had been forced
into doing something she would typically have been against. He
believed this, finally having met her after all these years. He
could see why his father would have chosen her. Maggie was a
beautiful woman. Yet, there was something grating at Brad
since he left her office. He couldn't quite put his finger on it
though. He pondered its roots as he left the office building,
stopping in the lobby for a cup of coffee.

This woman was partly responsible for what happened to
his mother: having been subjugated for six years in the hospital.
People had to pay. They had to be held up to the penetrating
sword of justice. Brad had long ago decided that this would not
be a problem for him, he knew his capabilities. He also knew
that what happened had been unfair to his mother and that his
actions, however grotesque were justified: they stole her life.
"And for what?" he thought. Each had a reason different than

that of the others. Each sold their soul to the devil *per se* and had to be held responsible for their actions; but this one was different. Maggie was set up from the beginning, at least according to his mother's diary. Brad's father had used Dr. Drewer for the sole purpose of gaining something for himself. She had been duped, yet she still had a choice. One she'd made on her own accord. She could have chosen honesty and paid the price. That price being a probable demotion, an Article 12, but nothing more than that. She would still be a doctor. She would still be able to practice her trade. The choice Maggie made affected his mother and resulted in her ultimate death. Maggie Drewer made that choice and it would lead to *her* own demise.

For some reason this was difficult for Brad. He had decided to meet Maggie before killing her. He wanted to know what type of person would make his father cheat. He had to know *her*. And now that he did, he felt differently about what route to take to end her life. He'd made a promise to his dead mother that those responsible would pay. He would take from them precisely what they'd taken from her so long ago: *life*.

Reading his mother's diary was to say the least a difficult task for Brad. He'd delved into it while flying back to Europe those many years ago. He found it impossible to lay the book down once he had started reading her words, her thoughts. The diary itself was quite extensive. Being locked up in a mental hospital for six years can lead to many thoughts. Some the paranoid ramblings of a woman backed against the ropes, but most coherent. As he read through the pages he found it written in chronological order; normal for a personal diary. Her writings began with feelings of despair, leading to feelings of loneliness and abandonment. His mother's final passages were of retribution. It had taken six years for Brad's mother to go from victim to wanting to victimize. He read the diary from front to back during his flight from Syracuse to JFK; then on to London.

Brad had to gain an understanding of his mother's state of mind when she'd penned her thoughts. The problem was that being in a mental institution, even if you're sane, as Patricia was, leads one to develop tendencies that disregard sane thoughts and disassociates one's self from reality, making it difficult for Brad to untangle his mother's thoughts throughout the diary. Patricia vacillated between reality and incoherent thought. He found himself having to decipher his mother's writings as if they were a language unto themselves.

While spending a week in Cleveland, Brad found himself re-reading the diary; especially the parts that included anything involving Dr. Maggie. He needed to clarify for himself what damage she had caused his mother, other than the obvious; being one of two doctors that involuntarily admitted her to St. Lawrence Psychiatric Center for the rest of her life. Brad needed to unearth a befitting death for Maggie. He'd read his mothers' diary many times since acquiring it from her acquaintance at Saint Lawrence Psychiatric Center so many years ago. It was worn and Tattered when he'd first received it, and now nearly fifteen years later, it was truly in dire condition.

He'd underlined and circled in red things and names that stood out. He'd decoded the "language" that she'd taken on while hospitalized. This led him to a thought; "How do doctors know when to believe what the patient is saying? How do *they* decipher the truth from ramblings?" Grimacing, he continued to read the diary while at the same time trying to think like a doctor in the Psychiatric field. He felt getting into the mind of another was not only difficult, but could prove perilous. One slip up, one miscalculation, or misunderstanding could have lifelong, or *life-ending* ramifications.

Brad set the book on his bedside table in his hotel room and closed his eyes. He tried to picture his mother in session with Dr. Maggie. From what he'd learned earlier in the week, he believed Maggie was a decent person who truly wanted to help people work out their problems. From Brad's memories of his mother he attributed her depression and feeling of despondence to the fact that she was an American on foreign soil with a husband that neglected her. She never fit in overseas, having been pulled out of her niche in life that was constructed carefully by her father; and then thrown headfirst into a life of constant moving, overwhelming change then finally isolation. Of course she became depressive. It would have been a normal response to such a situation, but not so overwhelming that she would have to be institutionalized.

Throughout her writings, Brad's mother referred to Dr. Maggie as being a major player in her eventual permanent admittance, however she also referred to Dr. Maggie as the only doctor that thought *short term* hospitalization could mend her depression and binge drinking. This did happen many times while in England, his mother would have one of her *'episodes'* as his father used to call them and be placed in a hospital for observation for a few days. Just enough time to correct any medication issues and detoxify her. In his mother's early writings she had referred to Dr. Maggie as "one of the good guys". But as his reading progressed he understood that his mother had only surmised as much. Maggie played a decisive role in Patricia's being locked away for good. Brad had a hard time thinking that the woman he'd met a few days ago played such a pivotal role in this conspiracy. "How could a doctor such as Maggie go against better judgment and ethics, locking away a person who could have been helped?"

The hour was late and he'd re-read enough for tonight. Brad called home and spoke to his child who had believed it was time to move on and get another dog. About six weeks before this trip, their family pet, a yellow lab named Winnie was killed by a car. This devastated the kids and the mere mention of getting another pet was traumatic.

"Daddy, I've decided that I think it's time to get another dog. I miss Winnie but she would understand," his daughter Lilly had stated. A smile crossed his tired face.

"Well if you think you're ready then when I come home next week we'll talk some more, okay?" he replied to his precocious three year old daughter. He'd tried to explain that out of respect for Winnie they would not be getting another pet for a while. Lilly's answer to that was "Well, mommy's a dog doctor and she can bring one home from work". At that Brad had to laugh, the mind of a three year old. After speaking with Lilly he'd asked to speak to mommy again.

Brad asked his wife for a favor: to overnight a package in the morning to his hotel. She agreed and said that as always, she missed him. He expressed his emptiness without her and called it a night, falling asleep with the open diary on his lap.

Monday came and Brad awoke with mixed feelings. He'd clearly respect his mother's request but having spent time with Maggie he'd come to like her, creating some frustration within the inner workings of his mind. He'd received the package from home on Saturday leaving plenty of time to prepare for the events planned. "This would be a difficult day," he thought. Not a great motivation to get out of bed, which he did reluctantly.

174

Brad arrived at Dr. Maggie's building a few minutes ahead of his scheduled session, walked through the main lobby doors on the first floor and migrated toward the coffee shop. It was raining lightly with dense gray clouds; making everyone in Cleveland more miserable than usual. He shook off the rain, ordered two coffees, and moved to the section of counter that housed the straws, napkins and whatnot. There were only a handful of patrons in the shop, so no one saw him pour the clear liquid into Maggie's cup, stir it then replace the lid. After picking up the backpack he'd set on the floor between his feet he was off to the central bank of elevators; entering the first one that had arrived.

Dr. Drewer wore a welcoming smile when she greeted him in the reception room.

"Good morning Brad," she said and placed her hand out in greeting only to find a cup of coffee being handed to her. She smiled.

"What's this?" she said in a pleasantly surprised voice.

"You're morning Joe," replied Brad with a grin. "Thought I'd get this session off on the right foot; a small bribe for my doctor so she'll take it easy on me today," he concluded with a handsome smile and a slight chuckle. Brad thought to himself that he'd probably have done the same thing if this were a normal session with a shrink; a fruitless attempt at being let off the preverbal hook. But this would be far from a normal session. Not even close.

"Thanks a lot Brad," Maggie said as she ushered him into her inner sanctum. She was sincerely pleased knowing this would save her a trip down to the coffee shop after her session.

"Don't give it a second thought Doc, but don't expect this treatment every week." Brad flashed another smile; this one was honest and without adoration.

"Well, have a seat Brad and we'll pick up where we left off last week". Brad sat in a comfortable oversized brown leather chair, crossing his legs and sipping his own coffee. He took the initiative.

"I'd like to start off by saying you make me feel very relaxed, making this whole ordeal much more pleasant, Doctor." Maggie smiled nodding her head in appreciation while thoroughly enjoying her hot beverage. "Maybe this will turn out to be a good day," she thought. And so began their second session.

Maggie started feeling tired about half an hour into the session, Brad had been speaking of his father when she became cognizant that something was terribly wrong. Her desk, Brad's voice, everything around her was fading in and out. Unsure of what was happening to her she knew that she was still in her chair behind her desk. Suddenly she was wondering why her patient was standing over her with his hands on her armrests. She surveyed Bradley from behind disengaged eyes. He looked at her like some kind of predator.

"You are feeling the effects of a drug called Ketamine Doctor Drewer. Maggie. Maybe you've heard of it, although it's actually a horse tranquilizer. It has however made it to the streets as a date rape drug; known as *Special K*". She was hearing everything that Bradley was saying but it had no real effect on her. She felt detached from what she surmised was reality.

"Maggie, I need you to tell me the truth, okay?" She nodded not saying a word; her head foggy. "You and my father had an affair while the two of you were stationed in England. This much I know is the truth. What I'm about to ask you is much more important" he continued. Maggie's mind began to wander as she sat slumped in her chair; feeling the full effects of the Ketamine now.

Brad supposed he may have inadvertently overdosed his victim. He was forced out of convenience, to use an intravenous form of the drug; supplied by his wife. She advised him that dosing for effect could be difficult when administering orally. In other words, he'd been forced to make an educated guess as to how much drug needed to be placed in Maggie's coffee.

Bradley gently tapped her cheek, then a second time a bit harder.

"Are you still with me Maggie? I need you to focus for me Doctor." The words were delivered with little to no emotion, his eyes transfixed on hers. He proceeded with his questioning.

"Why did you help him lock my mother away? You knew she wasn't crazy. She could have been helped. And she believed you knew that." By now Maggie was in a state of mind that caused her to want to please her captor.

Ketamine is a strong tranquilizer used by veterinarians, typically on horses, however it tended to cause mild hallucinations in humans often giving them a euphoric feeling. It had a place on the street as well; known as Special K. Brad could have found it easily if he wanted to, however but Linda agreed to help him and had a stock of the medication in her office.

Maggie shook her head in the affirmative and spoke in a low, garbled voice.

"I....I didn't know, Wesley wanted so much from me." Maggie began to feel a little more in touch with her environment. Bradley's questioning and soft slap cleared her head a bit. She continued feeling "disconnected" from herself but was able to focus better. "Maybe it's starting to wear off!" she thought. She began to speak; slowly at first, eventually reaching about half normal speed.

"I never would have slept with him if I knew..." She sobbed. Her head felt heavy as the room spun in circles. Bradley knew time was of the essence. The Ketamine he fed the doctor would last about an hour though everyone reacts differently to the medication. He needed a confession soon.

"Focus on my words Maggie" he was speaking slowly but louder than before. "Why would you do such a thing? Lock up someone like my mother. Do you know that she killed herself knowing she would never be released? How does that make you feel?" he howled, finally showing emotion.

Tears trickled down Maggie's cheeks which were noticeably reddened.

"I'm so sorry Patricia. Wesley, he made me do it. He said he would end my career if I didn't." she wept. I'm so sorry." Her words slurred even more as the drug took its full effect.

Bradley was satisfied. He'd retrieved what he'd come for; acknowledgement of her participation, but more importantly, that his father had coerced her into helping him by essentially threatening her future in the Army. This was his father's doing. Maggie was just another pawn in his game. The time had come however to end this chapter. To yet again make good on his promise to his dead mother. Maggie hardly felt the small bore needle break the skin and enter the brachial vein in her left arm. As Bradley depressed the plunger of the syringe,

Maggie's eyes widened with fear then froze in place within seconds.

"This is two hundred milligrams of Succicholine doctor," Bradley stated, showing her the syringe without emotion. Maggie's breathing quickened with his statement, then just as suddenly ceased altogether.

"It'll be over soon Maggie." Bradley continued, now holding Maggie's limp body in the chair. Her neck extended, he never took his eyes off hers; out of pity or concern he couldn't be sure. He did, however find her impending death intriguing.

"You'll be asleep soon my friend. Your part of the debt repaid." Maggie understood with horrible clarity that Bradley had given her a muscular blockade agent; paralyzing every skeletal muscle in her body, most importantly her diaphragm; the muscle used to expand the lungs, letting in precious air. Conscious thought was all she could control as the paralytics took effect and the Ketamine continued to wear off; her mind scrambled, unable to breathe or even blink. Maggie's final moments were spent staring into Bradley's cold, lifeless, eyes. Then as darkness swept over her like a shroud; she was gone.

PART VII

DR. MILES DUVAL

CHAPTER 37

The weather had taken a turn for the worse, Brad thought. The Grindstone Island ferry tussled with strong cross winds as dark clouds rolled in from the west, threatening a good soaking for anyone brave enough to stay on deck. The crowd thinned quickly, leaving Brad with just a handful of the hardier passengers and himself. Brad was thankful for the windbreaker he'd grabbed at the last minute before departing the Bed and Breakfast this morning. He quietly praised Mrs. Riley, the owner and operator of the establishment for giving him a heads up on the possibility of thunderstorms for the day.

Brad had driven up from Connecticut two days ago taking room at Riley's Bed and Breakfast in Clayton, New York. The B and B was bought by the Riley's ten years prior and had been renovated from top to bottom by Mr. Riley himself. The two had come to the Thousand Island area after Mr. Riley retired as a maintenance man for a large apartment complex in Philly. They had visited to the area as tourists every year for close to twenty years and had decided to run the Bed and Breakfast to help make ends meet while living in the house.

The house itself was located on Goose Bay off of route 12 a few miles north of the village of Alexandria Bay. The Thousand Island Park was located on the northern fringes of New York State, bordering Canada. Mainly a summer tourist destination; there were plenty of activities to participate in during all four seasons. Boating, fishing, and golfing. You name it and you can probably find it in the near area as far as summer activities.

It was now late August and the summer season was winding down with fewer and fewer tourists cluttering the streets. Brad had made reservations with the Riley's a couple of months prior and found no trouble in finding accommodations for this late in the season. The temperatures had been dropping the last week and there was the slightest hint of fall in the air. Brad had noticed that a few trees were already turning to the rich and beautiful colors of autumn.

He and the other passengers finally succumbed, leaving the open deck of the boat for the comfort of the enclosed area of the ship. He felt oddly uncomfortable being in such close proximity to the other passengers, noting one was particularly too close for comfort. Brad pushed, albeit slowly, through the crowd to the back of the small enclosed cabin. He had made this trip three times now and started to recognize some familiar faces of the local residents. The ferry closed in on its destination agonizingly slowly in the harsh conditions, the boat bumping the pier a couple of times before finally coming to a stop. The winds still rocked the large vessel while the mooring lines were secured but not nearly as badly as on the open water. The Captain announced their arrival and that foot passengers could begin departing at that point. Most of the passengers shuffled along the wet decking to their respective vehicles to await their departure as well. Brad sat in his car patiently waiting his turn to pull off the dock: three cars behind a blue Cadillac, the driver of the Cadillac remaining unaware of his presence. After all, there wasn't much that stood out when it came to Brad. He had come to the conclusion that he was pretty average in appearance. A trait that was very helpful at times like this.

The Cadillac roared off as soon as the tires hit the dirt road. Brad let the blue car pull ahead, staying a safe distance behind his mark. He knew where the car would end up anyway, having followed the Doctor home three times now. Brad was learning his ways, his habits. Dusk was quickly approaching as the cars departed the dock one by one moving to their ultimate destinations. Brad turned his headlights on and followed Dr. Duval, listening to soft jazz to help shorten the five mile drive to the doctors' summer home on Grindstone Island.

CHAPTER 38

The phone rang unanswered. Major Margaret Drewer, MD tapped her fingers on her desk impatiently as she let the phone ring a few more times before returning the phone to its cradle. She called out to her secretary in the next room to come in to her office.

"Jenna, can you try to get through to St. Lawrence Psych Center for me. I'm trying to get a hold of Dr. Duval. He's not in his office", she asked with pleading eyes. "It's kind of important," she concluded.

"Sure thing Major, I'll put him through when I get him on the line", Jenna replied turning on her heel and departing the office.

Maggie sat in her chair staring at an old vase that held fresh flowers. She retreated to the past in deep thought, going back to a time when there was little else besides her career and life seemed simpler; a time before she'd met Wesley. She'd cursed herself a thousand times for putting herself in this predicament. "*Asshole*", she whispered.

The ringing phone jolted her out of her stupor, making her heart skip a beat. She answered after getting her thoughts together.

"Yes?" she asked.

"Ma'am, I've got Dr. Duval on the line. Hang up and I'll put him through", Jenna replied.

"Thanks", Maggie simply replied hanging up the phone. Jenna transferred the call thinking that her boss had been acting strange lately.

"Major Drewer" Maggie said in a professional tone.

"Maggie! How in the hell are you?" barked a jovial voice on the other end of the line.

"Hello Miles. How have you been?" Maggie asked in a friendly voice.

She and Miles met in Medical school and had kept in touch professionally ever since. After Miles lost his wife to breast cancer two years ago the calls seemed to get spread out farther and farther. Maggie had gone to the funeral and had been there as a friend but Miles seemed to introvert his feelings and isolate himself from many of his friends and colleagues. It was good to hear his voice though.

"Miles, can I take you out to dinner tonight? I've got a favor to ask", she stated as boldly as she could.

"Maggie, why are you asking an old buggar like me out? You're surely scraping the bottom of the barrel!" he boasted. There was a short pause and then he heard her chuckle.

"Kiss my ass Miles! You've always had a special place in my heart." Maggie thought she may have crossed a line with that last remark. Miles however took it in stride, as he did with most things.

"I'm a one woman man Maggie; always have been." He paused before going on. "Besides, I'm too much man for you!" They both laughed at that. She continued quickly, hoping that her old friend would not pick up on the stress in her voice.

"I'll meet you at McCarthy's at six. And Miles", there was an awkward break in the flow of conversation. "It's nice to hear your voice again". She hung up and smiled. She did miss her friend but she needed him right now. She knew she'd regret it later but right now she had no choice. Her career depended on it. Maggie felt her heart skip another beat. She called out again.

"Jenna? Can you make a reservation for two at McCarthy's for six o'clock tonight? I've got a date with an old friend."

Maggie arrived at McCarthy's restaurant at ten minutes past six. She'd changed into a summer dress and a pair of flats. The restaurant was small and she had no trouble finding her colleague. Miles stood as she approached, the two hugging like old friends do.

"It's so good to see you Miles. It's been too long", she said as they embraced. Miles broke the hug off after an affectionate kiss to her cheek.

"Far too long my dear, far too long."

The pair sat at opposite sides of a small table in the far corner of the room. McCarthy's was a cozy place that had been in operation for close to thirty years. Many of its patrons dinned there at least once a week, giving the room an air of friendliness about it. That was the reason Maggie had picked this particular restaurant as opposed to the numerous choices available this time of year. She was about to cross a line, both professionally *and* personally and wanted as much ammo as she could get.

"How have you been since," Maggie paused wondering if she should go further, but she was spared the pain, having her thought finished by Miles.

"Since Elise passed?" he asked. She reached across the table and took hold of her friend's hand.

"You must miss her dearly. I know I do", she concluded. Maggie forced a smile and changed the subject.

"How is your practice going?" she asked making it quite clear that she did not want to dwell on the past tonight.

"Fine...fine", answered Miles. "There is rarely a shortage for the likes of us Maggie," he said as he picked up a menu opening it to the wine section. With a wave of his hand the waiter was at the table receiving an order for a light white wine. The two caught up on the goings on of the past two years and enjoyed a neatly prepared meal, Miles having a dish of locally caught Perch; Maggie having Salmon. Ninety minutes had passed before Miles' expression changed. He looked his friend in the eyes.

"So, my dear Maggie would you care to elaborate the purpose of this wonderful rendezvous? Or am I to sit here in the dark all night" a smile breaking the tension that seemed to be rising in his voice. Maggie returned his with a serious look and began her well prepared speech.

After fifteen minutes of listening, Miles sat forward and spoke.

"That is quite a story my dear friend. It seems as though you have found yourself between the preverbal rock and a hard place. I'm not sure what it is you're asking of me though. This woman Patricia, she's living locally now? Is she at Fort Drum?" He prodded. Maggie looked at the table, collecting her thoughts before leveling her eyes on Miles' once again.

"Yes. She's living with her husband and their eleven year old son. That is, when she is not in the base hospital. Her breakdowns are becoming more and more frequent. She's admitted two and three times a week for evaluation. The help she needs is beyond what we can provide however, if she's to make any recovery at all. Her alcoholism elevates her baseline depressive issues and often brings her into our Emergency Room.", her eyes once again drifted down to the table. She lifted her glass of wine taking a long drag of the liquid. "She needs to be institutionalized so she can get the help that she deserves."

Maggie told her colleague of her affair with Wesley. She felt telling the truth was best, at least most of it. Miles would pick up on it if she were to deceive him. He was good at his job, but so was she. After mentioning the affair she continued, telling him that at first she'd had no idea that he was married, trying to look as pitiful as she could.

"I broke it off soon after that. I didn't know there was a child involved as well until later", she continued. Maggie sighed expressively saying, "I'm such a fool Miles. I don't know how I got myself into this situation". Miles held out his hand, this time taking hers.

"Well I know how you got yourself into this situation but I'm not here to judge you Maggie. This woman needs help and I'll see her in the morning after I round on my own patients at St. Lawrence. I should get up to the post around noon at the latest. I have an ID to get on base already. I'll do anything I can to help. You know that Maggie. You were right in letting someone else take over her care. You should not have allowed yourself to be put in this situation in the first place", he paused, "God damn men. All they want is a good time then they screw you over! Maggie, we're all pigs. It's time you learned that!" She smiled at that, squeezing her friends hand tighter.

"Thank you so much for this Miles."

CHAPTER 39

Brad watched the sun set in the west, sparkling off the water. The sight was dazzling and he'd wished for Linda to be there with him to take in such a majestic sight. Somehow he felt closer to her than ever. These excursions were difficult on them, on their relationship, but the two knew what had to be done. That it would end soon and they could get on with their life together. The sun reflecting off light gray rivulets of water spraying in the air as the waves crashed on the rocky shore reminded Brad of her eyes on one of the many nights the two fell asleep in each other's arms. He felt a pang of loneliness he pushed through, reminding himself that they would soon be together again. Their love was strong enough to endure this path he was forced to walk. They would endure. They would overcome this and live happily.

Brad edged the thoughts to the back of his mind and set forth with the day's *activities*.

The access road circumvented the Island that was about ten miles in length. The road supported about fifty year-round residents with that number growing to well over two hundred during the summer months. Families from all walks of life, from all over the country came to summer on the Island, but their numbers were thinning as the summer faded quickly into fall. The transition from one season to the next was often overnight occurrence this far north, though Brad had to admit to himself that the area was indeed quite beautiful. The drive to the doctor's home would take less than fifteen minutes. As the road wound around the Island dusk overcame daylight and the road quickly darkened. Trees lined the right side of the roadway with intermittent breaks from the foliage on the left showing the waters of the Saint Lawrence River.

The Island stood between two countries; the United States to the south and Canada to the north.

Two cars ahead of Brad, the Cadillac Seville STS signaled and turned left onto a private drive heading toward a small peninsula that held the home of Dr. Miles Duval, Bradley's next victim. Brad remained on the roadway passing by the driveway eyeing the fading taillights of the other car in his periphery. His destination lay about a quarter mile ahead. Soon he was pulling into the parking lot of a small waterfront park that also housed a few seasonal camping sites. He knew that his car would remain unnoticed as he went along with his business for the evening. He pulled into a parking space and turned the car off popping open the trunk as he closed his door. "Time to go to work Bradley", he thought to himself. He stood looking at the water for a few minutes stretching his legs before pulling out an olive drab Army duffle bag and a smaller green rucksack he'd bought at an Army surplus store years before. Linda had always thought it somewhat sacrilegious, having never joined the military, but at the same time fitting for what Brad had coined 'my journey'. He closed his eyes momentarily thinking of his wife and how much he missed her during his annual 'outings'. Slamming the trunk shut he left the parking area for a pathway he knew led back toward the doctor's house. He strained under the weight of the two packs but quietly made his way toward his goal.

CHAPTER 40

Patricia sat quietly in a small room in the post hospital waiting with Dr. Drewer for the arrival of their guest. She noticed that Maggie was a little edgy today and decided to broach the subject.

"You know that this is not an admission of failure on your part Maggie." She had found it difficult to call Dr. Drewer by her professional name, feeling more comfortable using her first name instead. Maggie turned her head to look at her client and stared into Patricia's blue eyes, not saying anything. "In fact I think more highly of you for knowing and admitting your limits as a practitioner", Patricia jabbed, smiling. She leaned in closer to the doctor whispering, "I know you fucked Wesley. I'm not a fool. That's why you're dumping me onto this Dr. Duval", she said pointedly.

Maggie remained silent, swallowing saliva that suddenly filled the back of her throat.

"Look", Patricia continued, "I like you Maggie. You're a decent person. Wesley's a master of manipulation. He gets what he wants; every time. You don't know him like I do. Look at what he's done to me. *I'm* living proof that nothing good comes from that man!" Her voice echoed off the walls of the small room and Maggie noticed Patricia's face had reddened. Yet she remained silent. Patricia felt her pulse increasing and the veins in her forehead bulged ever so slightly. She wanted to get this off her chest and was unsure if she would ever see Maggie again. "I'm sorry he pulled you into whatever it is he's doing. I truly do feel badly for you. He only loves himself. I don't think he even loves Bradley. What an asshole!" She blared.

Patricia took on a look, one bordering between anger and worry. She interlaced her fingers, whitening her knuckles, staring blankly at the table. She regained a level of composure and looked meekly into Maggie's eyes, tears welling in her own.

"I don't know what this doctor is going to do and it scares me, Maggie. At least with you I was comfortable. Even knowing what you did with my husband. I don't blame you." She began weeping softly, wiping tears from her eyes with the back of her hand. Maggie reached into her bag removing a tissue and handed it to Patricia. Maggie cleared her throat fighting back the urge to cry along with her patient.

"I am sorry beyond words for what I have done Pat. I failed you and I've failed myself. That's why I want Dr. Duval to meet you. I think he can help you overcome what has ravaged your life for the past decade. He's very good, but more importantly he is a kind man". As the last couple of words passed her lips the door to the room opened. A large man with a broad smile stood looking at the two women. Noticing the look on their faces he reeled in his grin.

"Is everything alright ladies?"

CHAPTER 41

Brad walked the quarter mile along the trail with ease meeting no one else travelling the opposite direction. He made this same walk two times prior to tonight's expedition, noting that most hikers had left the Island prior to dusk catching the ferry back to the southern shore of the river. The trail itself consisted of a mixture of broken shells, crushed actually, and sand, all naturally found on the shores of the island. Brad's feet softly crunched along the pathway until see saw the lights of Dr. Duval's house peering ominously through the brush off to his right. The house was set on a small peninsula that reached out to the foreboding waters about four hundred feet.

Brad noticed the boat house at the end of the dock. The boat, a 21' River Tunnel manufactured by Schiada Boats was moored to the dock leaving the boathouse empty, just as Brad had expected. The boat house was two stories high allowing room for the boat to be hoisted out of the water for storage during the coldest months of the winter; when the waters were frozen solid. The grey building was dark against the setting sun. Brad doubted the doctor used the boat for much more than the occasional weekend ride on the river. He left the ease of the trail and walked about twenty feet into the thin underbrush setting his bags down softly noticing the smaller bag rustled slightly as it settled onto the freshly fallen foliage. Brad looked at the bag carefully, kneeling next to it as he bared his teeth, smiling. Tapping the duffle bag softly he whispered.

"Soon my friends, soon."

He would now wait until the full darkness that the new moon offered. It would be a good thirty minutes to an hour until his next move. Brad sat down facing the house leaning his back against a young maple tree, closed his eyes and listened contently to the waves gently lapping at the shoreline.

He sat idly and in total silence controlling his breathing, calming himself. He knew he would now go through a period of transformation when marking his prey for the kill, taking time to control any feelings of doubt in not only his ability to perform the task but also to rid himself of any feelings of guilt he may have for Dr. Duval. Reflecting on his situation, Brad knew he had to kill these victims, to make them pay for their role in his mother's misfortunes. Having read his mother's diary at least thirty times by this point he began to feel sorry for particular players in this game. There was Dr. Maggie Drewer, his mother's first doctor. A woman his mother had called "Friend" in her own writings. Making it quite clear that felt sorry for *Dr. Maggie*. Brad knew that she played an instrumental role in his mother's demise and therefore had to pay, but also had feelings that Maggie had at one point attempted to help his mother. In his readings about Maggie he learned that his mother often reflected upon her a graciousness and kindness that had made his mother think of her as a sister of some sort. A kinship had been forged in the time the two had known each other. A sisterhood in kind.

Brad found himself back in Maggie's office in Cleveland. He genuinely felt sad the day he had killed her. A battle waged between thoughts of necessity for her demise and the feelings his mother had brought forth in her own writings. He remembered telling Maggie that her impending death was particularly difficult, harsh even, to deal with in the days leading up to the event. He portrayed Maggie also as a victim of his father's evil but nonetheless had to pay for her role, having not had the fortitude to tell his father to "go bugger yourself". This last thought slapped a broad grin on Brad's face as he reflected his time in London. "That would have been quite fitting", he thought. "Too bad Maggie, you could have saved yourself by doing so" he softly whispered.

Brad, still drifting further thought of Lenny, his first target. He had befriended the man, not far from the very place he sat tonight, and then killed him. No ill feelings from that encounter surfaced, the thought of Lenny reminded Brad of the initial transformation he underwent the night of Lenny's death, and more importantly the incredible ease at which it overtook him. Leading him from the person he was to the person he'd needed to be for the actual killing. Brad remembered the anguish he fought with personally in the days leading up to that first kill. Not knowing if the transformation from Brad to Bradley would happen, remembering that it had not occurred until the last moments preceding Lenny's death. And more importantly if the change would reverse, allowing Brad his old self. That last thought sent a cold shiver down his spine. Had he not been able to, as you would say "flick the switch" it would have had devastating effects. Brad would be stuck in Bradley's world. A world full of hatred and darkness, one void of love and fulfillment, it was the last place a sane man would want to be stuck. He thought of other killers and if that was *their* problem. Had they reached that dark place, unable to leave? To be stuck in the muddy waters of hate and retribution, forever? He thought of losing the love of his wife and children. Linda witnessed the metamorphosis, from killer to the man she fell in love with, seeing first-hand he could "turn it off" and lead a normal life; a life to share. Brad snapped out of his introverted state of mind at the sound of a small boat passing the island, not far from where he sat; the waves smacking at the rocky shore louder than before. Looking up at the sky he noted darkness had befallen and stood up, once again stretching his legs. He gathered his bags and began the short walk to the house. His tranquility slipping away, it was once again that time.

CHAPTER 42

"Patricia," Maggie started, "I'd like you to meet Dr. Miles Duval. Miles, this is the woman we spoke of earlier." Standing up to greet the Doctor, Patricia held out her right hand, shaking his with purpose.

"Patricia Fordam, nice to meet you, Dr. Duval." They politely shook hands and both sat down.

"A pleasure to meet *you*, Patricia. I've heard you have had a rough go of it as of late," getting right to the point. Patricia plucked at her hospital band letting him continue without saying a word, however Maggie interjected before Miles could speak.

"Dr. Duval is a wonderful man Pat and it's my belief that he can truly help you".

Miles spoke softly. "I am one of the doctors that run the Saint Lawrence Psychiatric Center down the road in Ogdensburg. I think you would benefit from our expertise. The Army has never been *into* healing the mind. With the exception of Dr. Drewer and a few of her colleagues I have met through the years, I have come to the conclusion that the Army prefers to use Psychiatric Doctors to resolve other matters like PTSD", otherwise known as Post Traumatic Stress Disorder. It's a newer term in the world of Psychiatry. With the end of the Vietnam War we found that there was a phenomenon that was particularly disturbing when it came to dealing with soldiers returning home. They had serious problems, *mental problems*, in dealing with much of what they saw, and often *did* over there. The military has started to equip itself to better deal with that particular problem and have reallocated many resources that normally would have benefitted those such as you".

Patricia peered at Dr. Duval with narrowed eyes, "Crazy people."

"No, no my dear. In fact, I don't think you are", he paused at saying a word he greatly disliked, "*crazy!*" He eased the growing tension with a genuine smile. "Besides, I prefer the term '*whack job*' myself. Patricia smiled. Maggie, taking her cue from Miles earlier, sat quietly. This was his moment to win Patricia over and he needed to do it *himself*. "Patricia, if I may call you that, I help patients that cannot overcome certain obstacles they may be facing by themselves. I specialize in Depressive Disorders myself, but our facility has a wide range of help we can offer people in need. We help people overcome addictions such as your alcoholism, as well as many other addictive behavior patterns. These are usually not a quick fix, and they sometimes need to be dealt with as if they were one, often blending into each other as well as feeding off each other. I'm sure you understand how one affliction such as depression can be fed off the 'need' for alcohol or other drugs." The room remained quiet for some time, Miles letting this sink in. Patricia needed time to process the flood of honest information and either rebut or accept his offer. Weaving her fingers in and out of themselves, she made eye contact with Dr. Duval.

"How long do I have to stay there?"

CHAPTER 43

Bradley had been peering at the house from about a hundred yards away, just beyond the tree line of the yard. There were very few lights on but he could tell from the structures' silhouette that the house was closer to a mansion. Dr. Duval was one of the few inhabitants of the island that spent most of the year. He wintered south near Naples, Florida from mid-November to late February. He saw the doctor walk from room to room occasionally. After making himself a small microwave dinner the doctor went to his study on the first floor to read. Bradley noted from his earlier visits to the house that this seemed to be a nightly routine. Dr. Duval was now semi-retired lending his expertise to peers when called upon and helping with some of the administrative issues that arose from time to time at the hospital. The doctor knew that this mostly involved lending his good name to fundraising objectives and accepted his duties with grace. Miles knew that after Elsie's death he would never be the same. He was half the man he had once been.

Bradley retrieved his gear from a few feet behind his position and walked leisurely toward the house. There was no need to worry about nosey neighbors nor was there the worry of a pet alerting the doctor to his arrival. Miles lived alone in the five thousand plus square foot house he and his late wife, Elise built five years before her death. There was plenty of press surrounding her pre-mature death because of his standing in the community and her being co-chair of the local American Cancer Society chapter. She had volunteered her time *and money* to help the organization for years before her diagnosis. Her passing was treated much the same as a fallen fire fighter or police officer killed in the line of duty. The very thing she devoted so much of her life to, snuffed that very life out of her. Dr. Duval mourned her untimely passing deeply, shunning his practice for nearly six months before slowly reintegrating himself back into his career. But he felt hurt and loneliness when he sat alone at night. Friends attempted to help defray the feeling of destitution that he faced. He once had the fleeting thought of getting a pet of some sort, but knew that it would never fill the void that tore at his broken heart. Miles would have to accept his fate of being alone his remaining days on earth.

Bradley entered the house on the side farthest from the doctor's study. He removed the caulking of a basement window on his previous venture to the house. He needed to be inside the house before the doctor retired for the night and activated the alarm system. He would then wait in the basement until he heard the footsteps of this evening's victim taking the stairs to the upper level master bedroom. After silently climbing through the opening he replaced the glass then settled against the wall, closing his eyes in apprehension of the long night ahead.

October 17, 1975

My mind is reeling. I have no idea how they can do this to me.
I am not crazy. I do not deserve to be here. This is
unwarranted, unjust. My first days here were difficult. I had to
learn different ways to do the ordinary things I did every day.
My life is now institutionalized and I have very little say on
anything. My life as I knew it is over.
How could Wesley let this happen to me? Why isn't he here
fighting to get me home? Where is he? I've missed him for so
long now. Has he abandoned me? Left me here to rot?
Dr. Duval said I would get better here but all I see are people
that have no hope of regaining what they once had. I see no one
that has been helped by this place. Dear God what have I done?

The time spent in the depths of the doctor's house passed
slowly as Brad sat in the dark, damp basement quietly reflecting
on his life. Feeling guilty for not being the son he'd needed to
be for his mother. Taking the easy way out and turning his head
instead of stepping in and stopping the atrocities that befell his
mother, ultimately leading her down a path of loneliness and
despair, the path that led to her suicide. Brad could not help
feeling that in some part, his mother's demise was his fault. He
was too weak to stand up to his father. That was inexcusable.
He was aware of this but nonetheless had used his fathers'

motives as an excuse to look the other way. He had used his age to make himself believe that nothing he did would have affected the outcome of his mother's fate. Brad knew this was a weak attempt to distance him from what his responsibilities were as a son. He knew that no matter what he told himself, he was just as much to blame as the others. Sitting alone in the basement he wept for the loss of his mother, for the poor son he had been in the past, and in a whisper he swore on his own life, that he would be the man she'd needed him to be.

CHAPTER 44

Miles sat in an oversized armchair worn from use. He had taken to becoming somewhat of a recluse the past two years, since Elsie was taken from him. He was unaware during their marriage just what she'd meant to him. Just how much he had loved her, and how much he'd always hoped she'd loved him in return. He set the book he was reading, *The Three Musketeers* by Dumas on his lap as he wiped a tear from his right cheek. Doctor Miles Duval worked endlessly for decades with broken people from broken minds. He'd been privy to the inner workings of the human psyche having worked with mental illness for so long. He had seen people overcome their problems and survive, and yet he had witnessed the opposite, a broken mind *unable* to overcome obstacles resulting in a broken body. He'd dealt with patients hurting themselves many times over and even had a few commit suicide as a way to extinguish the flames of their personal hell. Miles had always taken these losses, what some in his field of work called "unavoidable", very personally, taking it as a failure on his part to help his patient heal. After all, that's what he did. Heal people. He laughed at this last thought speaking to the empty room.

"You can't even heal *yourself* doctor".

Elsie's death had been more than two years ago and he still felt the heated rush of emotions that overcome a surviving spouse. He would rather have died in a fiery car crash with his love than have to walk this earth missing her every day of his life. No, he thought, "I'll never heal. I'll never stop missing her."

Elsie Duval had spent her life helping others, much like her husband, but in her own manner. She'd met her husband shortly after graduating from college, having never used her degree in communications in a paid way. She turned her energy toward helping those less fortunate. She began a life of giving. The last two years of her life she worked closely with the American Cancer Society as a fundraiser and event organizer gaining popularity with the Society in a national light. Her work was invaluable to its causes. Elsie had a knack for getting even the most miserly give until it hurt. A term which she twisted and made it known that that hurt they felt actually helped others. She enjoyed raking in record amounts of donations in her short time with the Society. The community was stunned to hear the news that cancer was destroying the very person that had fought so diligently to create a public awareness that was unprecedented and sought to end the tyranny that overcame so many people every year. She had become a statistic overnight. The public outcry was enormous. Elsie however became a recluse in her final months opting for hospice care instead of continuing a losing battle after countless rounds of chemotherapy and radiation therapy. She had lost her hair, her dignity and finally her life to a nemesis that she'd fought for years from the sidelines. Her husband fought with her right to the end. He queried friends and co-workers about the latest treatments. He scoured over text books and the just invented and very difficult to navigate World Wide Web from a computer at nearby Clarkson University that had limited access. But most of all he'd held Elsie's hand and comforted her as she lay helpless, awaiting a fate he would not allow her to face alone. She died on a late spring afternoon. She died in his arms, the two of them alone. Just the way she wanted it.

After her funeral Miles himself became a recluse. Shutting himself off from the world, hiding in the bitterness and resentment that it seemed would eternally engulf him. People tried to reach out and help, but he refused anything other than support from their closest friends, but soon he wanted nothing to do with them either. Falling into a deep depression and alone in the world, he hit bottom in late summer. Miles sought out help from an old friend. The last place a Psychiatrist goes in search of help is another Psychiatrist. He reached her through a friend who had her private phone number.

CHAPTER 45

The phone rang only three times before a young woman's voice answered.

"Hello?"

"Hello Margaret?" He spoke softly like a child speaking to their parent.

"Who is this? How did you get this number?" Maggie was defensive in her nature; having reserved her private number for a select few friends and family. Not recognizing the voice at the other end of the line put her on edge. There was nothing but silence on the line while she waited for an answer. She was about to hang up when she heard the man's voice in a whisper.

"Margaret, it's me, Miles." Another prolonged silence filled the void between them while Maggie registered what she had just heard.

"Miles? Miles *Duval*?" she asked nearing a state of shock.

"Yes Margaret. I, I need your help."

The next hour was filled with the two old college friends and colleagues filling in the time lost over the years since they last saw each other. Maggie was in tears when her old friend told her of the death of his wife. Maggie had been at their wedding almost ten years before. Miles had been working for Social Services in New York State and Maggie, opting to pay her college loans, entered the Army, was travelling the globe. The two friends spoke rarely after the wedding. At the time of Miles' unexpected call she was stationed at Fort Dix in New Jersey and before she knew it, she was in front of her Commanders desk asking for emergency leave.

"Granted. Captain, go fix your friend. We'll get along fine without your services for a couple weeks." Maggie was on the road two hours later making the trek north. Miles had told her the directions to his office at Saint Lawrence Psychiatric Center. From there he would take her to his home for what would to prove to be the most enlightening two weeks of his life.

CHAPTER 46

Darkness surrounded Brad as he waited patiently in the basement. It was already later than the other nights he'd watched from the woods. "What was the good doctor up to tonight?" he thought. "Why is he still awake?" Lightly, Brad rapped the back of his head against the cold concrete wall where he sat. His legs ached from the dampness that was enveloping him like a dense fog. He closed his eyes and took himself back home to Linda, to *his* life. He missed her dearly. He always did and he too wiped a tear from his cheek. This madness would end and he would be able to go on with his life. Let his mother's soul rest in peace and move on. He pictured Linda. Her beautiful smile, her kind eyes, and he was home. The quiet respite of his memories, a welcomed old friend.

Brad's peaceful escape was disturbed by the sound of footsteps from above. The doctor was on the move. Brad remained completely still but was aware of everything Miles was doing. He worked to slow his breathing like a hunter taking aim at his prey; he had to control his body. His mind, as he had already discovered would control *him* when the time came. He *was* able to "flick the switch" and elude all emotion. *Bradley* was able to bridal his thoughts. It was his body he had difficulty controlling. He'd been parked on this cold floor for nearly two hours when the time came to act. His breathing quickened. His

212

heart pounded in his chest. The surge of adrenaline sent his body into a spiral that had to be garnered and kept under control. Bradley fought to keep his breathing in check. He closed his eyes and slowed his expirations with the convictions of a monk. His racing heart soon followed suit and began its' return to normal: homeostasis. That's what Linda called it. The need for the body to remain in its' normal state. A steady-state in which it can perform at its' peak. With the flow of adrenaline lessening, Brad felt himself transform into what he needed to be at this moment in time, a killer. With no emotion to hinder his thoughts, Bradley opened his eyes and looked straight ahead into the darkness. Once again it was that time.

Bradley arose from his sitting position and shook off the cobwebs in his legs. He heard the distant beeps of the security alarm as Miles set the code for the night. He stepped quietly to the base of the stairwell as he heard the footsteps of his prey ascend the stairwell leading to the second floor. The footsteps softened to silent thuds as the doctor padded his way across the carpeted hallway above and finally into the master bedroom. Bradley reached into his duffel bag and quickly found a flashlight in its exact location. The only sound heard was the sharp click resulting in the illumination of the stairwell above in soft red. Bradley used a military style flashlight he'd bought along with the duffel bag and ruck sack. The flashlight came with removable covers of blue, white, red, and clear. He'd chosen red due to its low visibility to the human eye. Soldiers used it routinely at night while in the field to avoid detection by their enemy. Now Bradley did the same hoping to avoid detection by *his* enemy. Slowly he ascended the stairwell to the door above, stepping at the outer edges of the stairs to minimize any squeaks. Arriving at the top stair Bradley gripped the doorknob slowly turning it until he heard a soft click then gently pushed it open. The first floor was dimly illuminated by a lone lamp in the foyer. It was enough for Bradley to see his way however and he decided to return the flashlight to its off position hanging it on his belt by a metal clip. With his hand now freed he was able to equalize the weight of the two bags he'd carried while navigating his way up the stairs. He stood in the kitchen for close to five minutes completely immobile while he once again allowed his vital signs to return to normal. The house was in complete silence with the exception of the faintest of sounds emanating from Bradley's ruck sack. He quietly hushed it and said but one word. *"Soon"*.

He set the bags slowly to the floor as softly as a mother laying her child to bed. He knew opening the bags would create an opportunity for detection, so he did so with soft, steady hands. He removed the contents onto the floor surrounding a large marble topped island in the center of the kitchen. Metal was wrapped in towels prior to packing the bag and enabled Bradley to set them on the tiled floor without so much as a clank. Satisfied with the setup, Bradley turned toward the kitchen exit that led to a hallway and the stairwell beyond and removed his boots leaving them near his now empty bags on the floor. Like a game hunter he followed the gentle scent left behind by his prey.

A hint of whiskey led the way down the hall and up the stairs to the second floor which ended in a small open area overlooking the living room below. Bradley ran a gloved finger along the cherry banister as he looked down upon the vast expanse of the five thousand square foot house, illuminated by the sole light fixture in the foyer. Bradley looked with a disconnected feeling. He didn't have to remind himself why he was here. Slowly he pivoted on his sock covered foot and turned toward the hallway leading to the four bedrooms that lay ahead. All were empty except for the last which was marked as the master bedroom by its double French doors made of solid cherry. One of the doors sat agape by six inches with no light from beyond. Bradley eased his way to the end of the hallway stopping a mere foot from the open door. His breathing and heart rate were amazingly controlled. He rolled his head in a small circle then from side to side readying himself, like a prize fighter readying for a bout.

CHAPTER 47

Miles slid into bed putting only the sheet over his body. The sun had warmed the room somewhat through the day but the sheets were cool and he welcomed the feeling. He took his reading glasses off setting them on the bedside table, turned the lamp off, rolled to his right side and closed his eyes. But not before pulling Elsie's pillow under the sheet holding it as if it were her lying in bed next to him. This was a ritual that helped him sleep more soundly. And again, tonight the whiskey would help. He calmed his breathing and closed his eyes wishing the pillow to become his bride, ending this nightmare. He was soon sleeping, his arm holding his beloved wife's pillow. He never heard Bradley's footsteps leading through the doorway and up to the side of the bed behind him.

Miles had no time to react after waking to a strong smell as a sponge soaked with chloroform was held over his mouth and nose. Startled, he thrashed under the sudden weight of his aggressor. His harms flailed but Bradley was able to remain in control, driving his own weight into the doctors' bare back. Miles' hands reached out for something to grab but found only thin air. Quickly, Miles succumbed to the overwhelming feeling the chloroform created. His arms felt heavy and he soon found it impossible to fight. His mind entered a dizzying downward spiral slipping into a state of semi-consciousness, then nothing.

Bradley felt Doctor Duval slump after what seemed a full minute. All remaining fight snuffed out for the time being. He felt for a pulse on the doctor's neck, more out of reaction than fear. He knew the amount of chloroform used was not enough to kill but he wanted to be sure. Bradley wanted this to be drawn out. He needed it to be. He lay atop the unresponsive doctor for a short time, feeling him breathe slowly. He seemed comfortable to him, peaceful even. He hoped Miles was dreaming of his lovely wife. The night was young however and Miles Duval was in for a long one. Bradley moved his prey down to the kitchen and prepared for what was to be the longest night of Miles Duval's life.

CHAPTER 48

June 12, 1978

They feed me pills I cannot stand to take. They make me say things I do not fully believe. This is not life. This is death. My body has yet to catch up with my mind. Some day it will and I will be free of this horrid place. Physical death is inevitable and I invite it.

"Hello. *Hello* in there."

Miles heard the words but felt disconnected, the words echoed as if he were in a cavern. He wasn't quite sure in what manner but he was sure something was wrong. There were soft words being spoken into his ear from close by. He could distinguish this much, but everything else was a blur. Opening his eyes slowly, blinking to focus, Miles could make out what was unmistakably his kitchen ceiling.

The voice echoed again, "Hello?" There was a long pause, only a soft breath on the nape of his neck. Miles was unable to move his head in either direction. His eyes were open, yet transfixed on the ceiling, he had no peripheral vision. His heart began to beat faster and faster. An unimaginable fear gripped, wringing him like a wet rag, draining any reality from his groggy mind. He thought "What could this be? What has happened?" His last memory being that of falling asleep while

218

holding his wife's pillow, holding Elise. What happened in the time after, where his memory ceased to register any events? He tried to move his hands to no avail. They were bound by some unseen force. Miles slowly realized that there was no part of him that was able to move. It was as if there was something lying on top of him, smothering him, yet there was no weight on him. Nothing actually smothering him. But still, something denied him any hint of movement. His breathing became more labored as he fought the unknown force. Then he heard the voice once again; quiet, calm and so very close. He shuddered at the sound.

"Hello Miles." The voice was a man's and he was clearly in control. "My name is Bradley. It's a pleasure to finally meet you. The words ripped through Miles like a bullet.

CHAPTER 49

The night was dark with barely a sliver of moon shining. The air had cooled considerably from the days' sunshine, a tell-tale sign of autumn in New York. A cool, brisk wind blew in from the northwest and gusted at times as a storm front gathered strength travelling across the warmer waters of Lake Ontario. Trees swayed with the increasing winds as leaves fell prematurely to the ground, rising into swirls before falling to their final resting place. Bradley could see lights dancing across the river. The Saint Lawrence was wide at this spot even though the Duval's house was on an island. You could make out the lights coming from Canada, but little else. The shipping lane was a good half mile from the island so there was little chance anyone would hear sounds emanating from the residence. There were a handful of neighbors left on the island but the properties in this area were large plots allowing a solid buffer zone between houses. Besides, there was a storm brewing.

Bradley stood on the back patio of the house leaning against a large white pillar which complemented the Greek architecture the Duval's had chosen for the yard. Elsie had placed a number of sitting gardens throughout the ten acres they bought after marrying. Friends and family were treated to a respite from the present when they entered the rear of the property, finding themselves lost in a world that faded long ago.

The landscaping alone on the property surpassed a million dollars and was the highlight of the island. Miles had to have buoys placed in the river directly behind the property having had a number of curious boaters finding themselves run aground on one of the numerous sandbars dotting the islands' northern shores. Passersby found themselves drawn toward the spectacular sight of the fabricated ruins. The pool itself was built as a reflecting pool and had never been used otherwise. Just beyond the pool sat a dock with a boathouse built as an exact replica of the house itself. An idea the Duval's thought of when visiting Boldt Castle, built by an Englishman for his wife just minutes up river. Lord Boldt's wife passed away unexpectedly during the construction of the castle having never set foot on the land her loving husband dedicated to his beautiful wife. The only structure actually reaching completion was a playhouse built on the river's edge matching the main castle stone for stone, however on a much smaller scale. A playhouse built for children never born. Lord Boldt, devastated by the sudden death of his young wife returned to Europe, never to return to American soil. The story captivated Elsie Duval, having just married, and she spoke of the commitment made by Lord Boldt to his wife and of the love he lost with her passing. Many visitors to the Duval home found themselves drying tear streaked cheeks after listening to young Elsie tell of the love affair the Boldt's were afforded and expressing the same feelings for her own husband. She told the Boldt story with such enthusiasm was as if it were her own. Inspired by the love felt between the young lovers Elsie dedicated her life to her husband.

Bradley turned toward the house as the screaming intensified. Shards of terror exploded from within but went unheard beyond the borders of the yard. The quiet night was forgone for one filled with horror and dismay. Bradley's work had just begun. He peered through the open French doors that led to the kitchen. The sight was horrific. Miles had been laid out upon a large marble island counter top. There were no visible signs of restraint but it was clear that he was being held in place by some unseen force; his muscles quivering from a mixture of pain and attempts at trying to free himself. Miles was stripped naked and lying supine on the cold, marble. Once again Bradley's victim mimicked DaVinci's Vitruvian Man; his hands turned palms up with obvious movement of his fingers. His legs were separated by a foot at the ankles and also showed signs of over excitement in the form of subtle tremors reverberating along the leg from thighs to toes; which were pointed straight and rigid. Bradley had placed the doctor's head in a box painted flat black creating a blinder; limiting his view to the ceiling of the kitchen. Although Miles' head seemed unbound in the improvised black box he was unable to lift his head. From his vantage point Bradley was unable to see the doctors face but was sure it was filled with tears of pain and the unknown. The underside of his victim pulled taut by the continual fighting to free himself, only to be denied by a liquid adhesive/epoxy mixture poured on the counter top before the doctors body was placed there. Bradley was forced to administer the chloroform a second and third time to allow the mixture to set thoroughly before waking Miles. The drying process took two hours longer than Bradley had anticipated but he was still left with ample time to perform what was to come.

Bradley walked into the kitchen closing the doors behind him as he went. Crossing the expanse of the enormous room he began to speak once again to Miles.

"I have waited many years to meet you doctor. I was blessed with the patience of a monk although I have to admit it was difficult not to move my time table up for our *meeting*. I blamed you mostly for what happened to my mother being that you were the doctor that accepted her into your care. I have come to believe that what you did, you did out of compassion for your fellow doctor. Maggie needed a friend to clean up a terrible mess she'd allowed to occur. Through her mishappenings you were reluctantly drawn into this web of deceit and conspiracy. What you did for your peer and friend is commendable but nonetheless you must pay for your participation".

Miles listened carefully trying without success to place the voice in the room with a face. He searched for something concrete to grasp; a weak attempt to grasp reality. His screams subsided substantially while he listened to his captor recite what seemed to be a carefully rehearsed speech. He groaned but held onto the faceless voice. He needed to be in control of this situation. He searched for the right words to confront his aggressor but waited for the right time to rebut Bradley's rhetoric. He searched his memory recalling no one named Bradley, none that he could remember anyway. He spoke in a whisper to Bradley using the knowledge and experience he'd learned throughout his years of being a Psychiatrist. He knew that it was vital to regain command of this situation he had been hurled into. He used his captor's first name in an attempt to tie the situation to him personally, making it harder for Bradley to view him as an object and forcing him to see him as a living breathing human being.

"Bradley", his voice trembled as he tried to regain some composure "why are you doing this to me? What have I done that is so heinous to deserve this?" Miles left that last sentence hang in the air before he continued. "I'm a doctor. I try to help people. I'm a healer of the mind." He stopped at that and let Bradley absorb it for its entire worth. He heard faint footsteps pacing back and forth in the room. He hoped he'd struck a chord. Bradley waited for the doctor to continue but decided to

224

speak after it was clear that the "healer of the mind" was remaining silent for the moment.

"I have no doubt that you think you are a healer of the mind. I know you're a good and decent man inside. You have quite the bio indeed, Doctor Duval. I know everything about you. I know more about you than you yourself may know." Miles thought he struck gold hearing those words. Bradley had placed him with his identity and was looking at him as a person. This was a very important tactic used not only by mental health doctors to control 'variables' with patients, but was also a known tactic of hostage negotiators. Miles had to think of himself as playing a dual role in this situation. He needed to be the negotiator as well as the hostage. If he could continue with this line of dialogue he may win over his captor and convince Bradley to release him.

"Tell me why you are doing this, Bradley. Why do you feel you have to hurt me?" Miles was optimistic of how this conversation was developing. He forgot about the pain he was being forced to endure and concentrated on making Bradley see this was not the answer to whatever problem he had.

"Humph", retorted Bradley. "There is a time to fight and a time to give in. Where are *you* doctor? How much fight do you have left in that haggard body of yours?" Miles swallowed hard and continued relentlessly;

"This is not a means to an end, Bradley. There are options for you to consider." Miles decided to take it to the next level, a risk he needed to take. He spoke slowly and clearly, "Do you intend on killing me, Bradley? Is that your plan? Are you ready to give up your freedom? That is not the answer. We can work through this, Bradley." With a click the room went amazingly dark, and with the darkness, an eerie silence. A low hum emanated from the refrigerator; just audible under Miles' labored breathing. He called out meekly, clearly having lost any advantage he'd gained. There was no answer, only silence.

CHAPTER 50

Having closed his eyes with the darkness forced upon him, Miles was jarred back to reality with a sudden burst of light. Bradley had returned to the conversation. Miles had anticipated correctly that he would resume talking with his captor. That Bradley had wanted to regain control of the situation by using the light, a variable, he would end up returning to dialogue as soon as he felt he was indeed back in control.

"Welcome back Bradley. Do you feel better?" Miles heard footsteps approaching him from the far side of the room; another accurate prediction. Bradley had never left the room. He only wanted to control the playing field. But Miles felt he had the home field advantage. He'd talked to many people in this frame of mind, de-escalating situations before they got out of hand. His eyes took a couple of seconds to adjust to the blinding light, but were now focused on the familiar sight of the ceiling. The footsteps stopped just to the right of him. There seemed to be impatience about the heaviness of Bradley's steps. "Talk to me, Bradley. What are you thinking? Keep talking, son." Miles knew that if he kept Bradley in a conversation he was likely to last longer. Miles was no fool. He knew that the odds greatly increased in his favor the longer he kept his aggressor talking openly.

Miles was ready to take the dialogue to the next level when Bradley cut him off, his voice calm.

"The time for talking is nearing an end doctor. We've reached the point where I let you know that I am prepared for your predicted tack. You're not dealing with an idiot Dr. Duval. In fact, I'm quite sure that your level of intelligence is a shade lower than mine. Bradley let out a long, exasperated sigh. He let his last statement hang in the air before resuming. In a lower, guttural voice he asked, "What is that *feeling* you've undoubtedly noticed in your belly? You know…the one that made you think there was something amiss but couldn't quite put your finger on it? Let me help you understand more clearly, Miles." A hint of sarcasm crept into Bradley's words. "Let me show you what that queer sensation is you've been avoiding while attempting to negotiate with me". A smile crossed his face as Bradley held up a mirror to Miles' and angled it just so; allowing the doctor to see his handy work. Miles was astonished at the sight. His eyes opened starkly.

"Oh my God! What have you done? What in the hell have you done to me?" he screamed. The sight was difficult to process. The angle at which Miles was forced to look *down* at his own body was foreign and it took a couple of seconds for the doctor to absorb and analyze what he was seeing. A mid-line incision along the center of his abdomen, from sternum to umbilicus that had been sutured closed peered back at him through the mirror; its' length about twelve inches with a small trickle of blood coming from the spaces between the sutures. Confusion replaced by fear, Miles' eyes widened even more with the horrific reflection staring back at him. "Bradley, what in God's name have you done to me?" Miles pleaded. His heart raced and his breathing became rapid and shallow as he watched in total horror. Bradley whispered in his ear.

"Welcome to hell Doctor Duval."

Miles watched, with a certain detachment, the horror unfolding before his eyes. His abdomen, large and pale was shaved clean of any body hair. His blanched and bloated body reminded him of medical school; working with cadavers: one of the reasons he became a *Doctor of the mind* and not of the body. He always had difficulty absorbing the ghastly sights of the human body in a surgical manner. He stared unblinking at his reflection then he felt that *feeling* Bradley had mentioned earlier. The feeling he was unable to place a finger upon. Movement caught his glazed eye, then again. Miles watched as a golf ball sized orb darted under his pallid skin, then another. And another! They moved in all directions. His eyes widened and a look of undeniable fear crossed his face. His rapid, shallow respirations sped and he developed a grunting noise. Snorting, he heaved as much as his unseen bindings would allow as he watched the foreign bodies tunnel through his abdomen. The sight was eventually too much to digest. His eyes rolled back as he passed out from shock. Light faded slowly until there was none, a respite from the reality he was forced witness. Bradley looked on as the doctor went limp, temporarily ending the battle with his restraints, thus marking the end of the session, for now. He set the mirror on the counter top and sat quietly on a stool he'd pulled alongside the island, patient as ever.

January 26, 1981
These monsters must each pay for their sins. They have kept me silent all these years and it is through my death that my screams shall be heard. Make them pay. Make them pay with their lives as I have done.

Miles slowly regained consciousness bringing the kitchen ceiling once again back into focus. He noticed that his heart had slowed and his breathing was normal. Suddenly the reality he'd been subjected to rushed back into his numbed mind. He spewed vomit into the air, acid burned his throat and he found himself coughing violently, initiating a second round of projectile vomiting. His mouth filled with a mixture of sweet whiskey and stomach acid. Panicked, Miles failed to clear his airway and instinctively drew a deep breath. He fought for air trying desperately to clear the stomach contents from his airway; but nothing happened. He heaved frantically realizing that he had aspirated his stomach contents, effectively sealing off his lungs from the precious air it craved. There was no more coughing. No more vomiting. Only silence as he craned his neck as far as he could. He was drowning in his own vomit. He heard tearing as he pulled his head away from the counter top desperately searching for air. A burning sensation flooded his already overloaded senses as his scalp ripped free from the black box. He wretched, fighting to regain an open airway, but nothing happened. His vision began closing slowly inward as the oxygen level to his brain plunged. He was fading back into the realm of quiet unconsciousness when he felt a hard object rammed into his oral cavity.

"Not yet, my friend. Not quite yet". Miles heard a suctioning sound as Bradley withdrew the obstruction with a turkey baster he'd grabbed from one of the kitchen drawers. After thirty seconds Miles was breathing again. Raspy, but effective enough to pull him back from the abyss. He coughed uncontrollably, clearing his airway more with each subsequent cough. Soon he realized he was able to breathe again and he drew in long, deep gasps of air.

"That was a close one Doc. I Thought I'd lost you there for a second," Bradley taunted.

"Fuck you Bradley!" Miles mustered in the course, raspy voice of a three pack a day smoker. "Why didn't you let me die? That's what you want isn't it, you sick little prick?" He continued to cough throughout the verbal exchange.

"Oh, I'm not quite ready for that Doctor Duval. We've work to do yet, don't jump the gun my friend. This is just getting started." Bradley countered, continuing the verbal sparring match the doctor had incited earlier. "Much to do", Bradley finished; whistling the song from Snow White and the Seven Dwarfs. *"Hi ho, hi ho its' off to work we go…"* all the while smiling.

Miles was now able to lift his head off the counter but was sickened knowing that he'd effectively scalped the occipital area of his head. He lifted his head trying to get a better look at the kitchen but was unable to see more than his body below the chest and of course the ceiling he'd come to loathe. Each time he set his head down atop of the counter he felt the wet warmth of his own blood. Swallowing hard he abated the overwhelming feeling of nausea that seemed to be coming in waves.

"What did you do to me Bradley?" Miles asked. "Why did you cut me?" The doctor's head spun while he attempted to postulate why anyone would do such a thing.

"Think hard doctor. Let all of your other senses drift away and focus on the problem at hand. What do you think I did? What logic is there in me cutting your abdomen open? What would that prove?" Bradley sat on the stool he'd pulled over earlier sitting next to the doctor's head. He whispered in his right ear. *"Feel* what I am telling you. Forget *thinking* about it and let yourself *feel* what I am telling you. Close your eyes

232

and let yourself just...*feel.*" Bradley spoke in a hush, his voice remained steadfast. Calmness fell over the doctor as he listened to his captor whisper in his ear. Miles did as he was instructed. He slowed his breathing and closed his eyes, shutting off as many senses as he could. He tried to do as Bradley had instructed and *felt.* There was a peculiarity to the situation Miles had not been able to identify. He had felt something earlier but because of his overwhelmed senses he'd placed it inadvertently in the back of his consciousness. Now he was once again able to feel what he had earlier. There it was again. It came and went seemingly with no regularity, chaotic in nature. He felt a light scratching, or so he thought. Yes, it was definitely a scratching but not always in the same area. It seemed to move from place to place throughout his belly. Then he felt something wholly different than that of the light scratching. But what it was, escaped Miles. He'd felt it a couple of times now that he was focused. Then the realization of what he felt stabbed at him like a dagger, something gnawed at him, from the inside. Miles' eyes suddenly opened with a fury and Bradley now understood that Miles understood. Miles once again began to breathe in a shallow manner trying his best not to vomit. His muscles tensed throughout his body and he could feel the epoxy holding him in place. Once again Bradley smiled.

"They were very hungry doctor. I've kept them for the past week giving them only a spattering of water to sustain themselves. You see, I detest rodents, having grown up in Europe they were everywhere you looked. Old Europe makes New York City look like utopia. I've even named them. Six mice, despite its overt simplicity proved quite daunting. You see I've always contended that these *excursions* of mine should be very personal and I had a difficult time placing six unnamed mice in your abdomen. I felt that they should all have been named out of respect to *you* doctor. Time was a factor, it always has been and for some reason even I cannot answer, I had to show you respect. All six were bestowed the privilege of identity. I realized it was *you* who gave me the insight needed! The beauty of it all is quite exquisite. Sometimes torture is not all physical. I thought you would appreciate the psychological aspect of the conundrum I was facing." Miles said nothing. He lay silent, remaining as composed as he could under the circumstances, only an occasional grunt crossing his lips; a muffled cry at best. Bradley continued, "I'll make you a deal Doctor Duval. If you can name all six mice I'll remove them from your belly. But you had better hurry. They were quite hungry when I pulled them from my bag. I have a feeling they are enjoying themselves in there; feasting on you as we speak. There's only one condition, however. The names must be old, very old. Call me crazy but I seem to have developed an unhealthy fetish for the old days. I guess that's what you get when you are left to raise yourself bouncing from European country to European, country with a father that ignored me for the most part and a mother that had been deemed dangerous to herself and forced to live institutionalized for the rest of her life." Bradley let those thoughts hover in the air, lingering before the silence was interrupted by the sound of skin ripping. It startled Bradley. Enough to force him to a standing position. The stool toppled to the floor. Bradley's heart raced for a brief moment while he fought to regain his composure. He starred at his victim, watching curiously as Miles tried to free himself from his hardened restraint. The doctor's right shoulder tore away from the countertop in what was best described as a wet, ripping sound. Blood spewed from the new wound as Bradley stood watching the man literally tear himself to pieces. Impressed, Bradley quietly watched the doctor fight, not saying a word to his aggressor. Guttural cries of pain emanating from deep within Miles.

"Names, doctor; that's all I need from you. But you had better hurry. I'm afraid the mice will cause permanent damage if left to themselves for too long. They are quite tenacious when properly motivated. I've read that hunger is a very effective motivator. All I need from you is six names. Now… concentrate."

For a brief moment the doctor suspended his fighting and lay quietly. "I...I don't know any medieval names asshole! Why are you doing this?" he demanded.

"Remember Doctor. You must concentrate on this and look at it from my point of view. Why I am doing this is completely irrelevant. I *am* doing this. *That* is all you must know for now. You do however have some say in the things to come. Give me six names Doctor Duval; that's all I ask, then I'll remove the rodents that are as we speak, eating you alive. Six names Miles." Bradley bent over to stand the stool back in the upright position.

"I can't think" Miles countered, his voice still hoarse. "How can you expect me to think? This is craziness!" Bradley took his position on the stool once again, leaning over Miles' belly.

"Better hurry my friend. They seem to be moving deeper as we speak. I'll tell you what," he said, I'll help you get started. Bradley looked up quizzically, one hand stroking his chin, deep in thought. Elizabeth. How's that? Nice and old; medieval you could say. Isn't that your late wife's name? Elsie? I do believe that is short for Elizabeth."

Miles fought at his restraint ever harder, tearing more of his shoulder free from the counter. This time however, it was evident that he felt the immense pain. He howled a deafening shriek feeling his skin rip from the shoulder. The cry was unimpressive to Bradley who slapped the doctor's face, taunting him. "There Miles, I gave you one. Now you need five more. Then I'll remove them from you. Hurry, hurry doctor.

Miles' mind reeled both from the pain he was experiencing and with having to think of names so he could bring this madness to an end. Crying now more out of stress than pain he blurted "Milady".

"Very good!" Bradley exclaimed. "Very good indeed. Not only did you name one of your newly found friends but you went with the one character Dumas used to fuck with the characters in The Three Musketeers. And to top it off, you came up with the one that had *herself* been branded for death with the *Fleur de lis*; very, very good doctor. Maybe I underestimated your intelligence!"

Huffing with the pain quickly becoming more prevalent Miles simply said "Fuck you!"
Time seemed to stand still. Miles had no idea how long this charade had been going on but he knew he was far from being out of the proverbial woods. "Athos!" he coughed.

"Sorry Doctor, but I'm going to make you use your mind. You've exhausted Dumas *and* the Musketeers; time to move on." Miles closed his eyes and thought deeply; trying to remember characters he'd read about in his lifetime. *Lifetime.* The word suddenly had new meaning.

"Alys", he said quietly.

"Hmm" Bradley responded. "Spell it" he countered.

"A.L.Y.S., asshole", Miles volleyed in defiance.

"Wonderful doctor, just wonderful! I am *truly* impressed! Now tell me what meaning that has to you at this time." Bradley prodded.

"What? I don't know what you want from me anymore." Bradley once again stood and paced the length of the island top with his hands clasped behind his back, again as if in deep thought.

"Doctor Duval", he started. "Let's look at this from the perspective of someone in your *profession*. What did you really mean by answering Alys? Of all the names of the time, you picked one that could release you from this; at least in theory. By answering Alys you were thinking of stepping though the mirror from Alice in Wonderland: a very interesting answer to say the least. I'm quite impressed. The question is 'Where do you think the mirror will take you? This all poses an interesting dilemma, but we must move on. I fear our little friends have moved on to the second course of their dinner." A wide grin crossed Bradley's face. He was in total control of the situation. He reveled at how easy he found it to steal the doctor's conceited attempts to control him earlier. He had removed that piece of the equation with ease. A Psychiatrist not in control is... *nothing*. Bradley knew the doctor was well aware of this.

238

The night was still young and there was much sparring to be done.

CHAPTER 51

Blood, bright and red, had found the edge of the counter top and trickled to the floor below, pooling just feet from where Bradley had set his duffle bag. Noticing this, Bradley pushed the bag away with his foot, not wanting to bloody it. Miles was quiet for now, pondering his next move.

"That's two, doctor. See, we're on to something. I do however need three more names from you." Miles remained quiet, refusing to open his eyes. He attempted to distance himself from the situation. Distance him from the pain, the degradation, and the humiliation that his captor was using against him. As he lay there the overwhelming feeling of his colon being eaten away stymied any control he thought he had mustered. Once again he started screaming as loudly as he could. Knowing that his neighbors were very unlikely to hear him the show was for the benefit of his captor. Bradley spun on his heel as he paced away. The screaming had startled him out of the trance like state he was in. "Now, now doctor. You mustn't waste your time with trivial things such as screaming. It is to no avail. There is no one to hear you."

"Sybil", the doctor finally choked out. That's four!" His breathing labored and wet; pink tinged spit dribbled from his quivering lip. Bradley allowed him go on without saying anything. He *wanted* to play this game. He enjoyed this, but was also on a schedule and needed to hurry things along. He let silence overtake the room allowing the doctor the luxury to think, teasing him. Making him think the game would end with the naming of the final mouse. Miles continued, as if an epiphany had struck.

"Lord Montagu". Miles smiled at having remembered these names from his past adventures in literature. "Five!" he announced as if he thought Bradley was unable to keep count. "One more asshole, then you take these fucking rats out of me!" he shouted.

"Mice", Bradley stated quietly.

"What?" replied the doctor, perplexed?

"They're mice. Not rats." Bradley sat down, waiting patiently, knowing that the Doctor was now in the game with all his heart. As if his life depended on it.

Once again, time seemed to stop for Miles. He searched the depths of his mind, scanning the hundreds of works of literature he'd read throughout his lifetime. Then a thought appeared. He was unsure if he'd thought aloud "Shakespeare!" He remained quiet not knowing if he'd actually said the words.

"Very good, doctor. I see we're moving from drama and action to humor. Keep going, you're almost there." Bradley was actually rooting for the doctor at this point. He was starting to like Miles, as one intellectual understands and respects a fellow intellectual.

241

"Does that count?" asked an exasperated Miles.

"Yes, I'll count it. Alas poor Yourik! One more *my friend.*"

"What? You gave me one you son of a bitch!"

"Yes, but I lied. I needed to give you a hint. Something to get your mind kick started. Now one last name Dr. Duval."

"Duke Solinus!" exclaimed Doctor Duval, proud of himself. Bradley began clapping as if he was at theater, the curtains falling, signaling the end of the last act.

"Bravo! Bravo! Doctor, you've outdone yourself. I have to hand it to you. You came through under fire; much better than I'd expected. To end on "A Comedy of Errors" was a nice touch; a nice touch, indeed." Bradley continued clapping softly. "You have done very well my friend. Quite well indeed." he concluded.

"Now get these fucking rats...*mice* out of me you sick fuck!" making sure he placed emphasis on the word mice in an attempt to grate on Bradley's nerves.

"You did well Miles. I am a man of my word. I'll remove the mice as promised, although it may prove too unbearable to stand. I'll give you the option of going to sleep while I do it, your call doctor." Bradley asked, having found a new respect for Doctor Duval.

"Just do it you bastard. You can't cause me anymore pain than you have already done. I'm not afraid of you anymore." Miles took a chance trying to gain some ground on his abductor.

"Okay doctor, whatever your wish..." Bradley removed a scalpel from his rucksack; the same he'd used to slice open the doctor's abdomen. Meticulously he severed each suture until Miles' abdomen opened, creating a gaping wound six inches at the widest part. "Hmm. It seems as if our little friends were more famished than I expected."

"What do you mean?" cried Miles, fear overtaking his consciousness.

"Well, it looks as if some of the mice bored through your mesentery in search of better eats!" replied an impartial Bradley. "It looks as though a couple have dug deeper than the rest. Quite intriguing I must admit. I'd have thought you would have felt that. I'm going to have to go in and get them out", replied Bradley as if he were a field surgeon removing shrapnel from a soldier.

"What? No wait!" yelled Miles. You'll do more damage than they already have!" clamored the doctor. But it was too late. Bradley had already pushed his right hand through the mesenteric lining of the gut, which was mostly intact. The mice had only bitten small holes to get through. The lining felt like a slimy web a spider may have woven over the bowel and it took both of Bradley's hands to separate it. Miles screamed in horror and agonizing pain; hearing the tissues soft tear made

Miles pass out. Bradley hadn't noticed as he was concentrating on removing the foreigners from the doctor's abdominal cavity. It took Bradley a good five minutes to gather all six mice. He placed them in a large boiling pot that had hung earlier over his victims head on a rack. The mice, bloody and reinvigorated having had a bite to eat scratched at the sides of the pot trying to get back to the doctors belly, wanting more of the delicacy they'd been given. One of the six was dead when Bradley pulled him out of the doctor's gut, having gorged himself to death. Bradley noticed that he was close to twice the size he'd been before being placed in the doctor's belly. He placed him in the pot along with the other mice and noticed that a few of the others had taken to eating their companion, seemingly having acquired a taste for flesh. "Interesting", thought Bradley.

After removing the mice, Bradley took to the task of closing the wound he'd created. A foul, bitter smell emanated from the wound. Bradley took note that one of the mice had eaten through the lining of the doctor's intestine and fecal material had begun pouring out into the abdominal cavity. He sewed as quickly as he could in an effort to extinguish the smell. He worked on the incision efficiently with the hands of a surgeon; expertly closing the wound so only a small trickle of blood seeped between the sutures. After completing the task at hand he washed his ungloved hands in the sink behind the island. As he dried his hands he noticed movement. The doctor was waking up.

"Time for the next part of our saga my friend".

CHAPTER 52

Doctor Miles Duval had gone to a pleasant place when he had passed out from the stress of the moment. He was with his beloved wife Elsie and they were young. It was a memory he cherished, the two of them on vacation in Europe just after they'd wed. They walked the narrow streets of Paris, window shopping, holding hands all the while and gently kissing the nape of her neck. Just the way she'd always liked. It was a perfect scene, then he awoke, rushing back to the horrible reality of present day. He muttered, "Elsie" quietly as Bradley turned from the sink drying his hands with a kitchen towel.

"Welcome back Doctor Duval. Soon my friend, soon you'll be with your lovely wife. But first we've work to do. We must close this chapter of the journey we're taking." Bradley picked up a filet knife he had brought. The blade was close to ten inches and bore an edge of incredible sharpness; its metal glistening in the light. "I need to ask you some questions Doctor Duval. I pray you'll respect me enough to tell the complete truth. This is very important to me. I must know that you understand *exactly* why I am doing this to you. You *need* to be honest with your answers. I will not tolerate dishonesty. You will surely die tonight. That I will not keep from you any longer, it is the grisly truth. The question I lay before you now is *how* you want to die. The answers will come as you answer the questions I am about to pose to you. If I feel there is any dishonesty in your voice, any wavering of the tone, then I promise yours will be an even more painful death. You know I make good on my promises. Earlier, I proposed a deal, and I made good on my end after you had made good on yours. I'm a man of my word, as I have already shown you. That will hold true for the remainder of the night".

Bradley walked to the edge of the counter top and raised his right hand; the one holding the filet knife. Showing the doctor the knife, he began to explain what was to be done. Miles' eyes went wide with the blade in front of him. He screamed.

"No!" repeating it as if it would sway the thoughts of his captor. "What the hell are you going to do to me?" he cried. "Get that fucking thing away from me!" Bradley pressed his fingers to the doctor's mouth.

"Shh. This won't hurt too much, I promise. I have to cut you away from the epoxy that is holding you to the counter top. There really is no other way to do this. The epoxy is probably stronger than the marble. There is nothing that will dissolve it. The only way to set you free is to *cut* you free." Bradley continued.

"No! Don't! I'm begging you Bradley. Please don't!" Miles countered in a desperate plea to alter Bradley's actions. He began sobbing uncontrollably. "Please don't."

CHAPTER 53

The knife felt cold at first as it sliced through the soft tissue of Doctor Duval's left calf. Bradley was amazed at how easily the blade slid through the tissue. He'd expected it to be much more difficult. The sharp edge cut through Miles like a hot knife slicing through butter. To Bradley's disbelief Miles remained quite calm. The pain was prevalent but numbed by the state of shock the doctor had slipped into. Bradley cut his way quickly through the lower extremities leaving very little skin behind. There was much blood but it seemed it was of a superficial nature and not life threatening. As he moved from extremity to extremity, Bradley began questioning the doctor.

"Miles, I know you have been put through quite a bit tonight but it's imperative that you answer a few more questions for me." Miles groaned at the requests and Bradley had hoped that he remained cognitive enough to follow his instructions. Then suddenly, shocking Bradley, Miles spoke clearly and concisely.

"What do you want to know Bradley? Ask your questions so we can get this over with."

Bradley, stupefied, stood next to Miles and said nothing. He took a moment to collect his thoughts then stated.

"Miles, I know that you placed my mother in Saint Lawrence Psychiatric Center against her will. Or was it completely against her will? Did she go voluntarily or did you have to force the issue? Having met you personally now, I do believe that you could have convinced her that you could help her." Bradley waited for a response but got none. "I also know that you did what you did as a favor to Maggie, sorry, Margaret. She already told me as much. I know you two were close friends and that she confided in you when she was faced with her dilemma. I felt bad for Maggie when I met with her. She was actually a very nice, personable lady. I do feel that she was coerced into this mess by my father. Unfortunately she'd made a decision that ultimately led to her demise. I did however take pity on her. She died somewhat peacefully. But the point is she died nonetheless. It was her payment for what happened to my mother". Bradley paused to see if Miles was absorbing his tale. The doctor lay quietly, staring at the ceiling as if he'd known all along that this would be his fate for having participated in this scheme. The only emotion he showed was pain as Bradley continued severing his restraint. "I think I know *why* you would have done what you did. Maggie was an old friend that helped you get through a difficult time in your life. She more than likely kept you from ending your own life. She was quite vivid in her telling of your woes and how she played a role in saving you. She was quite honored that you picked her out of all the peers you could have tapped for their professional capabilities. She had a lot of respect for you before your ordeal but was downright proud of you when you decided to take it upon yourself to seek help."

Miles realized tears had begun to accumulate at the corners of his eyes as he listened quietly to Bradley speak. He also noticed the tears were not in response to the pain he was feeling but to the chord that his very wise captor had struck. Bradley continued, "Maggie truly felt that you were suicidal and that her intervention saved not only your distinguished career but also your life. She told me your recovery was the highlight of her career. She said that she had always respected you, ever since you both attended university together and that your having asked her for help was the equivalent of winning a Nobel Prize to her."

Bradley stopped speaking and looked toward the opposite wall of the kitchen as if he were in another time. A tear formed in his eye and slowly grew until it descended his cheek collecting at the corner of his mouth. Tasting its saltiness, he snapped out of his trance-like state and cleared his head. It was the first time in this entire ordeal that he'd become emotional. He fought back the urge to let Brad out and walk away from what he *knew* needed to be done.

"I want you to know Miles that Maggie died a good death. There was no torture involved. She just went to sleep."

Hearing the news that he'd lost another woman whom he'd loved was overwhelming and brought Miles to tears.

"She didn't deserve to die", he stated between sobs. "She was a wonderful person. You shouldn't have killed her." Bradley stopped what he was doing and looked down at his prey.

"I know she was a good person, Miles. My own mother wrote of her positively in her diary, yet she fell into a trap set by my father. It's my belief that we all must pay for our sins. Don't get me wrong, Miles. I'm not an overly religious man and I make no reference to the sins against the church. I believe we are held to a higher power that lies within each of us. The *sins* Margaret committed were against humankind, not God. She had to pay for the choices she'd made. That's why I had to kill her. This has *nothing* to do with religion. It has *everything* to do with humankind and how we treat each other in our daily lives." A silence followed that both men unknowingly agreed to, out of respect for Maggie.

Miles was the first to break the silence. Choking back tears he simply stated, "Bradley, I want to apologize for what your mother had to endure. She was set up from the beginning by the actions of an overbearing, deceitful husband. She had verifiable mental health issues. I won't refute that, but it was nothing she needed to be institutionalized for. That was *my* doing. I thought I was doing a dear friend a favor, helping her out of a horrible situation. In reality I should have told Margaret to fix her fuck up herself. I took part in a heinous crime that hurt a woman that just needed a break, a new start. I took away her freedom and with that she lost the only thing she loved unconditionally. *You.* Your mother never recovered from the fact that she had lost you to the man you call your father. *That* is ultimately what led her to kill herself. She realized that I was never going to let her out of the hospital. She could not fathom the thought of living another moment without you."

Another trickle of blood escaped the corner of Miles' mouth. The room grew quiet again, neither man wanting to break the silence. After a couple of long minutes Bradley spoke.

"You didn't have to. You could have looked the other way. You could have said no to Maggie. She respected you enough to not let your decision come between your friendship." Bradley found *himself* crying now.

"I'm so sorry Bradley. What I took part of is truly a crime and I deserve to be punished. I have to tell you that not a day has passed since your mother killed herself that I haven't thought of her. She was a remarkable woman. Please Bradley, finish what you've come to do. I understand why you are here and I do not dispute it. In fact, I think of it as a way for me to pay my debt. I can only hope that I get to see my Elsie once again." Miles stiffened his jaw as if relishing what was to come. Bradley turned to him face to face.

"Thank you". I'll spare you any further pain. Go be with your lovely wife, Miles. If you see my mother tell her I miss her dearly."

With that, Bradley raised the filet knife and reached across the countertop drawing the sharp blade swiftly and deeply across Doctor Duval's neck severing his carotid arteries in one seamless movement. Miles' eyes opened wide then slowly closed as his remaining life flowed from his neck. Brad slumped to the floor, crying.

PART VIII

CHAPTER 54

The flight into Tweed-New Haven Airport, less than 5 miles southeast of New Haven, Connecticut was smooth as silk. Brad had booked a flight out of Syracuse the morning after Dr. Duval's passage into death. He wanted more than anything to be home with his family, missing Linda and the girls, Lilly and Ana, more than mere words could describe. The journey set forth by his mother was coming to an end and peacefulness blanketed Brad when he awoke in his room at the bed and breakfast that morning. A sense of reaching finality to a quest he had no choice but to endure. He lay in bed weeping tears of happiness knowing that his mother's wishes had nearly been fulfilled. It was now time to return home and resume *his* life. For the time being.

Linda and the girls arrived at the airport an hour early to retrieve the man they loved without conviction. They missed him dearly, as they always did during these annual summer excursions. Upon leaving, Brad had attempted to instill the thought that he'd only be gone for two weeks at the most but his daughters had always felt it would be an eternity before seeing their loving father. Lilly was far more insightful at the ripe old age of five and a half years than her younger sister, Ana who was just eighteen months. An enigma Brad had chalked up to a child's lack of comprehension for time. Brad did however love the feeling that his girls welcomed him home as if they'd not seen him for ages. These annual reunions had become both stressful and at the same time gleeful. A smile crossed Brad's face as the wheels touched down on the tarmac. He closed his eyes and silently thanked God. It was nearly over.

Sighting their father, the girls screamed and ran to greet him as he walked through the arrival gate. Brad bent down to get the full effect of their hugs and found it difficult to let go.

"I missed you two so much," he said as a tear trickled down his face, red with delight.

"We missed you too, Daddy!" they countered in unison as if they'd rehearsed it for the past two weeks. He kissed them both on the forehead and stood with a daughter clinging to each leg. Brads eyes met Linda's as he ascended and they stared into each other's saying nothing. They sensed each other's thoughts as if they had one singular mind. Linda moved forward taking her husband into an embrace that neither wanted to end. Brad whispered into her ear as they held each other.

"It's almost over". Linda began crying uncontrollably in Brad's arms. He too began to cry, overwrought with mounting emotion; he'd been to hell and back. The girls looked up at their mother.

"What's wrong Mommy? Aren't you happy?" Linda looked down at the confused girls, smiling.

"Oh yes girls. Mommy is very happy." Linda wiped the tears from her face as the four of them left the gate and walked to baggage claim. After retrieving his suitcase they left the airport for the hour-long ride home. The girls felt it was imperative to fill their daddy in on everything that had transpired during his trip.

"What did *you* do Daddy?" asked Lilly.

"Oh, daddy had to visit an old friend of the family. That's all." Linda took Brad's hand in hers as they drove home.

CHAPTER 55

It was early autumn in New England and the weather was changing, taking along with it the leaves in their entire splendor. Brad had been home for nearly two weeks and life had taken a welcome turn to the normal. He spent much of the time with Linda and the girls taking them to parks and playing in the yard. Lilly was readying for her first day of kindergarten; a very exciting, but distressing situation for her. Brad watched as she chose and re-chose her wardrobe for the big day. A bemused look crossed his face as Lilly turned scowling.

"Daddy, I don't have any good clothes to wear. All the other kids are going to make fun of me." As she finished her covert message meaning 'we need to go shopping', Linda walked in the room.

"Brad, I need to talk to you", a serious look on her face. Linda moved her gaze to her daughters eyes, "Lilly, why don't you hang these clothes up for now. We'll find something that won't make you look like a dork later." Lilly huffed a little but complied, carefully placing her clothes on hangers to be placed in her closet in an orderly manner. Brad laughed as he watched his daughter.

"You get that from your mother you know." Lilly looked up from her chore questioningly.

"What do I get from Mommy?" she asked.

"Being neat and prepared", Brad answered knowing that it was actually he who was the meticulous one in the family. Everything that had occurred to Brad in his life up until now had been carefully planned and executed leaving no room for error. He turned to follow Linda out of the room closing the door as they left.

Linda said nothing as she led the way to the kitchen, stopping at the refrigerator to retrieve a bottle of Evian. Brad decided to let her to say whatever it was she had on her mind at her own pace. She was clearly postponing the discussion as long as she could. He remained quiet as he sat on a stool near the kitchen island. Linda closed the refrigerator door and turned quickly on her heel as if she needed to say whatever it was she needed to say before she lost her nerve.

"I need to know if it is over", she simply stated. There was a look of disparity to her as she longed to hear her husband say *yes*. The room remained quiet for some time before Brad responded. He spoke to her as he focused on the floor.

"I have one more thing to finish. Then it will be over." Linda sank to the floor leaning against the cabinets. She opened the bottle of water taking a long drag. She stared at the bottle before addressing Brad.

"When?" she simply asked.

"Soon", he answered. "It won't take very long, less than a week." He finished.

"Why right now? Why can't it wait until next summer? Like the rest of *them*. Why do you have to do this now? There's so much going on here right now. I want you to be here for this", she said exasperated. "Lilly is starting school in three days! I don't want you to miss that. Don't you understand?" she pleaded. Brad crossed the room and sat next to Linda; reaching out taking her hands into his. The water bottle dropped softly, rolling across the floor.

"Look at me honey. I want this over more than anyone. You have to believe me." Linda dropped her head sobbing.

"You've missed so much as it is Brad. I need this to end. Now!" Brad pulled her into a hug saying without words that he understood.

"Alright."

CHAPTER 56

Brad decided to move up his deadline. Instead of waiting six months or even a year to complete his journey, he'd have to readjust and finish it now. In a way this was a blessing. He'd had enough also. This *alter* life was getting to him. He wanted it to end just as badly as Linda had, maybe more. Brad decided to wait until Lilly started school; he wanted to be there for that. He wanted some semblance of normalcy to gauge his life upon before initiating what would be his final part to this long drawn out play. Quietly he made arrangements to fly to Baltimore and begin what needed to be done. This however was his 'piece de resistance', therefore would take a bit longer to plan and set up than the others. He knew what he wanted to do. All that was needed was to scout a place and prep it. He then would need to sit quietly, in the background and watch. Watch and learn his fathers' life, his habits. Brad had spent a lifetime avoiding his fathers' life. Now his success depended upon knowing it. He pushed the thoughts to the back recesses of his mind. First he needed to tend to his own family. After all, they came first. *Always*.

CHAPTER 57

"Here comes your bus, honey," Brad announced. He and Linda both hugged Lilly topping it off with a kiss on the forehead. Lilly recently proclaimed that she was too old for her daddy to kiss her anywhere but the forehead; that it was embarrassing when her friends saw it. He felt he'd missed too much of his daughters life already, but was looking forward to the remainder of what he had left.

Smiling, Brad informed her, "Be safe. Don't get into trouble and for God's sake listen to your bus driver. If you do all those things then the rest will be easy." Lilly looked up at her father as if he'd lost his marbles but she appeased him.

"Yes daddy. I'll be the best little girl in the whole class." Linda wished her well as she buttoned up her coat to the neck; a move that Lilly would surely reverse after she was out of sight on the bus. Linda held Brad tightly as the bus pulled away.

"He's going to miss this stuff you know", he said to no one in particular pulling Linda closer as he did. His voice was an octave lower and flat.

"What do you mean by that?" Linda asked. She suddenly had a very concerned look on her face.

"Oh nothing, she's growing up too fast. That's all I guess." With his voice back to normal Brad dropped his head looking at the pavement. He kicked at a small stone as the two turned toward the house. "It's just that I missed so much of my childhood. I want to give the girls everything I didn't have." Linda pulled his arm around her neck.

"You've already given it to them. You are a wonderful dad, Brad. Don't ever think otherwise. I'm very proud of you". Linda had a smile cross her lips, slight at first then growing to a full blown 'I've got a secret' smile.

"What aren't you telling me sweetheart?" Brad gave her the look that told her he knew she was up to something.

"Nothing dear…why do you ask?" she giggled.

"Linda Fordam, I know you better that anyone and I know when you're hiding something." He stated with a smile. Linda took two steps back and cradled her belly as if holding a child. She looked down at her shoes scuffing one on the driveway as she did so.

Timidly she continued, "I'm not hiding anything. Not anymore", she looked up into her husband's eyes seeing he finally understood. Brad took her hands in his own grinning as if he'd just won the lottery.

"How long have you known?" he asked exasperated.

"A couple of days. I wanted to be sure before I told you. I was sick the other day out of the blue. I had a feeling then, but I had to be sure". She stepped forward closing the gap between the two in an instant. Brad took her in his arms and held her tightly saying nothing at first. They held each other listening to the others breathing. Brad lowered his chin and met her lips with his own and they kissed gently. Linda drew her head back first looking up into Brads eyes. "I wasn't sure how you would take it. It's only been eighteen months since Ava was born". Brad hunched over to look Linda straight in the eyes.

Unblinkingly he said, "I love you more than ever, Linda. You have made me so incredibly happy. He carried her to the bedroom making love to her passionately. When Linda awoke she found herself alone in bed. She found a short handwritten note on the pillow next to hers. It simply stated "I love you. I have to finish this *now*".

CHAPTER 58

Brad spent the rest of the day in his workshop at the rear of the garage, *his* space. Although the path he chose professionally was that of an educator, he had always felt that a man needed to have basic skills in carpentry, plumbing and whatever else a well-rounded man needed in his arsenal of useful skills. His students often poked fun at him because of his rough hands. He could pass for a mechanic some days. He was proud of his firm handshake, having always been taught that a strong grip is a sign of a strong man. One of the few lessons of use he'd received from his father. Today though was not a day for carpentry. He was doing a little welding tonight that would prove useful in the weeks to come. Linda allowed him his privacy interrupting him only for lunch. She had decided to take the day off from her veterinary service for the first day of Lilly's schooling. She was lucky enough to have a partner that had young children earlier in life and knew the importance of being a phone call away in case of an emergency. Brad had extended his summer vacation by two weeks citing personal reasons. No one asked him to explain his actions. He'd been one of Yale's brightest rising stars and almost never missed a day of work. His Dean advised him that he would arrange for one of the other professors to help cover the lectures as long as Brad would provide a syllabus. Brad had only one graduate level class this semester to teach and advised the dean to let the class take two weeks off in preparation for a most demanding semester. He provided some required reading and told the class through the Dean that the first two weeks of class were being suspended. Those students who knew Professor Fordam wholly understood that they were in for a tough semester as it was and gladly accepted the free time to prepare themselves.

CHAPTER 60

April 10, 1976

He will never let Bradley see me again. I now realize this.
What is he telling him? What awful things is my child hearing
about me? My letters are returned unsent. Where is my child?
Where is my Bradley? I have so many things to tell him. So
many things to explain. So many things to apologize for. So
many apologies.

Brad had decided to drive from Connecticut to
Baltimore. The drive would prove to be pleasant with the
changing of the seasons as the foliage was magnificent this year.
Trees seemed to explode with color all around him as he drove.
"Two weeks", he told himself. He'd be home in time for Lilly's
first school event. A parent night to showcase some of the
artwork the kids created. The thought of this made him smile.
He hadn't noticed the police cruiser behind him until it was too
late. The bright lights alerting him to the fact he was being
pulled over.

"Shit!" he'd said aloud. Brad was a safe driver never
getting as much as a moving violation in his lifetime. His heart
raced as he set his directional to pull off the roadway. He had
decided to take a more scenic route and was staying off the main
highways as much as possible. There was no reason for this

other than wanting to see the countryside. Looking through the mirror he noticed it was a local cop that had pulled him over as he rummaged through his center storage in the car for his insurance card and registration. There was a knock on the window before he found the required items, startling him.

"Sir, please roll down your window" stated a police officer no more than twenty five. As Brad complied with the order he dropped the insurance card on the floor between his feet.

"Shit!" he exclaimed again.

"Anything wrong sir", asked the officer.

"No, no I just dropped my insurance card. That's all," replied Brad noticing his hands were shaking. The officer also noticed his shaking hands.

"Do you know why I pulled you over sir?"

Brad shrugged his shoulders saying, "No sir. I didn't notice my speed when I saw your lights go on."

The officer, his left hand on his revolver replied, "Well sir you've got a brake light out. That's all. Can I see your registration and insurance card please? How about your license while you're at it." Brad leaned to the left to pull his wallet out of his rear pocket and also leaned down to retrieve the insurance card laying at his feet.

"Here you go officer". The officer took the documents.

"Wait a minute while I run these through the computer. Anything I should know about before I do that?" he asked with a fake smile.

"No sir. Nothing that I know about anyway", replied Brad with his own fake smile.

The officer took what seemed to be an eternity to return to the car. When he did he had Brad's documents in his left hand. This small sign brought instant relief to Brad. His heart slowed knowing the officer saw him as no threat.

"Well it looks as though you're telling the truth", the officer divulged. "Your record is clean as a whistle. Where are you headed anyway?" Brad's heart raced again. He could feel the color leaving his face. Then he realized there was no need to not be truthful. After all, he wasn't doing anything illegal, was he? *At least not yet.*

"I'm headed to Baltimore to see my father", he answered.

"You coming from Connecticut?" asked the officer.

"Yeah, I thought I'd stay off the highways though. The drive is too nice", Brad attested.

"Hmm. A lot of drug runners do the same. You know?" replied the officer.

"No, I didn't officer; never thought about it. I'm in no hurry and the highway didn't seem any fun", Brad replied truthfully.

"Well, I'll tell you what. I'm gonna let you off with a warning this time. Just promise me you'll get that brake light fixed soon". He handed Brad his papers back and tipped his head. The officer was just about to turn around and head back to his cruiser when he spoke again.

"What do you do for a living if you don't mind me asking?" Brad looked back up at the man and told him he was a professor at Yale in the Linguistics Department. He also said his father was the same only he was with the Army. Albeit retired.

The officer shrugged his shoulders and said, "Army brat, huh? Me too. Hated every second of it; never got used to moving so much. Shitty life for a kid. Don't you agree?" Brad smiled.

"You have no idea. I think I had it the worst." The smile leaving his face he continued, "What are you going to do? Life goes on, right? I'm actually going to see my father that I haven't seen in fifteen years because of that life. I'm just getting around to crossing that bridge".

The officer reached in the car and patted Brad on the left shoulder. "Good luck my friend. I hope you have a fruitful trip. Get those issues resolved. Life's too short." With that the officer returned to his vehicle and pulled away turning his lights off as he did so. Brad sat there in amazement.

"You have no idea my friend. No idea." He returned the documents to their rightful places and pulled back onto the road shaking his head as he did so. "Life *is* too short", he repeated aloud.

CHAPTER 60

The remainder of the trip was uneventful. Brad thoroughly enjoying every minute of it. As he drove further south the fall scenery became steadily less evident, but enjoyable nonetheless. The time alone allowed for Brad to formulate his approach to this final chapter. He entered Baltimore around seven that evening driving straight to his hotel.

The Biltmore Suites were located on West Madison Street not far from the University of Maryland and more importantly Druid Hill Park. The Biltmore Suites were built in 1880 having the feel of a 19th century Victorian era building, reminiscent of old Europe; a most suitable hotel to spend a couple of weeks. After checking in with the front desk he rode the elevator to the third floor that housed his suite. He then took a long awaited shower. The suite housed a separate bathroom, sitting room, small area with a mini-refrigerator, and microwave oven. He slept on the queen bed without even pulling the sheets down.

When Brad awoke the next morning he noticed he was in the same position he'd fallen asleep, still naked. The musty smell of his damp towel was the first visage of the day. A day he hoped would prove fruitful. As it was, there was much to do.

The Biltmore was located in an historic area of Baltimore with many restaurants within walking distance. There was also the famed Antique Row around the corner. The entire area held the aura of strolling along an old side street in Belgium. The hotel was also conveniently located for Bradley's upcoming events. Brad found a small café on the same block as the Biltmore and enjoyed a refreshing cup of coffee along with a hearty breakfast. He felt re-invigorated after a good nights' sleep.

Mentally planning out the mornings activities, Brad decided to pay a visit to the University of Maryland; time to learn his father's habits along with his normal routes of travel. Brad hoped he would be able to discern his father's face, not having seen him in over fifteen years. He was able to find a picture of him a couple of years prior from a lecture the senior Fordam had given at Harvard University. Brad attended the event but remained in the shadows. There was a time and a place for Wesley Fordam's contribution to this saga. The lecture was part of a combined series involving the top five universities in the United States that had PhD. programs in Linguistics; more precisely Semiotics. A field that Brad's father had excelled. He had been recruited by the University of Maryland to start up their newly developed program, feeding into his father's ego perfectly. Brad actually enjoyed the lecture having participated himself through Yale. He recently gave a speech dealing with the research aspect of semiotics and how there were advances occurring almost daily dealing with understanding how individuals learned a language through symbolism. Their respective paths generally paralleled each other only occasionally intersecting. Brad had been lucky so far never having to deal with his father directly.

CHAPTER 61

The University of Maryland was founded in the late 1800's primarily as an agricultural center. By 1920 the college became the property of the State of Maryland becoming part of the State University System. In 1988 the state of Maryland designated the University of Maryland as its flagship institution among all others in the state system, acting as a magnet for Wesley's ever growing ego...but now someone else was in charge.

Wesley awoke slowly, his mind garbled from drugs administered after he was tasered in his cell. He found himself sitting in a bare-metal chair, naked. Cold, he began to shiver, unsure if it was the chill of his environment or fear and uncertainty coursing through his veins. His vision was blurred making it difficult distinguishing forms in his sight. A pain shot through his mid-chest when he attempted to move his head to the right and retreated when he'd straightened his posture, but stung as a reminder that maybe he ought not to try that again. His hands were bound securely behind his back, it seemed with duct tape but he couldn't be sure. His feet bound tightly to the legs of the chair.

The last cognitive thought he'd had was that of the door opening to his cell; a dark figure shadowing the overwhelming blast of light that emitted from the entrance. He remembered feeling, meek and had trouble forming words aimed at his captor, but still he staggered to a standing position. Just as he began to speak a jolt slammed him to the floor. His skeletal muscles contracting in a rage, he'd fallen back to the cold concrete with a mind-rattling thud. He was able to think clearly, unable to focus his attention on anything but the spasticity of his muscles. As a feeling of dread held him in its grasp the flow of electricity lessened then ceased altogether. He remained in a state of fear and confusion lying on the cold, hard floor; helpless. He had never in all his years felt such a loss of control. As his rigored body slackened he remembered feeling a sting in his arm. Slowly the darkened figure blurred until finally the sight was gone; momentarily erased from his mind.

Whoever had done this had done so with great efficiency and ease. Groggy, his vision slowly improved and he was now able to decipher different shapes and shades of darkness in the room he'd been placed. The room itself was much larger than the one he'd remembered being held in earlier. How much earlier he was unsure of. His loss of time frightened him even more now. Had anyone noticed he was missing yet? How long had he actually been missing?

Slowly he was able to see a door frame with light sneaking through the cracks. A bench about four or five feet directly in front of him also appeared out of the darkness. Metal, with no paint, it looked like a park bench. He tried to look to the left only to endure the same excruciating pain he'd felt turning to the right. He thought, "What could be causing this pain?" There was pressure pushing downward on his sternum. This answered no questions and distracted him from the task at hand; trying to see where he was and what else, or who else for that matter was in this room.

Slowing his breathing, he pushed the thought of pain from his mind as best he could. Moving his eyes only he was able to make out the vague shape of the room in his line of vision. The room itself was larger and more elongated than that of his previous. "Probably about fifteen feet wide", he thought. This time he was able to see a ceiling, thanks to the light trickling in from the door jam. It looked as if it were about ten to twelve feet high and had something protruding from it every three feet or so, but still he couldn't be sure.

Visual clarity came quickly with Wesley's tears wetting his eyes, and now he saw that there were ropes tied to metal loops in the ceiling. The ropes seemed to just dangle to the floor and he was unsure if they were attached to anything. Lowering his head to look at the ropes created a pain even worse than that of side to side movement. He could feel a warm sensation that undoubtedly was blood trickling onto his chest from under his chin. He fought to release his hands from their bindings to no avail. At least there was no pain involved with this maneuvering. His senses were slowly coming back to him and he smelled something burning in the distance; just a vague sense of the smell once in a while wafting through the stale air. There was also a crackle of possibly a fire. Wesley was amazed at how much he had relied on his other senses when he was essentially blind. These other senses seemed to fade with his new found sight. He spat out a small chuckle at this thought. Then he heard *him*.

"What seems to be so funny Professor Fordam?" a deep calm voice asked from somewhere behind him. Wesley jolted to attention in his cold metal seat with the thought that he hadn't been alone all this time. His heart pounded in his chest and stomach acid crept up his throat, burning. He was, at last, facing the unknown force driving this insanity. Instinctively he'd turned his head to the left to see where the voice came from only to be reminded that a horrible pain would soon follow. He immediately straightened his head and cleared his throat readying himself for the fight of his life. As he attempted to speak however there was a sharp pain emitting from under his chin. He quickly discovered that if he opened his mouth to speak he'd be faced with yet another gruesome shot of pain. At that he snorted out a laugh realizing that he'd gained his sense of sight back only to lose his ability to speak. His laugh quickly turned into a cry. This loss of control over his body was overwhelming and overloaded his sense of cognitive thought. He subconsciously defaulted to crying. He muttered

"Why?"

There was a low pitched chuckle from somewhere behind him. Then he heard footsteps. There was suddenly a deafening quiet that eerily reminded Wesley of being held in his other cell. A feeling of despair overwhelmed him and he muttered once again, "why?" In a low whisper in Wesley's right ear his question was addressed.

"Soon Professor, soon. First I have to take care of something."

With a deafening roar of metal on metal Wesley was wrenched backward, still seated firmly in his chair. His head slammed on the floor behind him as his feet flew up in to the air. As he tried to regain his breath he felt his feet being pulled taut. Possibly one of the ropes he'd seen in the ceiling was now being put to use. A shearing pain caused Wesley to groan as the pulling increased. The force was so strong that Wesley could feel the chair being drawn toward whatever was pulling him; the loud screeching of metal across concrete rang in his ears.

Suddenly, there was silence. The scraping of the chair along the concrete floor ceased and Wesley was aware only of his own heavy breathing. There was an indescribable pain stemming from chin to chest: much worse than before.

"The pain you feel in your chest is that from a device called the Heretic Fork. It is a two sided fork. Each end with two sharp points. One end is dug deeply into your sternum.

278

The other is wedged under your chin. As you have undoubtedly figured out it causes extreme pain if you attempt to move your head or speak. Such a lovely device." the voice quietly said as if speaking to a lover.

Wesley tried to lift his chin away from his chest in an attempt to loosen the device but without success.

"Try all you want Professor. The device is kept firmly in place with a leather binding around your neck. Trust me, it's not going anywhere. Not unless I say so."

Wesley stopped fighting and tried to regain what little composure he could in such a situation. His head was pounding from the blow it had taken when he was slammed to the floor.

"Why?" he muttered question went unanswered.

"The Heretic Fork was used quite frequently in medieval times. Mostly by the Spanish during the inquisition by was also adopted by the Papal inquisition. Its purpose is to make the wearer of the device recant his sins to the church and accept God. The accused was told to repeat but one word over and over: *Abiuro*. Which, when translated means 'I recant'," the voice recited in a cold manner; as if teaching a lesson to a student. "You see Professor; this is an orchestrated attempt to get you to confess *your* sins to me. I know you're asking yourself what you could have done to bring this upon yourself. Well, we both know the answer to that but one of us apparently needs some prodding." Wesley could sense the toothy grin on his captors face as he finished the sentence.

"You're a linguist Professor. Quite famous in academic circles from what I understand. You speak Russian and German as if they were of your native tongue. You've had many years to develop this skill as I understand. There was a seemingly endless pause. "Do you know any Latin, Professor?" Wesley's eyes narrowed and he furrowed his brows as if proclaiming "why in the hell does that matter?"! "Listen carefully Colonel", the voice said calmly. "Nunc Scio Tenebris Lux". There was silence between the two adversaries. Colonel Fordam nodded. "I thought you would. *Now I know that from darkness comes light*'," whispered the unknown voice.

At that moment Wesley's head was covered with a black cloth bag and cinched around his neck. "Lights out" he thought.

"You see, Colonel, one cannot find his way out of the darkness until one is immersed in it. You are essentially on trial for crimes committed in your past. This trial began more than six years ago; however you were not invited to the initial proceedings.

Once again Wesley heard the faint sound of footsteps, this time moving toward the bench which was, until recently in front of him. The man with the mysterious voice sat down silently.

"I spent many years developing a knowledge base that I once thought of as a mere hobby of interest but now I know it can and *will* be put to proper use. You see Colonel, medieval cultures have always fascinated me. I had the advantage of being immersed in academia at a very young age and absorbed the information I was given like a withered sponge."

"Who?" Wesley started to ask before he felt the stinging of the fork pierce his chin and embed itself in the fleshy under part of his tongue.

"All in good time, Colonel."

Wesley couldn't figure out what he reacted to first, the loud crack or the raging pain he felt on the soles of his bare feet. The pain was incomparable to anything he'd endured thus far and he let out a deep resonant moan.

"That Colonel is called canning. This little form of punishment was used until quite recently and is still used in some parts of the world, although rarely." Another loud crack and yet another shard of pain. "I actually found it somewhat difficult to find bamboo green enough to endure what *you're* about to without breaking. You see the object is not only to cause an immeasurable amount of pain," another crack this time breaking some of the bones in Wesley's feet, "but to also cause permanent physical damage."

Colonel Fordam tried to lessen the pain he was feeling by forcing his mind to replay his life in an attempt to unravel this mystery. His time in the military was spent translating Russian and German into English for someone else to decipher. He was the middle man. He was of no beneficial use to anyone. He brown-nosed his way up the ladder of success. Later in life, he left the military and started teaching languages as a professor at Indiana University. There he rarely found himself in conflict with others. He'd kept to himself mostly. Things were not adding up.

After the sixth canning came a very calm silence, the only sound coming from Wesley, who was gasping for breath between muted cries.

"Six should suffice, don't you agree Colonel?" Six." Then a pause. "Six." Yet another pause, "Six!" screamed Bradley. Before he realized what happened Wesley was jarred into the upright sitting position once again. The rapidity of the motion had a dizzying effect and it took him a couple of seconds to gather his balance. "There seems to be a connection here, don't you think Colonel Fordam?" Bradley removed his father's hood.

A dim light came on from somewhere behind Wesley and he was once again able to see the bench in front of him. This time however there was a man sitting calmly. The stranger had dark, shortly cropped hair with a hint of grey. His features reminded him of someone although Wesley couldn't place who just yet. The stranger simply sat, coldly watching Wesley for any signs of recognition. The older man, feeling the coolness of the concrete floor under his badly damaged feet fought the need to moan. Wesley tried to look down at his feet but was entrapped in his neutral position by the Heretic's Fork; forced to look directly at his abductor.

"Six." The man said coolly. "Six years." Another pause. "Six dreadful years. You kept her there for six horrible years. You sick fucking bastard!" His mind spun uncontrollably as Colonel Wesley James Fordam sat face to face with his captor, his son.

"Bradley?"

There was no answer, just a cold stare; a forced silence; son versus father: a final showdown.

Bradley Wolfe Fordam smiled as he relished the fact that all of this had been a surprise to his father. Years of planning. Years of revenge. Years of torture and murder had culminated to this final moment. All Bradley could do was smile. Wesley could see it now. His son had always had Patricia's smile.

Bradley could see recognition in his father's face. His smile broadened and a short laugh exploded into the quiet room.

"You seem surprised Colonel. Are you surprised at the fact that it's me or by the fact that I knew all along it was you behind mothers' death? Father, and I use the term loosely, it was you that made all this happen. Your doing. Please don't ruin this for me by playing the fool. I know you're smarter than that." With that Bradley gave his father another toothy grin. "Today", Bradley stood holding his arms stretched out in front of him as if praying, "is the culmination of your life's work. It represents the irony of a fool's life; to place yourself before your own family? How dare of you!" Hatred now filled Bradley's otherwise stoic face. "And to think that I believed that mother was crazy! That I believed you."

Wesley sensed the rage brewing in his son's voice and attempted a scream for help. A loud *pop* resonated in the room as the heretic's Fork finally worked its way completely through his tongue and lodged itself in the upper palate of his mouth. The muffled screams made Bradley smile again. To see his father in such pain brought forth a long awaited joy.

"Ouch! That's gotta hurt old man!" he snickered. "As I said earlier, this is a very useful toy. It helps the aggressor keep total control over his victim. The latter being you father."

The surprised look draining from Wesley's face indicated to Bradley it was time to move on.

"You see...*Dad*, before Mother died she had made an arrangement to have her personal diary delivered to me. You see...*Dad*, Mother set you up from the beginning. Knowing that she would never be released from the Psychiatric Center she'd noted all of the happenings between the two of you. She had also made a list...a shopping list of sorts for me to follow. *She* in essence brought you to this place." Bradley showed no emotion when speaking of his mother. Wesley started to weep once again.

Most of the physical pain now went unnoticed. The fact that he had absolutely no control over this situation frightened Wesley the most. He was used to being in control. He'd commanded people. He was *always* the boss. Even now as a professor he was completely in charge of his pupils. A life of ownership had abruptly become a life owned. His future held in another's hand.

Wesley started to cough uncontrollably, choking on the blood accumulating in his throat. He spat blood out as best he could but would not stop coughing. Suddenly the chair he'd been tethered to lurched forward as if it were on hinges. Wesley readied himself for the blow surely to follow when suddenly the chair stopped, leaving him looking down at the concrete floor. His face merely inches from the cold, unforgiving surface. He coughed even harder from the jolting but his new found position allowed the blood to run from his mouth emptying the back of his throat. Wesley looked down at the floor watching the pool of blood grow larger by the second.

"Handy chair, eh Pop?" joked Bradley. He'd tried to make himself sound crazy, luring his father yet deeper into the trap he'd set to spring. Bradley let out a loud roaring laugh that echoed off the walls of the room. He placed his father in the upright position once again; his face only inches from that of his father's; a wolf-like sneer on his face. "You have a tendency of making people crazy, Dad. Don't you think?" Wesley violently shook his head back and forth screaming in pain as he did so. Trying to show his son he couldn't be broken. "Now, now my dear father, let's not intentionally hurt ourselves. We all know where that'll land you!" Another horror filled laugh bellowed out of Bradley.

His son's voice was as calm as a pond, "I felt a lot of self-resentment for not being there for mother all those years. I felt I had a hand in her misfortunes. But I also could not stand being around either of you. You fed off each other's emotions, like starving cannibals. You had to control her and you knew she'd let you. She didn't have the fortitude to end your wrath so she took everything you dished out. You forced her into alcoholism. She'd turned to the bottle to escape *you* and that made you push even harder. Depression set in and went hand in hand with the booze. One feeding off the other. Eventually you realized there was no way of hiding your little secret from the Army so you played it out like the perfect husband. Very caring and wanting your loving wife to get all the help she could. You told your superiors that everything was under control, that she was just homesick.

Eventually they told you that if you didn't get a handle on her behavior that it would affect your future in the services. You had been mired as a Captain far too long and knew that you would never make it to Major with this *problem* looming over your head like a storm cloud." Bradley rambled on as if not sensing that his father was still in the room. He spoke as if he'd rehearsed this speech a hundred times in his head and now that he had a stage there was no stopping him.

"This next part took some doing to figure out but I'd found that people *will* talk if properly motivated." At this last statement Wesley's eyes widened with fear. Just the reaction Bradley was anticipating. "You then made arrangements with some of your "buddies" to get orders stateside.

This was tricky being that you were a linguistics specialist in Russian and German. But from what I'd learned, you had some friends in helpful positions. Not to mention a Commander that owed you a favor or two. Rest his soul". Wesley began to moan inconsolably. Bradley was beginning to unravel his father's web of betrayal ever so slowly. A torture unto itself he thought, smiling.

"General Tanner was very instrumental in getting us to this point, father." Bradley said pointedly. "He was pretty hard to track down though. He'd been retired for some time by the time I learned of his whereabouts. Had a nice little ranch down near Alamogordo, New Mexico. Just he and his wife. She's also dead, although she had nothing to do with this debacle. She became collateral damage. Caught in the cross-fire, wouldn't you say? Sound familiar, father?" Bradley prodded. "Was *I* collateral damage, Dad?"

He remembered General Tanner most vividly of all his prey. The General made it all possible by reassigning Wesley stateside. Joshua also had a doctor, one he'd never met reassigned around the same time Wesley was. Her name was Captain Margaret Drewer, a Psychiatrist stationed in England. What General Tanner hadn't known was that she was Wesley Fordam's mistress. Wesley then blackmailed her into signing the papers.

Bradley had showed some leniency toward her because of this and the fact that she reminded her of his mother in a way. She had to die nonetheless but he made her death quick and relatively painless. General Tanner, on the other hand was a grumpy old bastard that reminded Bradley of his father. This allowed him to feel nothing for the man but resentment and pure hatred.

He'd started telling his story when he realized that his father's mouth was once again filling up with blood from his wounds. Wesley, once again had to endure being tipped forward with all its involved pain, although he welcomed this in comparison to drowning in his own blood. After a couple of minutes Wesley was once again sitting upright and able to breathe, relatively unlabored. Bradley resumed his story.

"General Tanner kind of fell off the grid after his retirement. There seemed to be some sort of incident between the United States and the U.S.S.R that he was involved in. This *incident* forced a few high ranking officers into a somewhat hastened retirement. It all looked perfectly normal because they all had their twenty years under their belt. The incident had something to do with misinformation given to the intelligence community by our good friend, the late General Tanner.

He found a small ranch in New Mexico close to where he was stationed years before at White Sands Missile Range and he and his wife settled down with a few horses and a fat pension check the government gave him to make up for his early departure from protecting the world from Communism."

Bradley continued, "I have to say he was quite surprised to learn the reason I was there. He'd all but forgotten his role in this ordeal. After some exercises in persuasion he told all he knew. I'll hand it to the old bastard; he was one tough cookie to break." Bradley smiled at the metaphor. "I'll get to that soon enough, *Pop*". Rubbing his hands together in a circular pattern, Bradley continued. "All those years of having a neglectful father really paid off when it came time to implement all of the eccentricities of torture. At first he was very strong, especially for a man of his advanced age. I used a method of torture that was developed long ago by the church during the inquisition, of course. It is appropriately called "The Wheel". I have to admit

this approach did not come directly from me but rather from the
fact that General Tanner lived on an old ranch. It's quite funny
if you look at it from my perspective. He and his wife had
found an old wheel from a carriage or something similar and
displayed it in their front yard, in a flower bed no less. I first
noticed it when I checked out the place a week prior. It
practically called out to me!" Bradley sneered. "I took the
wheel from its resting place and rolled it to the barn, fastened it
to a strong piece of rope, then collected the unconscious General
from the living room where he'd been slumped over his dead
wife.

The barn was a good three hundred feet from the house
so it took some doing to drag his almost lifeless body there.

"You see father, all of this is *your* fault. I almost felt a
pang of guilt for what I did next but then remembered that you
are the one to blame; no one else. I explained this to the
General after reviving him with some cold water from the well.
He couldn't grasp why he was being punished so severely. I
told him that what he was about to endure was nothing
compared to what my dear old dad would undergo." With that
Wesley was once again lurched backward, slamming his already
pounding head into the unforgiving floor. After a couple of
minutes he'd noticed that Bradley had stopped talking.
Wesley's eyes darted left to right to left again trying to recapture

the sight of his crazed son. Nothing. Still though, he swore he could smell something smoldering in the enclosed space

Wesley's senses had to keep readjusting whenever there was a change in condition thrown at him. His sense of sight was limited because of the Heretic's Fork; his sense of smell was weakened due to the strong smell and taste of copper in his mouth from the copious amount of blood he was losing. His sense of hearing was unreliable. He continually thought he heard things that were, in reality not there; thus diminishing his self-trust. Wesley Fordam was lost in consciousness. He was awake, but unaware of very little around him. Only small strands of reality slithered through what Wesley was sure was unreal. Footsteps, smoldering charcoal, and the occasional breathing from somewhere in the distance. Wesley knew his grip on reality was weakening with every passing moment. He feared he would soon be unable to distinguish between the two.

From somewhere beyond Wesley's limited sight came the now familiar voice of his son. A son he hadn't heard from in over fifteen years.

"You know, father." Bradley said condescendingly. "I have to admit that there was a great deal for me to learn after I read mothers diary: The wonderful world of Psychiatry!" He exclaimed. Interestingly however, one thing that I did learn was that there is an actual sign for the field of Psychiatry. I took this *sign* and incorporated it with my earlier teachings from Europe.

That's where I was all the time, father. I was learning. Making myself smarter than you could imagine. I went along on the ride you took us throughout Europe but while mother was drinking and you were advancing your career I was absorbing everything I could about their ancient cultures."

"I had always been fascinated with the writings of Alexander Dumas. You know…The Three Musketeers, Count of Monte Cristo and on and on and on. Well anyway, He'd branded those condemned to death with the Fleur de Lis; a symbol father, a *sign*. One just like that which you are about to receive!" Bradley's voice seethed with anger and hate. His eyes widened as he turned to face his father, and plunged a red hot poker into the arch of his right foot. As Wesley tried to scream in response to the pain shooting up from his foot to his brain along a trail of billions of neurons, a warm spray of blood covered Bradley's chest and face. Bradley joyfully started crying. Wesley passed out almost immediately after the branding, unable to withstand the overload the intense pain had caused. Bradley tossed the steaming iron into the smoldering coals and dropped to his knees hunched over his father's still smoking flesh.

CHAPTER 62

Wesley found himself in the sitting position once again as he awoke slowly. His breathing had become labored and raspy. As he became more alert his heart began to race. He looked around the room as well as he could looking for his captor. Looking for his son. Looking for Bradley. There was no one in sight. Wesley tried to calm his breathing in order to listen for any sign of Bradley. There was nothing. No *sounds* like before. No breathing other than his own was audible. He was alone.

He contemplated calling out to his son. Trying to reason with him but thought better of it. He didn't want to attract any more attention to himself at this point. He knew it was not over but at least for a short while he had somewhat of a reprieve. Wesley sat quietly thinking of his circumstances. He knew that he was in some sort of chair, albeit an odd one. He was naked, cold and in severe pain, to say the least. His feet hurt when he placed them on the floor but the coolness of the concrete made it bearable. His hands were bound behind his back and he was able to feel the wooden backing to the chair. Something felt odd about the chair however. The backing was narrow but sturdy. He was pretty sure it now extended above the height of his head. He was able to lean his head back and rest it on the wooden backing although he tried to avoid this act because of the pain he felt. His head had taken quite a beating with the forward and backward jerking the chair made earlier. The back of his head felt sticky as if it had bled earlier but was now somewhat congealed.

There was only room enough to move his head a couple of inches, some sort of strap ran across his forehead to the back of the chair. He could not however turn his head from side to side for fear of bringing on the onslaught of pain from the Heretics' Fork Bradley had placed under his chin. His ankles were strapped as well to the legs of the chair in the same manner as his head. The legs of the chair seemed warmer than the floor so Wesley assumed that the entire chair was made of wood. The chair had proven its strength earlier withstanding the devastating maneuvers Bradley had put him through. Any feelings of hope diminished as soon as Wesley realized that the chair was constructed to take a beating.

Time passed slowly for Wesley, alone in the room he'd been placed. He still could not see the room in its entirety. There only remained a soft glow from somewhere behind the chair. Wesley thought he noticed a faint flickering like one given off by a burning candle. His sense of smell however had been extinguished with all of the blood running down the back of his throat. He felt a sudden urge to vomit at the thought of it. Then as suddenly as before he heard Bradley speak from behind.

His voice was soft at first. Like that of a child telling his parent a secret. In a whispered tone Bradley spoke to his father.

"As long as I have known you, I have hated the very thought of your existence. I honestly have no good memories of you, father. None what so ever. I find that odd", he continued, "Did you know I have two daughters? No of course you don't. Why would you? You haven't one parenting gene in you. Do you? I have lived my life feeling that I was not only a mistake in your eyes but also a liability. That is until you realized that you could use my existence to your advantage. Maggie told me all about it. About how you told her you were essentially a single parent and how hard it was to raise a child on your own." Bradley stopped to let out a snort of laughter. "You know she fell for it hook, line, and sinker. She told me herself." He paused to see what effect that had on his father. None. "She was easy to find. She never tried to hide her identity. I don't think she ever thought her past would haunt her like it did in the end. She was a very pleasant woman I thought. I could see why you had picked her. She must have been very attractive when she was younger. She reminded me of my mother in the old photos I'd kept after you <u>sent</u> her away". Bradley noticed his father's breathing get a little more labored. You sure pulled a blanket over my head on that one father. I believed you at the time; that my mother was crazy and therefore a danger to herself, and to me. I hated the very thought of it but I had no reason not to believe you then. After all I was only a teenager. Why would my own father lie about something as important as that? You were so easy to believe. You should have been in sales". That got a laugh out of Bradley.

Wesley sat motionless during the barrage of accusations that flew his way. He knew it would be no use to trying to reason with Bradley right now. He held onto a thread of hope that his son would let him defend himself. He was sure that he could talk his way out of this. Make Bradley believe him once again.

Minutes passed before Bradley continued.

"She never stopped loving you, you know. My mother, that is. She wrote it in her diary. She had held onto the belief that you would come and rescue her from that dreaded place; like in a fairytale. She was a fool in that sense. She was unable to see you for what you really are. A self-centered, manipulating fuck." Wesley closed his eyes and lowered his head as far as the Heretic's Fork would allow. "You cared about no one but yourself. That much is clear. What is not so clear is why you thought you were going to amount to anything. The Cold War was fizzling out. The need for a Russian Linguist was fading. There was little else you could do for the military". Bradley remained quiet as if contemplating the events of the time. "I don't know. Maybe you did have the foresight of what was to come in terms of your career. Maybe you thought you needed to advance to a point where you had some use. Who knows? Unfortunately for you, you'll never have the chance to tell your side of the story. Unless...you had the foresight to write your life story." Bradley could sense the shot of emotional pain this had inflicted. He smiled.

CHAPTER 63

Wesley heard footsteps approaching from behind making his heart leap into overdrive. His breathing became labored at the thought of something horrific about to occur. His body tensed as the inevitable approached. The only thing Wesley didn't know was what the inevitable was. A sense of foreboding doom loomed in the air. It hung there like the trail of a burning stick of incense. With a sudden jerk Wesley's head snapped back striking the recently placed head board. Bradley was tightening the leather strap used to restrain his head. There was a loud popping that followed as the Heretic's Fork withdrew from where it had embedded in the roof of Wesley's mouth. Surprise and pain shot through Wesley's mind and body like a bullet. His cries muffled only by the sound of blood he spat with every labored breath. His mind wanted to turn itself off. To conceal itself from the onslaught of pain that raced through every fiber of his body. He wanted it all to end. It didn't matter how, just that it did. Wesley was unaware that this evening's proceedings had just begun. That his death would be painfully slow. That his son was not even close to redeeming his mother's name.

"Sorry about that father. That sounded like it may have hurt". Wesley was barely conscious as he listened to his only son speak. He was however, aware that the tone exuded in Bradley's voice was one of pure pleasure.

Bradley resumed his position in front of his father, sitting on the bench. He relaxed, leaning back crossing his legs at the ankles. His hands were clasped together in a relaxed display on his lap. He sat quietly staring at his nemesis; writhing in pain and agony. He wanted badly to end this charade but knew that this was to be his masterpiece. Bradley knew all too well that the man who sat in front of him was the primary reason his mother suffered so badly. He sat opposite his father for a good ten minutes; saying nothing, just watching: watching his father suffer, more so than any of his other victims.

May 13, 1976

This is not the life I knew. This is not fair. I do not deserve such a dishonorable end. Wesley is not coming back. He left the country. He stole my child. How could God let this happen? My depression deepens daily. There is no hope. My child is gone and I have lost faith in God.

Bradley shifted in the bench. Leaning forward he rested his elbows on his knees and cupped his hands over his worn, blood splattered face. He took a few deep breaths then peered over his fingertips at his father. He hesitated speaking at first not knowing if he should go where he was about to. Then suddenly he spoke having felt that he had no other choice. Bradley spoke to his father in a calm, unwavering voice that sent chills through Wesley. Their eyes locked on each other.

"Father, I must admit that there was a time that I felt I would not be able to go through with this. After I graduated High School and headed back to the states to attend college I thought I'd lose the hatred I felt for you. My years in college and then in Grad School were spent on *me*. I wanted nothing more than to be better, smarter than you. I was fueled by that very hatred to be the very best at whatever I did. I finished in the top one percent of my class at Yale, but I'm sure that you knew that. I'd impressed them so much that they offered me a position right out of school. I was unable to take them up on their very surprising offer at the time, however. I had a date with someone that summer. It was where I began this journey I am about to conclude. I met two very influential people that first summer out of school."

Bradley clasped his hands together, still on his lap, and then continued. "The first was my beautiful wife Linda. She was a student in a class I taught at Potsdam State University. We fell in love that summer and it was at the end of the summer that I asked her to be my wife. You could say that we found each other. I was having a very difficult time with the inner conflict that involved reclaiming my mother's good name. I'd promised myself that after I graduated school I would tend to her needs. As the years progressed though, I toiled with the thought of dropping the whole thing; getting on with *my* life.

It was Linda who made me see that I could never have dropped it. The love I felt for her made me realize that my mother had loved you that much, and that you had pushed her aside for you own needs. Linda made me realize that when you truly love someone *your* needs come second. That what I had to do was right. No matter what mixed feelings may have crept into my mind. Linda made me see that I must fulfill the promise to my mother I'd made all those years before. I do believe that had I not met Linda we would not be here today. Too bad you'll never meet her. She was very much like my mother before you brushed her aside." Bradley paused at that; remembering his mother in her happy years. He was very young but those had been the fondest memories he'd held on to. Wesley could see tears welling up in his son's eyes. The thought that he may get through this alive crossed his mind, however fleeting it was.

When Bradley continued, the tone in his voice had the slightest edge to it. "The second person was a chap named Lenny. You'd never met Lenny, although you caused his path to cross with my mothers. Lenny was a very simple guy. I found it proved very difficult to befriend him though. Our backgrounds were very different to say the least. He, like you was in the Army, but never shared your aspirations. He "did his time" as he once told me, and then got out. With no education he was forced into a life of petty jobs that never amounted to anything resembling a career. One fateful night however he made the distinct mistake of raping and sodomizing your wife. You see, it was before your divorce was completed. Word of this event never left the hospital as they brushed it under the carpet and asked Lenny to leave without question. At least Lenny was able to see a good deal when presented with one. He left, never coming into contact with my mother again.

She wrote of the occurrence *vividly* in her diary, though. She even wrote of filing a complaint with the hospital administrators. Nothing ever became of it though and as far as I know you were never contacted about it." Bradley's eyes narrowed and shot daggers through his fathers'. "*Did* you know about it father? *Did* they contact you? You were still married at the time. Did you know what Lenny had *done* to my mother?" Wesley's eyes widened and he shook his head back and forth trying his best to ignore the intractable pain it was causing. He began to whimper as he attempted to say "no". The Heretic's fork found its way back into the holes gouged out earlier, once again embedding itself into Wesley's upper palate. Even though there was no loud pop as before, the pain was the same if not more unbearable. Blood once again filled Wesley's mouth making him cough violently. Each jerking motion created by a new cough sent blood splattering from his mouth spraying Bradley who sat idly in his bench seemingly completely removed from the fact that it was his own father 'bleeding out' in front of him.

Slowly Bradley wiped the blood from his face with his hands. Then he continued as if nothing had happened.

"No, I guess you didn't know anything." He looked impassively into his father's eyes once again. Wesley was transfixed on his son's eyes. Once again Bradley continued, "There were, as far as I know only a handful of people that knew of that nights happenings. Mother wrote about telling her friend, the lady who handed me the diary and of telling the administrators. One of whom was a man named Dr. Miles Duval. Dr. Duval and I met a couple of weeks ago in Upstate New York. Soon thereafter he had seen the error of his ways. But I digress. Back to good 'ol Lenny. He and I hit it off famously. After I figured out what his likes were it was easy to befriend him. He too found that what he had done to my mother was what inevitably led to his demise."

"It was with Lenny I began to second guess whether I had the fortitude to go through with killing another human being. I had long deliberated in my mind the different outcomes that would ensue after the actual act. What would happen after the outcome had been reached tentatively grated on my soul. It wasn't born out of a fear of being caught but rather how I would be judged both in this life and the next. In a sense, I was afraid I wouldn't be able to do it. That I'd 'chicken out' in the end.

Lenny was my first kill. I wanted him to be the first for a number of reasons. Firstly, he'd played the smallest role in all of this. His part lasted as long as *he* could, you could say. But on the other hand his actions were so indescribable that he literally pissed me off enough to win the pole position. Although you played the biggest role in all this I'd reserved your death for last. Tonight is a special night for me. I had to give you your due respect.

CHAPTER 64

When faced with impending death many people become very calm and accepting of the inevitable. It's as though they understand and lose their will to fight it. But with Wesley it was different. He fought the urge to give in. A couple of times there had been a fleeting thought that there was no more fight to give but it was merely transient thought. Wesley continually pulled on his restraints in an effort to free himself of what was surely to come. His will to live though was not simply derived from the desire to exist but was drawn from a deeper fear of what would come after death. He knew that what he had done in the past was far from angelic. He would have to pay for his sins eventually. Clarity is easily found when faced with death. What was once clouded thought was becoming clearer as the night went on; as Wesley came closer with death.

He avoided religion most of his adult life but as time passed in this cold heartless room Wesley had grown *closer* to God. He was sure that this was the end of his time, but what came next was unclear. Does God existed or not. That lack of knowledge fueled most of his fear of death. Bradley sensed that his father was contemplating the afterlife. He noted a dazed look about him as if his mind were elsewhere. Bradley suddenly jumped to his feet arms stretched out with the palms of his hands pointed upward; toward Heaven. He spoke loudly and slowly as if he were a preacher delivering his sermon to his flock. "Oh dear Lord! We have found us a sinner! Look down upon us with Your forgiving eyes and help me help this man!" Bradley grinned as he continued. Wesley looked as though he were seeing aliens land on earth. His eyes bulged in their sockets, unblinking. He didn't know how to decipher what he was witnessing. Was Bradley mocking God or was he truly asking for His forgiveness? He watched, mesmerized as Bradley continued. "This man, who sits before you, oh Lord, begs for your forgiveness. His sins truly undeniable. Take him as your son. Accept him in your flock."

There was silence. Bradley remained standing with open palms looking up at the ceiling of the dark room. His breathing well controlled. His hands steady as a rock. Nothing happened. Bradley quietly dropped his head to his chest shaking it slowly back and forth. He slowly took his seat on the bench and stared at his father.

"I tried. It looks as if there will be no one to help you tonight. You'll have to stay with me for a while longer."

Wesley had pure terror showing in his eyes. He witnessed something so unbelievable he had had a hard time deciphering if it was a show for benefit or the real thing. He looked at his son as if Bradley were truly crazy. Refusing to blink his eyes they began to water.

"You see father", he paused for effect. "There is no God. You have nothing to worry about. With no God there can be no Devil. You're safe." He grinned barring his teeth. "The only thing you have to worry about is what I am going to do to you before I kill you. By the time we're finished tonight you'll rather have wanted to meet God's Fallen Angel."

CHAPTER 65

Bradley was sitting calmly once again in his bench directly in front of his father. Hands clasped together, elbows on crossed knees. He stared at the floor wondering if the blood would ever come off. He snorted quietly to himself thinking how he could be thinking of something so trivial at a time like this. Then he looked at his hands, thinking the same.

"I'm not sure I'll ever get this blood off my hands. You know?" He spoke to know one in particular all the time rubbing his hands together. It reminded him of an old MASH episode where a newer doctor *snapped* one day and could not get the *blood* off his hands. No matter how hard he scrubbed the blood was immovable. Bradley tried to push the thought from his mind. He would not suffer the same fate as the doctor. He, Bradley was the killer, not Brad. Confusion boiled over in his mind as he attempted to differentiate Bradley from Brad. He spoke in a hushed tone to his father.

"You know… when I was about to kill Lenny there was a point that I actually thought I'd have to back out. That it was not in my nature to kill another. And I was correct. It is not in my nature to kill. I'm a normal, functioning adult. I have a family now; two little girls at home sleeping as we speak. Dreaming dreams that little girls do. I will go home to my wife that I love so dearly and our lives will resume their normal paths." He continued to rub the blood on his hands, smearing it as he did so. "Then something happened to me. I don't know what it was exactly but it was like a light switch. One moment I was Brad; normal Brad. Then the next I was this person who I'd never met before. Something flicked the switch in my head and I became Bradley: the product of *you*." As he said these last words he slowly raised his eyes until they met his father's. There was no expression on his face. No hatred, no fear. Nothing.

"You created Bradley. You molded him with your lies, your deceit. He exists solely because of *you*. My whole childhood is filled with memories of you despising the fact that we existed. You proved daily that we were not part of your world." Bradley's eyes never left Wesley's. His head remained tilted down but his eyes looked upward. It impressed a feeling of fear upon Wesley. He'd never seen anything like this before. He felt a chill rise through his spine.

"I would ask you why you did what you did but I don't think you would answer me. I have attained a confession from everyone I've killed up to this point. But I don't think I'll get one from you. Everyone involved other than you had a valid reason to do what they did. They paid dearly for that decision but they nonetheless had a good reason. Even Lenny. He had to prove to himself that he had some control over his pathetic life. He was unable to get that from the military; in fact they probably quashed any individuality he'd had before enlisting. He had a chance to prove to himself that he could control something. He'd been looking for *anything* to control. Finally the opportunity presented itself in the form of your wife; lying on a bed, restrained. He exuded complete control of her as he raped her. As he sodomized her. For that short period of time no one controlled him. That was his reasoning for doing what he did.

In a way I can respect that. Man needs to remain in control of his own destiny. It is a mechanism our species uses to prove that our lives are not controlled completely by some other entity. And although I respect that Lenny had to do what he did, he still had to pay for his choice. Dr. Duval, Maggie, and even Joshua all had valid reasons. Although Maggie and Joshua did it out of self-preservation, Dr. Duval did it out of loyalty to an old friend. You however had your own reasons. Just what those reasons were continues to elude my thinking but I do believe that it was simply out of greed. Because of you I have had to endure these killings. I was given no choice in the matter when my mother picked *me* to fulfill her wishes. I don't blame her however. That rests solely on your shoulders, dear father. None of this would have happened if it were not for you and your petty greed." Bradley began clapping loudly. "My hat is off to you Sir. Well done Coronel!"

Wesley had had enough. He was unable to take any more of this lashing. He began sobbing. Tears ran down his face leaving little streaks where there had been blood. With every sob came a jolt of pain radiating into his head from the Heretic's Fork. He was unable to stop himself, he was broken man.

CHAPTER 66

When the police entered the maintenance building two days later they were shocked at the sight before their eyes. After receiving a tip that a murder had taken place they quickly dispatched the nearest units to the scene. The first to arrive were two Baltimore PD patrolmen that had been on lunch break at a sandwich shop just outside of the parks boundaries. The two, a rookie and a veteran of ten years were on scene within five minutes of the initial call. They found the front door open a couple of inches and entered. The building was built in the late 1800's and was made of solid stone. There were two floors to the building. The top floor was used for storage of lawn cutting equipment along with numerous other tools that were used throughout the park during more temperate seasons. The top floor was level with the surrounding landscape and had a small entry door to the left as you entered the driveway. There was also a double door on the same wall that allowed for the movement of tractors and such in and out of the building. The officers entered with guns drawn, cautiously. The room was dark and damp, smelling of decomposing grass clippings. They searched from one end to the other also searching the gables above. The building had once been a horse barn and although the hay loft had long since been removed, the exposed beams were still present. They found nothing out of the ordinary stave for the door left ajar. What they were about to find would haunt them the rest of their days.

The only place left to look was down the stairs at the rear of the building. The stairs themselves were circular and near an opening in the flooring that had a pulley system arranged so that equipment could be moved from floor to floor. The area was darker than the rest of the top floor with no windows on the rear wall of the building. The two officers did however see a faint light emanating from below. The flooring around the immediate area of the opening showed evidence of recent activity. The thin layer of dust that had settled on the wood plank floor over the past two months was scuffed in many areas surrounding the hole.

The younger officer, a twenty two year old Baltimore native named Mike Bannon barked.

"Police! Is anyone down there?" Only silence ensued. The two officers looked at each other pensively. The veteran, a man by the name of Clarence Johnson nodded to the rookie to start his descent down the stairs. The two moved slowly and carefully with Officer Johnson keeping a trained eye on the floor below. His Mag light shone only on the immediate area of the bottom steps and was of little help to Mike, who now had his flashlight out alongside his fire arm. Officer Bannon slowly circled the stairwell descending as he moved the flashlight from side to side.

"It looks clear down here" he yelled up to his partner who was now following down the spiral staircase. Clarence spoke first.

"Where's the light coming from?"
Mike answered without taking his eyes off the room before them. "I can't tell yet. It looks like there is another room though."

The two reached the bottom of the steps shining their lights around the empty room. A faint light came from a partially open door across the room. The room itself was merely ten feet by ten feet and by their estimation was about one fourth the area of the first floor. Mike spoke.

"Someone's been down here recently. Look at the floor." There were multiple areas' that had been disrupted by movement. Most of the dust had been disturbed between the stairwell and the door in front of them. Patrolman Johnson spoke.

"Cover me. I'll go in first." He repeated in a firm voice. "Baltimore Police Department! We're coming in!" He moved quickly to the door then pushed it open the remainder with his right foot. A quick glance behind the door through the crack revealed nothing noticeable. He trained his light through the door. There was a single light on in the room. It came from a recessed fixture that was covered with plexi glass making it flush with the ceiling. The walls were painted a dark gray and smooth to the touch. There was nothing else in the room. It was completely devoid of anything, including a single light switch.

"This room's clear!" Clarence barked to the junior officer who was just entering the room.

"What in the hell is this place?" questioned Mike. He paused lowering his gun while he absorbed the odd room. He tapped Clarence on the shoulder pointing to the door they had just passed through. "What do you make of that?"

The door was made of heavy wood and was clearly not an original fixture to the building. Clarence thumped the wall with a balled fist. A dull thud was audible.

"Soundproof" he stated flatly. "Something tells me there's more to this than we see." The two officers searched the room one taking the left and the other the right. There was nothing out of the ordinary noted by either of them other than the door and the light fixture. Both officers noticed a pile of feces in one corner of the otherwise empty room. It stank of urine. They continued until they met in the middle of the far wall.

"What do you make of these?" asked Clarence.

"Dunno."

The two had discovered minute lines in the wall reaching from the floor to the ceiling separated by about five feet. The lines were hardly distinguishable and went unnoticed until the two were practically on top of them.

"This is fucked up Clarence. What is this place?" Confusion filled Mike's face. "Look at the floor." The two took a knee. There were the faintest of scratches running perpendicular to the door. The two looked up at the ceiling in unison noticing for the first time two small metal runners following the same perpendicular direction as that of the scratches on the floor. The runners were made of a dark gray metal and blended almost seamlessly with the color of the ceiling which was the same as that of the walls and floor.

Clarence backed up a couple of feet holstering his weapon. "Cover me Mike". Clarence took a couple of steps toward the wall with both hands reaching out at chest height. When he reached the wall he placed both hands firmly and pushed. Nothing happened. Again he tried to push the wall to no avail. The rookie had a confused look on his face.

"What in the hell is this?" he questioned walking up to the wall; he pushed and released his hand as if slapping the immovable wall. The section of wall pushed in a fraction then the two officers heard a light clicking sound. They simultaneously leapt back drawing their weapons. The wall slid out about three inches after being released by some sort of latching mechanism. The officer's nervously looked at each other; their hearts pounding in their chests.

"Holy shit!" exclaimed Mike as he holstered his gun. "Get my back partner" he said as he approached the wall grasping each exposed end. He pulled the wall along the rails in the ceiling until he hit the end leaving a three foot gap between the sections of wall. Clarence moved to the right aiming his weapon in the darkened room. He leveled his flashlight with his Beretta, frozen. His mind not comprehending the sight he was witnessing. Mike saw the perplexed look on his partners face and moved to the left drawing his weapon and light at the same time.

"Dear God in Heaven" mumbled one of them as if they were both thinking it.

CHAPTER 67

Brad was nearly halfway home, this time taking the freeways, when he placed a call to the Baltimore Police Department at a rest stop. His message was simple.

"Listen carefully. There has been a murder."

He gave the desk officer the location then hung up the phone. While stretching his legs he bought a soda from a vending machine and returned to his car. After turning over the engine he sat there for a couple of minutes staring out the windshield at nothing. Smiling, he quietly said to himself "Okay", then drove off heading north. It was close to midnight when he pulled his Toyota into the drive.

"Home sweet home" he thought aloud.

When he climbed into bed he startled Linda awake.

"Oh my God. You scared the living hell out of me!" She said exasperated as she rolled onto her back staring up into his eyes. The two lay there saying nothing at first; Brad's expression said it all. It was over. Linda smiled. Brad broke the silence.

"I love you Linda." She had her husband back. It was finally over.

"I love you too Brad. I love you too." They lay there the rest of the night in each other's arms. Brad slept like the dead. It had been a long road travelled. He was finally where he belonged.

Brad awoke with a start. There were two beautiful young ladies jumping on the foot of the bed screaming "Daddy's home!" over and over, giggling as they did so.

"Come here you hooligans!" barked Brad smiling as if he'd met his two little angels for the first time. "Give your daddy a hug." Lilly and Ana hopped over to where he lay and collapsed on their favorite guy.

"We missed you daddy" stated a suddenly very serious Lilly.

"I missed you too honey". They hugged and kissed Brad until he ordered them off the bed and downstairs so he could get dressed. The girls gleefully jumped off the bed and ran downstairs screaming, "Mommy! Mommy! Did you know? Daddy's home!" This brought an ear to ear smile to Brad's face. He slowly got out of bed and walked to the bathroom where he ran the shower. He soaked in the steaming shower for a good fifteen minutes before getting dressed in a pair of jeans and a rugby shirt donning his alma maters' logo. When he arrived in the kitchen he found his three favorite people in the world preparing a pancake breakfast with beacon and scrambled eggs. It looked as though Ana had worn most of the batter having convinced her mother that she was old enough to help with the cooking.

It was Sunday and the four of them decided to go to the park and have lunch out. Brad was elated to be back in the mix of things. The girls got him caught up on all of the neighborhood gossip and rambled on constantly about everything from going to the mall the day before with Mom to how Maggie-moo tore the sofa while playing with them. The day was perfect and nothing could change that. Linda and Brad said very little to each other throughout the day, not that the girls would allow them to speak. They did however stare into each other's eyes like they did when they first started dating. They often said words were overrated and that more could be said with a simple look. Linda had always teased Brad about that with him being a Language Professor. He'd quickly rebut saying "Language isn't always used with words my dear". They put the girls to bed at eight o'clock and spent the next couple of hours doing their own thing. Brad had to prepare to meet his classes the next morning and Linda was reading a new journal of Veterinary Medicine that had arrived the day before. At eleven they decided to call it a night and went to bed. They did not make love. Tonight was about holding each other in their arms as they fell asleep.

Linda awoke noticing something was amiss. She turned to find an empty bed and the light on in the bathroom. She rolled back on her side closing her eyes once again. After five minutes or so she rolled on her back realizing that Brad was still in the bathroom. There was water running from what she assumed was the sink. Slowly she got out of bed. She was naked as she was every night she and Brad slept together; both loving the feel of each other's skin against their own. As she neared the bathroom door she felt something was wrong. The water was still running and she could hear Brad muttering something under his breath. When she entered the room Brad looked at her in the mirror then went back to what he had been doing. Linda put her hand on Brad's lower back watching him scrub his hands. They were raw with lather everywhere. The water was steaming hot and his hands were red and excoriated.

"What in God's name are you doing, Brad?" asked a still groggy Linda. There was no reply. Brad continued to scrub his hands even harder than before. "Brad?" Still nothing. It was then that Linda realized he was asleep. Her heart began to pound in her chest. She stood in the doorway with a hand over her mouth staring in horror. Brad had never slept walked before. This was entirely new to her. She was terrified. The sight of him practically washing the skin off his own hands was overwhelming. She stood there not knowing what to do. Should she try to stop him or should she let him keep going? She decided that she needed to do something. His hands were starting to bleed in spots. The foamy lather from the soap turned a light shade of pink. Linda's mind raced. She felt helpless.

Brad stopped scrubbing when Linda reached across him and turned off the water. He stood looking down at his hands not saying a word. Linda quietly addressed him.

"Honey? Can you hear me? I need you to wake up. Okay?" Her husband of five years remained silent. She gently patted his hands with a towel trying not to do more harm than good until they were dry. Still Brad just stood there staring at his hands. Linda reached across him once again. This time she grabbed a bottle of lotion and gave herself a couple of squirts. As she was applying the lotion Brad seemed to snap out of his sleep and looked at her in the mirror again, his eyes impassive. For the first time in their relationship Linda felt a pang of fear of her husband. This was not like him. Even with all he had done and seen he was never like this. He was always able to turn off the bad emotions and resume life as if nothing had happened. Brad pulled his hands away from hers and leaned on the sink for a moment never taking his eyes off her.

"What are you doing?" he asked in a flat tone. He waited for an answer. Linda sensed that she had better say something.

"I thought you might need some help in here. That's all." She gave Brad an impish smile. "Let's go back to bed sweetie. Come with me." She took his hand and led him back to bed. They lay there in the dark both awake now.

Brad turned to Linda and said, "I can't seem to get the blood off my hands". He then closed his eyes and fell asleep. Linda laid awake the rest of the night unable to sleep. Something was dreadfully wrong.

CHAPTER 68

The Monday edition of The Baltimore Sun headlined:

"Gruesome Scene Discovered"

There was a picture of the stone maintenance building with a number of cops and bystanders mulling around. The picture was in color and the yellow Police Scene tape was evident everywhere. The sub heading read:

"Body of missing Professor discovered after anonymous tip received by police"

The article was a preliminary one at best and had few details of what the two officers discovered.

Officers Clarence Johnson and Mike Bannon had been in a briefing room for more than two hours. They'd been summoned from the crime scene by their Captain. They recounted everything they'd discovered to a pair of FBI field agents that had been assigned the case. One of the agents spoke.

"The victim was a professor at the University of Maryland that had been reported missing by a friend about a day before you guys found his body. He was a decorated Army officer who spent his career mainly in Europe during the Cold War. His service record is, to sum it up, impeccable. He retired and began teaching Linguistics at the U of M, specializing in…you guessed it… Russian. We have no idea why someone would abduct this individual. He possessed no military value having been retired for more than seven years. He was renowned for his excellence in Linguistics research but still that gives us no motive." The other agent took over the conversation.

"What I'm concerned with is the manner he was killed. In my 15 years at the Bureau I've never witnessed a scene like this one. The man was tortured for what looks like two days before he died. The coroner is performing the autopsy on the victim as we speak. I want to know if he died from his injuries or if it was his injuries that killed him. Does that make any sense to you guys?" The two officers looked at each other and nodded. "To me, at least initially, it looks as if the killer was making a statement. I'm worried that we may have a serial killer on our hands. I need you guys to walk us through the scene again. Don't leave anything out. Even the smallest detail may prove invaluable".

Clarence walked them through the scene in agonizing detail aided occasionally by his younger partner. They left nothing out. They told of the first room they entered and the weird vibe they initially got from it. Then they delved into the discovery of the secret door and how they figured out how to gain entry, leaving out the fact that it was opened by mere luck.

"There was a strong odor of blood. We smelled it even before we entered the last room. There was also a foul odor looming under the smell of blood. We weren't sure what it was at first, Officer Johnson continued. I entered first followed by the rookie here. Johnson suddenly stopped talking. His mind fixed on the scene.

The agents looked at each other, then to the rookie who was also transfixed somewhere other than the debriefing room. The rookie's hands were shaking as he held a cup of coffee. It was evident to the federal agents the two officers were admittedly affected by what they witnessed.

A dim light shone from the back of the room creating a silhouette of the body. He remained in the makeshift chair that was attached to some sort of pulley system. The floor was a dark maroon color and had a sticky texture to it. In most cases the officers would have stopped there not wanting to contaminate the crime scene but they were unsure if the victim was indeed dead. The lighting was too poor to be certain. So they approached the body in a single line to keep their foot prints to a minimum. Clarence Johnson was the first to get to the body. He turned his flashlight to examine the body and suddenly wretched making him vomit explosively. He'd been on the force for ten years and thought he'd seen everything. Prior to becoming a cop he was a paramedic. What he saw was by far the most evil thing he'd witnessed having been done to a human being. The rage that must have gone into such an act was unfathomable. He ordered his partner to back off between dry heaves having already emptied his stomach contents on the floor. Mike abided and back-stepped, watching his veteran partner heaving on his knees. Instinctively he flashed his light on the victim and immediately saw what had caused his partner's sickness. "Oh" was all he was able to mutter before removing himself from the room completely. Clarence was beside Mike in a matter of seconds in the *gray* room regaining his composure. Mike turned to his partner,

"What was that? How?" Mike found he could not complete a sentence. His mind reeled at what it was trying to comprehend. There were no words to describe the horror that occurred in that room. This was beyond mere murder itself. It was like nothing the two had witnessed.

Mike asked the FBI agents for a short recess and he left the room in search of something cold to drink. The smell of the room had come rushing back and had left the taste of blood in his mouth. He needed to wash it down quickly. His brow covered with sweat. His fellow officers looked at him as if he'd seen a ghost. Nobody dared ask him if he were all right. Mike felt every pair of eyes in the station watching him at that moment. He sensed what they were thinking. It was as if he were somehow a different man than he was just hours ago. He ran to the men's room and splashed cold water on his face. Looking in the mirror he saw a stranger. He remained there, paralyzed for another ten minutes before returning to the debriefing room. All three were sitting at the table when Mike returned, all were silent. Clarence gave his partner an "it'll be okay" look as he took his seat.

"Sorry 'bout that guys. I'm just a little fucked up right now. That's all."

Out of respect no one spoke for a moment. They had all felt what Mike was feeling at some point in their careers. Clarence was the first to speak.

"Look guys. This is serious shit. Just listen to what I gotta say before you interrupt, okay?"

Both agents nodded in unison.

"The Vic…it wasn't just a kill, ya know? The guy was alive while this sick mother fucker skinned him. He musta been out for the most part, far as I could tell. The cuts were clean, but not clean, ya know? Cleaner than clean."

Although asked not to, one of the agents spoke.

"Meticulous."

"Yeah, that's the word, meticulous. No jagged marks, no multiple slicing. Clean as a mother fuckin' whistle. Never…never have I seen anything like it." Clarence shook hard then looked directly in the eyes of the lead agent, Davidson.

"This guy you're looking for…this guy has…*had* serious issues with the Vic. He took two days to torture, and then skins the poor bastard. Never seen nothing like it."

Agent Davidson spoke again, "Stick to what you saw officer."

"Yeah, sure thing. No problem. I'm no Doc or nothin' but the Vic's skin was peeled off like…fuck! I don't know what to say. You ever try to peel an orange without ripping the rind? It was kinda like that, 'cept cleaner. The Vic's face was pulled back, like at an autopsy I seen once. Right over the head. But the perp didn't pull hard enough to rip the skin. He cut as he pulled." Clarence paused to light a cigarette.

"It looked like he sliced the Vic right down the middle of the chest to pull the skin off like a fucking coat or somethin'. The hips, legs…fuck! Everything, right down to the ankles and the wrists were sliced…no, flayed like some fucking fish! The most fucked up thing I ever saw."

The junior agent, Murray stepped in. "You said 'he'. Why do you think a man did this?"

Clarence snorted. "Fuck man…I seen some pissed off ladies before, but none that coulda done what I seen in that fucking room!"

Murray held up an index finger as he flipped the tape in the recorder. "Go on officer."

"I mean, it's like we said earlier. This poor fuck was still in the chair when we entered the room, but his skin was pinned to the wall. Like a fucking map or something."

The agents looked at each other for a moment the Clarence went on.

"The chair, or whatever you wanna call it was nothing like I ever seen before. Jerry-rigged to move forward, backward…you name it…this fucking chair could do it!" Clarence sat shaking his head in disbelief. Mike burst from his chair, throwing it against the wall behind, startling the others.

"A map! That's it you son of a bitch!" He bent over and kissed Officer Johnson's balding head. "You're the smartest mother fucker around here!" Mike slammed both hands on the table palm down making everything on it hop a few inches.

"The skin was hung like a map! A fucking map of the United States!" Davidson's eyes lit up like a Christmas tree.

"We've got to get another look at that wall."

PART IX

CHAPTER 69

Her tail wagging relentlessly, Maggie Moo chased a stick wildly thrown by Lilly. She ran down her wooden nemesis as if she had a personal vendetta, plucking it off the grass and returning full speed to young Lilly for another go at it. Brad and Linda watched with joy as Ana and Lilly tried to out throw each other in a friendly competition to win over the dogs love; both knowing full well that Maggie Moo loved each of them equally. The collie had been in the family four years now and made it her mission to be as much a member of the family as anyone else.

Her long hair was wet after having retrieved the stick from the small pond the family chose for their picnic. The stick went wide after an erratic throw by Ana but the collie took it in stride entering the cold water with a lunge; her tail wagging with even more fervor than before. As she approached Ana, Maggie shook herself off, flinging water in all directions. The girls howled with excitement running for cover. Maggie took chase; thinking it another game.

"Ana!" Brad yelled "Don't throw it in the water!" Ana froze, startled that her daddy yelled at her. It wasn't something she'd experienced. The dog turned toward Brad as if sensing something was different. Some minute difference in the tone of her masters voice. Maggie gave Brad a perplexed look until Lilly threw the stick once again; ending any worries the dog had just seconds before. Linda looked at Brad as the two lay next to each other on a blanket, shaded under a tree from the late afternoon sun, his face masked in shade.

"Why did you yell at Ana?" she asked. "She didn't mean it". As quickly as Brad's anger arrived, it dissipated.

"I'm sorry honey. I know she didn't mean it." He leapt to his feet walking in Ana's direction. Linda watched closely as Brad approached their youngest daughter bending at the waist to look her eye to eye. She had her head lowered at first, but quickly rose to look at her father as he spoke. Linda saw her nod her head a couple of times then jump into her daddy's arms smiling. Brad returned to the blanket as the two girls resumed their playful game, and slumped back onto the blanket with a thud.

"There, all better. She accepted my apology." He said to Linda. She smiled back wondering what made him snap like that.

The rest of the afternoon flew by without incident; the four went to Friendly's for dinner as it was Lilly's turn to pick the restaurant. After an agonizingly long and arduous decision on which ice cream to get for dessert they went home. The girls were asleep long before their arrival at their house. Brad carefully unbuckled Lilly from her booster seat as did Linda with young Ana taking them directly to their beds. The girls awoke long enough to fight getting into their pajamas and to brush their teeth. They fell asleep at once.

Maggie Moo went to her bowl finding it empty and patiently waited for Brad to fill it with food. She too went to sleep at once having run far more than her normal. Linda walked into the den, where Maggie Moo's bed was and plopped down in the oversized couch, watching as Brad powered up his computer.

"She needs a bath tomorrow", she stated to no one in particular.

"Who?" Brad said looking at his pitifully tired wife.

"Mag." "She smells like wet dog. I need to go to the office in the morning. Bob asked if I'd take all the sick calls and any emergency calls for the day. It's the least I can do. He's covered my end for two weeks now. He's got to be exhausted. So I guess it's you by default," she said with a coy smile.

"Thanks. What did I do to deserve this?" Brad asked as he climbed onto the opposite end of the couch with Linda, sliding his cold feet under her ass.

"Oh my God, your feet are freezing! Get a pulse for God's sake!" she exclaimed lifting her butt off his feet. Slowly she lowered herself back onto Brad's cold feet not having the fight in her to complain further.

"I've always known how to warm my feet." He said smiling broadly, a sparkle in his eye. She glared at him, one eye closed.

"What do you mean by that?" His smile grew with delight.

"I know you think you've got a great ass: too hot to handle!" he said wiggling his toes for effect.

It worked. The pair went upstairs, and after a hot bath they made passionate love. Linda quickly fell asleep in her lovers' arms drifting off to her dreams. Brad lay quietly holding his wife as her breathing slowed. He rested his head on her upper back and fell asleep listening to the steady, rhythmic beating of her heart. As Brad drifted away terror crept from his subconscious.

CHAPTER 70

Linda awoke groping for the protective arms she'd fallen asleep in but were no longer wrapped around her naked body. She turned to find Brad once again missing. She sat on the edge of the bed feeling the coolness of the room; reaching for her bathrobe she stood wrapping herself in the soft cotton. Her heart sped as she saw the bathroom light ablaze. Water was once again running and she found it difficult to bring herself to the bathroom door. She was sure she wouldn't be able to take the sight of Brad standing in front of the mirror like before. Linda pushed the door open and froze.

Brad was not in front of the sink this time, but rather curled in the fetal position at the base of the cascading water of the shower. Shivering from the cold water spilling over his pale body a steady, sickening stream of bright red blood flowed down the drain. Linda's hand covered her mouth as she gasped at the scene.

In the blink an eye Linda saw her entire world unravel and time stood still for the briefest of moments. The sound of running water was drowned out by the blood coursing through her head. The edges of her vision blurred, giving a surreal feeling to the moment. It was when she fell to her knees that Linda was jolted back to reality. The *doctor* in her took over and pushed the *wife* aside. Linda systematically assessed the situation. Brad was cold, *very* cold, almost to the point of shock. She turned the water off with her left hand as she reached across her husband's limp and pale body.

He was lying in the fetal position on his left side with his back facing Linda. It was if Brad wanted to watch as his life trickled down the drain. Blood was life no matter who controlled your actions. Remove the blood and you remove the life, remove the monster. After all, monsters have blood, don't they? Curled, he looked younger, almost childlike to Linda. She grabbed his right arm in her hand and pulled it out from under his knees. There was a deep fleshy laceration across his inner wrist. Bright red blood poured out of the wound as she moved his arm. The red liquid occasionally spurted telling Linda that he had only partially severed his radial artery. She held his wrist tightly in her hand acting as a tourniquet to lessen the flow. Brad's left wrist was cut less severely but still leaked copious amounts of darker blood. Diluted by the water in the shower, the amount of blood lost looked horribly worse than it actually was.

Linda fought to control her emotions as she cried Brad's name. He showed no signs of arousal. Linda then did the next best thing she could muster and reached under the sink to where their first aid kit was stored. With her right hand occupied she fought with the clasps with her free hand to gain entry to the kit. When it seemed she wouldn't be able to unclasp the box,

everything inside spilled out in an explosion. She sorted
through the pile until she found a packet of 4 X 4 gauze.
Ripping it open with her clenched teeth she then placed it under
her right hand atop the laceration.

Linda barely noticed her husband's lifeless body move. *But it
did.* She gently lifted his head in her free hand smearing blood
under his chin as she did. She bent over the edge of the
combination shower/bath and spoke directly into his right ear.

"Honey? Brad? I'm here baby. I'm here." Tears
flowed easily down her face; pale with fear. Brad responded to
her voice by opening his eyes slowly. Linda's heart danced at
the thought of her husband coming back to her. She could no
longer contain the wall of tears she had so bravely shored up;
gasping for air between cries. "You son of a bitch! Where do
you think you were going?" she yelled. Brad's eyes slowly
closed as the room went silent once again.

Linda, realizing Brad was once again unconscious, knew
she had to get him help. As she lifted her head to gather her
bearings the small fragile silhouette of Lilly standing in the
doorway came into focus. Pushing aside her instinct to remove
her daughter from the tragic scene she yelled to Lilly.

"Get the phone for Mommy sweetie! Hurry! Daddy's
hurt!" Lilly moved as if being pushed by Linda's convictions,
bolting across the bedroom to the bedside table on Linda's side
of the bed. It had been moved there about a year ago when Brad

began to complain about the late night Vet emergencies that routinely came. Lilly plucked the handset off the receiver and rushed the cordless phone to her mother, staring at her daddy. Linda fumbled with the phone dropping it to the ceramic tile floor jarring the battery cover from its place. She picked the phone up with her free hand once again and prayed for a dial tone to come. With a protracted delay it resounded in her ear causing Linda to let out a deep sigh. Frantically, she dialed 911 looking up to see Lilly sitting against the door jamb crying in fear. Then suddenly a voice came on the line.

"911, state your emergency?"

Linda's life slowly began to flow back into view knowing help would come.

CHAPTER 71

Linda lifted her weary head when she heard her name. A man no more than thirty years old stood in front of her. He wore blue scrubs and had a surgical cap on his head. Black curls finding their way out from underneath the cap. He was smiling.

"Mrs. Fordam?" He sat next to her, "Your husband is going to be fine." Linda forced herself to breath. "We had to repair his right radial artery and a few ligaments but otherwise he'll be okay." Linda bent over, setting her heavy head on her hands which were propped on her knees. She began to cry.

"Can I see him now?" She asked through sobs. The young doctor reached out a hand for her, which she took.

"Come on, I'll take you to him." The two walked into the Surgical ICU leaving a cold, empty waiting room behind.

Linda left the girls in the care of Jane, a neighbor who came to the house after hearing sirens in the otherwise quiet cul-de-sac. Lilly was a friend of Jane's five year old son Zachary, so she felt at ease waiting at home. Luckily, Ana was asleep during the entire ordeal. Linda told Jane she would call the house when she knew what was happening with Brad. She called forty-five minutes later with the news that Brad was being taken into emergency surgery because they couldn't stop the bleeding from his right wrist.

"Take as long as you need honey", Jane told her neighbor. "I'll get the kids dressed later and take them to my house for breakfast. They'll think it's an adventure." And they would, thought Linda.

"Thank you so much for this Jane", Linda finished then hung up the phone, leaving Jane to clean the bathroom as best she could when Lilly fell asleep on the couch. There was a blood stain left where the Paramedic's moved Brad's limp body to stabilize him for transport to the hospital.

Brad was asleep when Linda walked into his room in the Intensive Care Unit. There was a stranger sitting next to the bed reading a magazine. The young girl with long blonde hair and green eyes stood as Linda approached, setting the magazine on the chair. The doctor spoke.

"He'll have a sitter with him until he's cleared by Psych in the morning". Linda looked at the young girl, her name tag saying Terri G. Patient Services, and smiled.

"Thanks" she simply said.

"No problem Mrs. Fordam. He's been sleeping since he got out of the OR". Linda smiled again at the young girl as she stepped up to the bed. She reached out for Brad's hand as he opened his eyes. Linda looked down not yet ready to make eye contact when she noticed the bandages on his wrists. His skin was an amber-brown from the iodine prep they used in the operating room. His wrists were also tied to the bed. This took Linda's breath away, snapping everything back into focus. She'd been in a trance since arriving in the Emergency Room. She remembered people asking a lot of questions and signing some papers. A couple of people came up to her filling her in on what was happening. A police officer also asked her some questions. She hadn't even realized that the police were at the house when in fact they were the first on the scene. Everything happened so quickly, she thought in retrospect; it was all a blur.

"Hey there?" said a harsh voice, bringing her back to the present. Linda looked down at her husband. His eyes were slits, still feeling the effects of the narcotics the nurses had given him. He had oxygen tubing in his nose and two IV's running in his left arm. His hair was matted from where she held it with her bloody hand, and his skin seemed a couple shades lighter than normal.

"Hey you". She was smiling.

The doctor took a step toward the couple.

"We had to give him three units of packed red blood cells. He lost a lot of blood. Once we were able to repair the radial artery everything else was mostly cosmetic. We did however, have to re-attach two tendons. He'll be in a cast for a couple of weeks to immobilize the hand and let everything heal. He's lucky you found him when you did, another fifteen or twenty minutes and you might have lost him." He turned toward Brad setting a hand on his shoulder. "I'll see you in a few hours pal. I'm going to get some shut eye. Someone woke me out of a pleasant dream tonight", he finished, smiling.

"Okay. Thanks Doc," replied Brad. Linda looked up at the sitter.

"Can we be alone for a minute?"

"I'm sorry Mrs. Fordam. I can't leave the room. It's hospital policy for patients who attempt suicide".

The words struck her like a freight train. Linda hadn't thought of this as a suicide attempt. She hadn't actually thought about it at all. Too much had happened, too fast. Her head started to spin, she grabbed at the side rail on the bed for support, but not finding it she began to lean to the left. She felt two strong arms grab hold under her arms and guide her to the chair Terri had been using earlier. Soon there were three nurses in the room with them. She couldn't get her bearings; everything was spinning out of control.

"Slow your breathing, Hon. You're alright".

Slowly the room came back into focus. The ringing in her ears receded, and she was able to face the terrible truth.

"I'm okay; I just got a little dizzy. That's all." The nurses left the room one by one over the next five minutes until it was just the three of them again. Linda remained seated holding her husband's hand. "I'm sorry Brad. I need to be stronger right now. It's just that...... I didn't see this coming". She paused taking long slow breaths, fighting back waves of nausea. "Or maybe I did and didn't want to deal with it. I don't know anymore. All I know is that I want things back to normal."

CHAPTER 72

Eleven days later, Linda hurried the kids along in their morning routines. "Hurry Ana, eat your breakfast. Lilly can you get Ana's bag for me? We have to get going." Lilly ran up the stairs of the Colonial style home, racing to retrieve Ana's Diaper bag from her little sister's room. She returned within seconds huffing.

"Mommy? Are you dropping me off at school again?" Lilly liked "drop-off's" and "pick-up's," as her daddy called them. Linda looked down at her oldest as she wiped the remnants of Ana's oatmeal from her face.

"Yes Lilly I'm dropping you off then taking your sister to daycare. I'll go see daddy before I go to the office for a couple hours", she finished.

"Why can't we see daddy yet?" pouted Lilly.

"The doctors say soon honey, very soon. Take your stuff and Ana's bag to the car and get buckled in. We'll be right out." The three Fordam ladies drove off after putting Maggie in her pen. Linda was readying for a busy day. Brad's doctors finally said he may be able to go home today; they would set him up as an outpatient for group meetings twice a week, and get him a one on one with a Psychiatrist once a week. Brad had asked them when he could return to teaching but they let that hang in limbo for the moment. He'd spent over a week and a half in the hospital; first in the ICU until he got medical clearance to transfer to the Mental Health Unit for "closer monitoring" of his medications. He and Terri hit it off well. Brad had been admitted on the first day Terri started her work week, so the two of them spent four nights together before he was transferred to the MHU.

Linda entered the hospital room at 3 pm, just as Terri clocked in for work.

"Hi Terri, Linda said passing her in the hallway.

"Hi there!" replied Terry, clearly excited. "How's *our man* doing?" she asked with a grin. Linda responded with her own.

"He's good, might be going home today," she said crossing her fingers in front of her face.

"That's good news Linda. I hope you guys do okay." Linda smiled once again at her new friend.

"Thanks Terri. You've been great. I'm glad we got to meet you." Terri hugged Linda quickly.

"Me too, just would have been nice to meet under better circumstances", she said. "Well, I've gotta go. My shift starts in a couple of minutes, take care hon." The two parted and Linda resumed her track for the Mental Health Unit.

Once cleared to enter the unit, Linda passed a few of the residents on her way to her husband's room. The first was a down trodden young man who looked as if he were lost. He was about twenty years old Linda thought, but may as well have been fifty. His hair was a mess. Clothes were mismatched and he wore hospital socks; one red, one yellow. There was a green and yellow band around his wrist. The green indicating that he was a flight risk; the yellow matched the one on Brad's wrist. It indicated "potential harm to self": in other words, *suicide risk*. A shiver jolted Linda out of her trance as she watched the young man pass her in the hallway. She continued down the hall taking a left at the next junction; jumping as she was sideswiped by an older lady pushing a walker with gray hair and steaks of white. The old woman brushed off the near-collision with a stern look in Linda's direction. Linda heard her mumble something under her breath then set about her way, the walker leading her to her destination. She had a very serious look about her as she travelled the byways of the unit nearly running over people as she rumbled down the corridor. Linda leaned against the tiled wall and shook her head in wonder. This was a foreign place to her she realized at that moment; cold and unapproachable. Poor lighting and tiled walls that were cold to the touch reminded her that this was an *institution*. She let out a deep sigh and turned on her heel to continue toward her destination: Brad. Before she completed the turn she was grabbed by her arms. Linda shrieked, startled as she looked up into her husband's eyes.

"Hey there good looking!" Brad said as he released her arms.

"Shit Brad! You scared me half to death!" Linda said catching her breath. As sudden as the adrenaline had coursed through her veins the look of exasperation had faded into one of loneliness. Linda wrapped her arms around her husband's neck pulling him in for a much needed kiss. She whispered in his ear "I love you". Brad tightened his grip on her waist replying.

"I love you too honey." The couple walked back to Brad's room and shared a few minutes together before being interrupted by a nurse.

"Hey Brad", the nurse called out turning toward Linda. You must be Linda, he's told me a lot about you." Linda reached out her hand in greeting.

"Hi. It's nice to meet you…" Picking up on the fact that she had not introduced herself the nurse replied.

"I'm sorry. My name is Anisha."

"Anisha, is *Mr. Wonderful* going to get to come home with me today?" A hopeful smile crossed Linda's face.

"I think the Doctor is on his way in to round on the patients. We'll have to get the okay from him", she replied, guardedly.

Brad and Linda spent almost an hour together before the doctor stopped in. Brad had asked how the girls were doing and grilled Linda as to what they had been doing in his absence.

She filled him in on all of the details of the last few days trying to hold back the tears that had so badly wanted to escape their restraints and flow down Linda's pale cheeks. Brad sensed this and held her hand tighter.

"It's going to be alright Linda."

CHAPTER 73

It was four thirty in the afternoon when Linda pulled into the driveway of their home with Brad in the passenger seat and two very excited young ladies in the rear seat of her car. Maggie Moo trampled Brad as he entered the house, barking with delight at the sight of her long lost master. She ran around in circles playfully allowing the girls to join in her excitement. Linda followed Brad up the stairs to the master bedroom. He walked to the side of the bed and sat quietly. Linda stopped short of the bed as she discovered her husband starring at the faded spot of blood near the bathroom door. She stood, immobilized as she waited for Brad's reaction at seeing where he lay while the Paramedics worked to save his life; his life spilling onto the white carpet. He looked up catching her stare. Blinking twice Linda broke off the eye contact the couple had made. She starred down at her feet before Brad broke the silence.

"I'm sorry I did this to you." His voice crackled under the strain of holding back his emotions. Cautiously he continued, "I didn't mean to hurt you. I...I just collapsed on the inside. Everything that I've done in the past six years came to a head all at once. I couldn't see any other way out", there was a long, silent pause. "It was a pitiful way out of the situation."

Linda collapsed on the floor in a broken heap. She began to cry uncontrollably. Brad raced to her, pulling her into his arms holding her tightly. She began to speak in a whisper weak voice between sobs, "I should have been here for you Brad. It's my fault. I should have known the burden you were bearing would be too much to handle." She let out a wail crying loudly in her husband's arms. "I shouldn't have let you continue all these years! Why did I allow it? I should have made you stop!" she finished.

"There was nothing that would have stopped me, Linda; you know that. It was something I had to do. I just couldn't let it go. I should have been ready for this." He spoke softly in her ear as he rocked her on the floor. "I never thought about what I had to do *after* it was over. It never struck me that I would have to deal with *him*. I guess I thought that I would be able to just walk away from everything. Leave it all behind, but I was wrong. And I brought you and the girls into it. I'm so sorry baby."

The two sat on the floor overlooking the dark red/brown stain that represented Brad's only failure. The girls eventually wandered up to the landing at the top of the stairs but were wary of entering the bedroom as they listened to their parents cry together. Maggie was the one to break the moment as she tore up the stairs rupturing the silence with the sound of her nails grabbing into the carpet as she turned the corner and broke for the master bedroom at full speed. The girls gave chase in a vain attempt to stifle the dogs' characteristic playful aggressiveness, without success. They were drawn to their parents and took a seat next to them on the floor; both girls offering hugs in absence of words at the sight of their mom and dad in tears.

"It's okay daddy. We'll take care of you." Lilly offered to the accepting nods of Ana.

The evening took on a more normal tone as the foursome made breakfast for dinner and sat down to watch a movie of the kids' choosing. Quietly, Linda watched as the clock slowly ticked away unsure of what the night would bring. She kept her anxiety hidden from Brad but was unable to push out the thought of finding him in the shower. At nine thirty, they carried the sleeping girls up to their room, carefully changing them into their pajamas.

Afterward they kissed the girls gently on the forehead and exited the bedroom. Brad turned to Linda.

"I'm going to soak in a hot bath. Want to join me?" he asked with a boyish smile.

"Maybe in a little while sweetie, I'm going to pick up the kitchen first. You go ahead." Brad kissed her on the cheek and turned toward the bathroom quietly padding along the carpeted floor. Linda descended to the kitchen after Brad closed the door behind him. The sound of running water upstairs momentarily stole her breath.

Linda awoke with start. She felt her heart pounding in her chest, heaving to regain her breath. There were beads of sweat appearing on her face, her hands clammy; a grim reminder of events past. She opened her eyes to discover bleak darkness. Groping, she quickly found Brad's body lying next to her in quiet slumber. Her head slumped. She began to weep.

Brad slowly awoke from his sleep finding his wife slumped over her side of the bed. Shifting his body toward her he discovered the wetness on the sheets from her sweat.

"What's wrong?" he asked stroking her bare back, still glistening from perspiration. Linda trembled under his hand; her breathing labored, uncontrolled, and panicked. She responded in a soft, jittery voice. Brad had to tilt his head to catch her words.

"I can't stop", she said faintly.

"Can't stop what?" he asked as he continued trying to reassure her through his gentle touch.

"I…I can't stop…I don't want to lose this Brad. I don't want to lose what we have." She sat up lifting her arms to her chest, clutching her hair that cascaded over her bare shoulders. "This. I don't want to lose this" Linda waved her arms in a sweeping movement around the room. "I don't want to lose everything we've worked so God damn hard to get." Once again Linda broke into tears. Brad moved his hand up Linda's spine reaching her neck, which he gently rubbed before pulling her down to the softness of the bed. Drawing her close, Brad held his wife as she cried.

"It's going to be alright. The worst of it is behind us. I promise." Linda cried herself back to sleep as Brad held her close protecting her from whatever evils dare encroach.

CHAPTER 74

The morning was gloomy at best. A storm front had blown in through the night depositing dark and ominous clouds over New Haven and most of the northeastern United States. Brad was up first, beating the ladies by a good hour. He felt good despite the horrific weather; his mood had lifted since starting on anti-depressants, giving him a presence of hope. Maybe there was a *"light at the end of the tunnel"*. After dressing in a pair of khaki cargo pants, a blue denim shirt over a black tee, and his under-used hiking boots; he worked his way to the kitchen to prepare breakfast for his three favorite girls. Linda was much less enthusiastic, forcing herself out of bed. She trod barefoot down the hallway to wake Lilly and Ana; she found the girls fully dressed and cleaning their room.

Smiling, she entered, "Well, well what are you two *fiends* doing?" The girls jumped, startled from their chore. Both ran to the doorway at full speed.

"Mommy, Mommy!" they said in unison as if saying well-rehearsed lines. "Look what we did!", Ana said as she twirled around in a circle showing her mother her school clothes as if for the first time. "We got ourselves dressed!" "Daddy made us clean our room", said Lilly, with a pouting grin on her face.

"Well", Linda said widening her smile, "it must be Mother's Day... or maybe my birthday! Where's Daddy?" Lilly handled this question.

"He's making us breakfast", she simply stated.

"Well, you guys finish your room then come down and eat. I'll go help Daddy." Linda turned and left the room letting the girls finish their cleaning.

Once downstairs Linda could hear the sizzle of bacon on the stove and smelled the aroma of fresh coffee. She slipped into the kitchen and grabbed hold of Brad's waist.

"Morning big boy", she said. Brad, ready for the surprise spun around and pulled Linda in close for her first hug and kiss of the day. Linda cradled her head on Brad's chest, leaning in to hear the thump, thump, thump of his heartbeat. The pair stood quietly for a minute before Brad broke the silence.

"The bacon is going to burn". With that he turned reluctantly to work on the meal he'd been preparing. Linda stood clutching him from behind, her arms wrapped around his waist.

"Thank you for last night", she said softly. Brad said nothing in return, but gave her a secretive grin.
The quiet respite was ended in a rush with two hungry girls materializing from upstairs; Lilly leading her sister by a good second in what could have been mistaken as the race of their

lives. With a crash Lilly placed herself in her chair waiting for what she expected to be nothing less than a spectacular meal. Ana realizing she had lost the race ran past the table landing right at her father's feet.

"Daddy, Lilly cheated! She pushed me into the bathroom!" Brad looked at his youngest daughter with a serious face.

"Well, all is fair in love and war!" he said grimacing. Linda jumped in to give her two cents worth.

"And breakfast!" she blurted.

"Ha, ha!" exclaimed Lilly, glowing with pride.

"Okay ladies. Let's play nice. Lilly apologize to your sister".

The bantering went back and forth for a few minutes until they were all occupied with eating. Ana would shoot her big sister a foul look only to receive a tongue wagging back at her. Maggie Moo curled next to Ana's chair awaiting the food she would ultimately drop on the floor.

Everything was perfect for now, Linda thought. Smiling she watched her family interact with each other the way they ought to. Brad had regained his appetite after starting on his medications; his doctor warned they may make him lose the urge to eat for a while until his body got used to them. He looked at Linda while piling more eggs on his plate and ruined the moment.

"Are you going to go with me to see the doctor today?" The color instantly left her face.

"Do you need me to go?" she asked sheepishly.

"No, I should be okay", he answered honestly. "This is something I have to face". Linda looked down at her coffee cup with a disconcerted look.

"I've already let you go through too much alone. Are you sure you don't want me there?" Brad reached across the table taking her hand in his, rubbing the back of hers with his thumb.

"I'm certain. You relax today. Aren't you going into the office tomorrow?"

Linda simply replied, "Yeah", covering her anxiety with a false smile.

Brad left with the girls soon after breakfast was finished. After dropping Lilly off at school he drove the two miles to Ana's daycare. Ana wanted to stay home with her mother but Linda insisted she get back to normal also and spend at least half a day at daycare. With everyone gone Linda went upstairs to dress for the day before tackling the dishes and mess Brad left at her request. She decided to dress in jeans and a white tee for what was to be a relaxing day at home, alone. Looking in the mirror she decided not to do anything with her hair. "Maybe a hair tie" she thought aloud. Maggie had trotted into the room carrying a beat up old tennis ball in her mouth. She dropped the ball at Linda's foot in an attempt to let her know it was playtime. The ball struck the top of Linda's foot rolling under Brad's side of the bed.

"Good job, Mag" said Linda to the collie that was too slow to catch her prey before rolling under the bed. She plopped to the floor with a sad look about her, knowing she was too big to fit the cramped space. Linda finished pulling up her long straight hair then bent to one knee to retrieve the ball for Maggie who had assumed a pathetic look on her face. Linda peered under the bed noticing that the ball had traveled to the middle of the space resting against a shoe box under the bed. Unable to reach it on one knee she went down on both and stretched her hand as far as it could extend. She was about to tell the Collie that she lost her ball when she decided to give it another chance. Linda reached as far as she could as she wedged her head under the side of the bed to gain a couple of inches. She grabbed hold of the green ball successfully and began to withdraw her arm when she noticed a rip in the under lining of the bed about a foot from the edge of the bedside.

Maggie bolted to fetch the slimy ball after Linda tossed it across the room. She decided to take a look at the tear to see if it could be mended, then she noticed something out of the ordinary between the torn fabrics. Linda pushed her head further under the bed until she reached the hard metal frame with her shoulder. Her face was beginning to turn red from the blood rushing from her inverted body; the veins on her forehead were bulging from the extra fluid. She reached into the slit, grabbing hold of the foreign object, slowly withdrawing her hand trying not tear the hole any more. Her efforts revealed a small bundle of letters bound by a lone heavy duty, red rubber band. Sitting with her back against the bed she stared at the bundle in her hand. Part of her was mesmerized with intrigue at not knowing the origin of the letters, another part panicked at what she might find.

CHAPTER 75

Brad arrived at the outpatient clinic fifteen minutes ahead of schedule; an old habit of his. He entered the office noting they had modeled it with an old European feel. The walls were a dark cherry wood with inviting leather chairs and couches in the waiting room. The side tables were of a simpler design but the center table was what caught his attention.

"Beautiful isn't it?" The voice, soft and feminine came from behind a desk to the left of Brad. A petite woman in her forties was seated behind a large mahogany desk in the corner. A green lamp was illuminating the nook in a soft light. The woman was thin with a body much younger than her years. She wore a red dress with a V-neck that led to what Brad thought could only be surgically enhanced breasts. She had a soft inviting smile that drew him in her direction. She stood as he entered and reached across the desk accepting Brad's hand in hers. "You must be Bradley Fordam", she said in an engaging manner.

"I am", he replied simply taking her hand in his. She held his hand rather than shaking it showing Brad that he was safe in her presence. Brad pulled his hand away allowing his fingers to slide along hers for an extra second. The woman smiled at feeling this small sign of attraction from the man who stood before her.

"I'm Doctor Calista Wright. And *you* are early", she said with a smile. "My secretary Jeanette left for a few minutes to run an errand. Please come into my office and make yourself comfortable. We can take care of the paperwork after our session when Jeanette has returned." She waved Brad through the solid double doors located just to the right of the desk. The interior office was well appointed with articles that had to have been imported from Europe. The carpet was a blood red that complemented the dark walls and built in bookshelves that stood a good ten feet; lining three of the four walls. The shelves were filled with medical texts as well as a plethora of literature interspersed with knick knacks. All held an aura of medieval Europe. Brad was speechless as he entered what could have passed for any number of decadent reading rooms located in the oldest of libraries scattered throughout the old country. His mind travelled back to his childhood as he took in the vision before him. He made a full circle as he looked around the room, which he guessed was at four hundred square feet. There were two floor-to-ceiling windows on one wall, fittingly situated opposite the doctor's desk. Doctor Wright followed Brad into the room, passing him on the left when he paused to absorb the room in all its majesty. He felt completely at home among the artifacts and books. He heard the doctor speak from behind her desk.

"I take it you approve of my office, Bradley?" His mind was pulled back to reality upon hearing her soft voice. He smiled as he approached her desk taking a seat across from her.

"It's quite impressive, doctor. I feel as if you've thrown me back into my childhood". Doctor Wright gave Brad a puzzled look as she continued. "

Please elaborate, Bradley." An inquisitive look crossed her face.

"It's Brad", he replied. The doctor raised a brow asking, "What is?" Brad crossed his leg over the other leaning back in the well cushioned chair. It was made of soft leather that had a worn, but not worn out, look about it. "My name; it's Brad, if you please. Only my parents called me by that." He returned the Calista's smile with one of his own.

"My apologies; I wasn't aware…" Brad cut her off in mid-sentence not wanting to travel that road just yet.

"It's quite all right, Doctor Wright. Please think nothing of it." With a nod the Calista stood.

"Would you care for some coffee *Brad"* He smiled again, seeing that she was embarrassed.

"Tea would be nice", he replied, testing her.

"Very good Doctor Fordam" she said. "I'll be right back. Earl Gray?" she asked as she walked to a small side table to the left of the desk.

"One sugar please", he answered, obviously pleased with her choice.

After returning to her seat across from the desk, Doctor Wright opened a manila file and read in silence for a brief moment; a sign the pleasantries were over and it was time to address what the meeting was intended to address.

"You have been sent here as a follow-up to your hospital stay I see". Brad understood what the doctor really said was "so you're here because you tried to kill yourself, I see". He appreciated her candor.

"That is one way to put it, Doctor Wright. Or you could just say that I am back from an extended vacation." He smiled at that.

"You joke about the fact that you tried to end your life", she stated rather than questioning.

"Well, I've seen the error of my way." She looked down her narrow nose at Brad.

"You're not going to get off that easily my friend". It was her turn to smile. "You joke at my expense?" Doctor Wright's face gained a certain professional look suddenly. "We have a serious problem Brad. You're here because you wanted to put an end to something. It's my job to help you see that suicide is not an end, but rather a beginning. Suicide may seem like a way out of a situation; a convenient one at that, but what the person doesn't realize is the affect their actions have on others. Quite often it triggers a ripple effect you could say. You're more likely to kill yourself if someone has already done so in your past. It's my job to break that cycle, Brad; to ensure your safety, as well as your children's." She placed the folder back on the desk letting it remain open as if to pique Brad's interest.

"Your file is very interesting to say the least. It's not often I get to treat a fellow Doctor. And quite an accomplished one at that." Brad lowered his head in humility.

"Please Doctor; I'm but a lowly college professor; and a mediocre one at that. You're the *real* Doctor." Doctor Wright scoffed at that remark.

"I made a couple of calls on your behalf Doctor Fordam. I have a few colleagues at Yale in the Psychology Department. You are quite well known around campus. They all had nothing but high marks for you. A couple may know you in passing, but all of them know your work. Linguistics and Psychology are closely related as you are well aware. Your work in Semiotics is well established and closely watched by my peers on campus." Brad said nothing. Doctor Wright had evidently done her homework. He liked her.

CHAPTER 76

Maggie circled around Linda's feet as she remained frozen in place on the floor. The collie knew there was something amiss with her owner. She sensed Linda's anxiety and showed her own as well by circling Linda's feet whimpering from time to time; concern showed on her face over her master's sudden change in behavior. Linda sat holding the bundle of letters in one hand as the other held her chin, her fingers dancing around the edges of her mouth. Maggie finally gave up, deciding to lie at her owner's feet and rest her head with a whimper. She never took her eyes off Linda for a moment. The family dog was very aware that things were not as they should have been for some time now.

Linda looked up from the letters to Maggie, realizing for the first time that she was at her feet.

"What do you think girl?" she asked waiting for a response. Maggie lifted her head continuing to look directly at Linda. Her tail wagged at hearing "girl" but quickly ceased when it was not followed up. Linda took in a long deep breath releasing it slowly. "Well, here goes nothing." Linda slipped the red rubber band off the letters as if she were dismantling a bomb; her fingers nimble and steady as a surgeons'. Her mind was however, racing. "What could he be hiding? Why would he hide this?" These questions raced through her mind, finding no resolution.

The letters were old; the envelopes faded and yellowing with age. They were turned into each other leaving no visible writing. Most of the corners bent this way and that from frequent handling. Linda took the envelope on top of the bundle and turned it over slowly revealing where it had been and who sent it. The letter was addressed to Alice Redding Fordam at Saint Lawrence Psychiatric Center in Ogdensburg, New York. Linda knew this was the hospital to which Brad's mother was committed. She moved her gaze from the recipient to the sender in the top left corner. It was from Brad; Bradley; Bradley Fordam; with the address of an Army post in Germany.

Linda sat quietly staring at the faded envelopes, questions circling in her head. "Why hadn't Brad shown these to her before? What could they tell her about his childhood?" And most importantly, "should she read them?" The questions kept her from opening the aged envelope until a voice from within told her it was okay and that her husband had no reason to keep these from her. She timidly pulled the letter from the faded envelope. It was handwritten in what was clearly Brad's meticulous penmanship. She looked at the date on the post mark. It would have been when Brad was a sophomore in high school. He was sixteen at the time. She set the envelope on her lap with the rest of the letters and carefully opened the letter.

There was one page with writing on either side. She held her breath as she began reading.

Dearest Mother,

It is late August and very warm here. The days are getting shorter as fall approaches. I have been visiting the local libraries more often as of late and sometimes feel I should move into one of them! I don't see father very much anymore. He's always working and I feel there is no place for me there. We are in a small two bedroom cottage just off base. It's a short bus ride into the city where I spend most of my time. There is so much to learn about past cultures that walked the very streets I do. I am intrigued as well as astounded at the vast difference in our times. Sometimes I wish I had lived back then. I think I would have like it.

There is a girl I have taken a liking to. Her name is Penelope and she lives here with her parents and younger brother. Her Dad is in the Army as well. They are from New Jersey (I think). We have gone to a couple of plays and recently went to a renaissance fair together. It was actually fun and I enjoyed being with her.

School is going well. I have A's in all my classes but would rather be in a library reading. I walk the streets in the evening before returning home to our empty cottage. The sounds of the old cities I think are my favorite; the narrow cobblestone streets

give off a feeling of Old Europe. Sometimes I just sit in a coffee
Shoppe listening to the city bustling with life.
I hope you are well. I think of you every day.

With Love, Bradley

Linda read quietly through the first few letters. She attacked them one at a time, keeping them in order; they had been arranged chronologically. So far they all had been from Brad to his mother and they all carried similar tones but it was evident the disdain Brad felt for his father increased as the letters progressed through time. They were spaced out every two or three months and all had been addressed to the Psychiatric Center. Linda collected her thoughts before continuing. She noted there were about twenty letters in all. Maggie kept Linda's feet warm as she drifted off to sleep calmly; finally taking her eyes off her distressed master.

CHAPTER 77

"Tell me what led you into the area of Linguistics", Doctor Wright asked. She was now crossing her legs beneath the imposing desk. Her hands set neatly on her lap.

"I don't know exactly. I've always had a great appreciation for language arts", Brad replied. "I thought I'd be good at It." he concluded. Doctor Wright placed her hands back atop the desk folding her fingers into each other.

"Well, I'd say you certainly have an aptitude for it. From what I have learned about you in the short time I've had, people tell me you're in the top ten linguists in the country. That's quite an achievement. Your parents must have been proud of you".

There was an eerie silence in the room. Brad shifted in his seat containing his feelings as best he could. Dr. Wright let him off the hook by continuing.

"I heard about what happened to your father. I'm very sorry for you. Your mother passed away some time ago?" She kept her face as neutral as possible in anticipation of Brad's response. The two held onto each other's gaze as Brad formulated his canned response. Clearing his throat in an attempt to let the doctor know he was uncomfortable broaching this subject, he answered.

"Yes, she passed away while I was in high school. My wife and I are still in shock over what had happened to my father." He took a tissue from her desk for effect, crumpling it for effect.

"You were close; you and your father?" Brad was suddenly unsure how to answer this question. How much did she know? Was she trying to get him to open up about their torrid relationship or was she just poking around in the dark? He collected his thoughts before responding. In a careful tone he answered.

"My father and I had a very..." he paused in an attempt to seem strained, "complex relationship". The answer raised an eyebrow on the Doctor's face, yet she remained silent. Pointing an innocent finger at her, Brad continued, "You're very good at this Doctor Wright." She uncrossed her legs, leaning into the desk from her chair.

"What do you mean by that Brad?" He slumped back in his chair as if pushing away from her and answering any more questions. He suddenly felt very uncomfortable speaking to her. Brad needed to be careful not to lead the questions down a path that may divulge too much of his past. He sat looking at the Psychiatrist, studying her expressions with great care. *What did she know?*

Brad suddenly found himself standing in the kitchen of a house he and his parents occupied in London. He is about ten years old. As he stands there, his parents are engaged in an all-out verbal confrontation. His mother is drunk at two in the afternoon. It was a Saturday and his mother had been drinking heavily most of the morning. Bradley's father, to no one's surprise had been working that morning. His mother was slurring her words, fighting the urge to fall over. This unfortunately was not uncommon to Bradley; as his parents fought often during their stay in London. It was near the end of their relationship, about three months before they were reassigned to Fort Drum, New York.

Their shouts had become enraged as Bradley stood consuming the hatred as if he were a starving child. He began to feed off the hate. It fueled his passions in life and also gave him reason to abandon his parents, seeking refuge in the quiet, musty corners and alcoves of the many libraries he frequented. This period shaped Bradley into the man he eventually became. He craved the quiet respite that would soon follow. His father would storm out the door heading back to post and his mother would be slumped over the arm of the couch crying herself into an inebriated slumber. Bradley never left a note saying where he would be, although his mother always knew. He would pack a light dinner and hike the two miles to the Library; always unsure of what he would come home to. Would his mother vomit in her drunken stupor, aspirating the vile fluid into her lungs? Would his father come home at all? There were nights that he hadn't. Bradley never questioned his father as to where he was those nights. At the age of ten he knew already of the temptations that stalk a man of his father's greed.

"Brad?" The voice was soft and lured him out of his past. He opened his eyes to realize that he was back in Doctor Wright's office. His eyes were wet with tears. Calista had come from behind her desk and was holding a tissue for him. Her right hand lay on his shoulder, "Brad? This is good. You need to start healing. You need to help yourself recover from the abuse you went through." Her voice was gentle, calming. He regained his composure, breathing in deeply through his nose and out his mouth, before attempting to talk.

"I'm okay".

The tears began flowing as if a dam had been released. He couldn't hold it back anymore. Through the tears he spoke; the words foreign at first. Words he'd never thought he would speak. He cradled his head in his hands. This was foreign territory for him. He'd never thought he would have the feelings that were now tearing at his emotions. Uncontrollably, he sobbed, hiding his flushed face from Calista.

"I hated that son of a bitch so much! He deserved everything he got! That bastard killed my mother!" Brad had never spoken these thoughts before. He was always able to tuck them away. Compartmentalize his feelings; at least until now it had worked for him.

He thought to himself, *"What the fuck is happening? Get a hold of yourself. Fix this!*

CHAPTER 78

Linda read nine letters so far. She sat in the same position, transfixed on the words she'd read. Seeing for the first time a side of her husband she'd never had access to; a boy who was forced to become a man too early in life. Her reading was interspersed with bouts of tears as she grew closer to the man she'd fallen in love with. Why hadn't he shown her these letters? What did he think he had to hide? His letters to his mother were filled with sorrow and emptiness, pain, and suffering. She was reading the thoughts of a boy who had lost his mother. The lies he was told by his father had corrupted his ability to see the devastation that was done. Maggie remained dedicated to Linda, lying at her feet in a show of support. She was always the friend for someone in need.

The tenth letter was the first written to Brad from his mother. It was sent from Saint Lawrence Psychiatric Center. The date preceded that of Brad's first letter. Linda gently opened it, unfolding the faded paper as if it may disintegrate with the slightest touch. She read to herself:

My Dearest Bradley,
The days here are the longest of my life. I miss you so much. I think of everything you had to witness and cry myself to sleep. I am so sorry for what you had to endure living with the two of us.

374

I am dealing with my problems while I remain here. Someday I will be able to hold you again; if you will let me, that is. I won't blame you for not wanting me in your life. I was not there for you for so long. I know you are hurt.

Not a day passes I do not feel the deepest regret for the decisions I have made. I abandoned you and I have to live with that reality, as do you. I only hope one day you'll forgive me for my actions. They were selfish and petty compared to my duty as your mother. I pray for my release as I am compelled to be with you again. I have so much to tell you; about your father and the people who aided him in his quest to relieve him of my presence. But that is for another day my dearest Bradley. Today I begin making amends with the child I neglected.

With all my love, Mother

Linda sat in silence. This was where it all started she thought. It was the beginning of the end. Her heart was heavy after reading the passage. It was the first time since reading the diary that she had the thoughts of Patricia Alice Fordam in her head. She remembered that night so many years ago; walking into that shed. Seeing what she had. While yet being able to see through Brad's mothers' eyes. Claiming stake on Brad's heart and giving hers to him as well. It all came back to her in a rush. Things she hadn't noticed or dared to notice swirled through her mind all at once. The dim lights, the pungent smell of fresh blood, Lenny's dying body, impaled. Linda, for the first time realized that she had spent half her lifetime forgetting that night. She'd spent these years loving Brad with all her heart, but a glimmer of doubt had anchored itself in the recesses of her mind.

CHAPTER 79

Brad's mind was foggy. His ears ringing in the presence of the ever increasing pressure in his head. There was a burning in the corners of his eyes from his salty tears. Heart pounding, breathing labored he slowly, cautiously pulled himself out of the spiral he'd found himself. He felt the warmth of Calista's hand on the nape of his neck; her fingers gently caressing his skin. Minutes passed as he worked to control his emotions. Yet she never stopped. She never left his side. Head still cradled in his hands he muttered, "I'm so sorry mother".

Soon after, Brad found himself lying on a comfortable couch in a far corner of the office. "How fitting", he soberly muttered to himself.

"I heard that," Doctor Wright shot back. Brad craned his neck to see that she had taken up position just out of sight near his head in a quaint Victorian era covered chair.

"I feel like such a fool", he said wiping his face dry for what seemed to be the thirtieth time in as many minutes. Under the cover of his hands he grunted loudly. "I'm not usually like this". He heard the Calista quietly let out a laugh.

"I kinda got that impression Doctor Fordam". Brad looked at her, smiling at him. He inadvertently began to laugh as well.

"It's good to see you laugh, Brad. You've a lot of baggage to get rid of. There's a lot of history to muddle through. But rest assured *we will* get through it."

Brad lay on that damned couch for another twenty minutes, answering the doctors questions as honestly as he'd let himself. He found it increasingly difficult to answer her and not reveal the past he was hiding. The thought of divulging the truth flitted in and out of his conscious as she asked how it made him feel when his mother had killed herself. And then once again when asked about his father's murder.

"It must be difficult knowing that both your parents died in unconventional manners," she stated. Seeing no response to her rhetoric she decided to push a little further. "Before I ask you why you decided to try to kill yourself; let me ask you the first thought that went through your mind upon hearing of your mother's suicide? What were your initial feelings?"

Brad sat up staring blankly at the far wall, taking himself back to that horrific day. He vaguely remembered arriving home from school before heading out to the University for a lecture on medieval cultures. The phone was ringing when he entered the apartment. He answered it only to hear a dial tone. The phone rang immediately after he replaced the receiver on the hook. This time there was a man's voice on the other end. It was his father. Readying himself for the verbal barrage he was surely to receive, he was confused, hearing a softer tone in his father's voice.

"Bradley; there's been an incident". It was as if his father were debriefing him on an aircraft crash.

"What do you mean father?" he asked.

"Your mother killed herself yesterday." There was a delay in Brad's response. He could feel the cold indifference in his fathers' voice.

"What do you mean? What happened?" he demanded.

"She was found by a nurse. She cut her wrists." There was no emotion in his father's voice. His tone remained steady; unwavering.

Brad's mind was reeling. "How do you react to such a statement?" he thought. He had felt a certain detachment from his mother for some time now; she had been gone for over six years with relatively little correspondence. He had been left, for all intent and purpose, to raise himself. His father was what you might call a *"hands off"* dad. What little parenting he did came in the form of providing for his basic needs; anything beyond that was Brad's responsibility. At an early age he became self-reliant in many facets.

Brad spoke slowly at first.

"When did you find out?" He felt his pulse pounding in his temples, his face flushed. Brad reached for a chair before crumpling to the floor.

"About an hour ago; there was no one else to call. They need someone to go over there Bradley". Wesley was about to tell his son that he was too busy to break free when Bradley spoke up.

"I'll go. I'll take care of everything." The line went quiet, Brad barely hearing the static.

"I'll hook you up with a hop over the pond to Dover, Maryland in the morning. From there you can catch a commercial flight to Syracuse International. I can have a driver from Fort Drum meet you and take you to the Psych Center so you take care of her things."

Brad sat on the edge of the couch staring blankly at Doctor Wright. She could tell he was somewhere else as he looked through her without blinking. She snapped her fingers loudly in front of his eyes commanding him to "snap out of it". It was as if he was able to hypnotize himself. Brad blinked repeatedly then shook his head. After a few seconds he was able to focus on the doctor.

"Sorry about that. I was somewhere else for a moment". Doctor Wright nodded impassively, hiding her concern from her patient. Brad continued as if by command, "I was back in Europe with my father. He had just told me about my mother killing herself." Doctor Wright noticed something different about Brad. He spoke with a flat voice, almost monotone. She decided to take it a little further, yet again.

"Brad, why don't you ever call your parents Mom or Dad? Why is it always Mother or Father?" He tipped his head to the left slightly, looking at the doctor as if she were a bacterium under the microscope. She felt a shiver run down the nape of her neck causing the little hairs to stand erect. His eyes shot daggers with their blue coldness. She knew something had changed about him, transference from one thing to another. Doctor Wright was sure she'd never met the man sitting on her couch. Her fear took a back seat to inquisitiveness. She knew she was about to cross into a different realm. She was drawn to him. She thought hard, trying to tie Brad in with whoever this new person may be. What little nuances had he shown earlier? He must have had *"the tell"* of a gambler. Then it hit her. She let out the slightest smile and pushed back in her chair. He remained fixed in his position, unblinking.

"Hello Bradley; my name is Doctor Wright. It is a pleasure to meet you."

CHAPTER 80

The sky was turning dark gray, Linda sat on the edge of the bed. Maggie was now lying at the foot of the bed; something Brad had never approved of. She held the bundle of letters tightly with both hands, white at the knuckles. Time seemed to stand still as she thought of the horrible past that she so easily dismissed so many years ago. The images of Lenny and the scene itself seemed surreal, but came back to her with the growing momentum of a tsunami. Waves of deeply embedded memories rushed at her over, and over, and over until she started to cry. Maggie's ears perked at the sound of her mother crying. She whimpered and buried her nose under Linda's arm, the whole time keeping a wary eye on her owner.

The harder Linda wept the harder she gripped the letters. She set the bundle on the bed, freeing her hands in an effort to grab a tissue to wipe her eyes. As the letters settled on the bed; uneven under Linda's modest weight, one slipped past the rest landing on the floor at her feet. Maggie instinctively jumped from her vantage point to retrieve the lone envelope for her master. Linda laughed at the sight of her dog pouncing on the letter, her tail wagging. She patted the dog's soft head saying, "Thank you sweetie. You're such a good girl. Mommy loves you." Maggie resumed her post on the bed laying her head down once again. Linda held the single letter in her right hand as she dried tears from her eyes. Something stood out, however as she looked at the unopened envelope.

She frantically pawed through the bundle of letters pulling out specific ones as she went. Soon there were two piles of envelopes lying side by side. The first were the letters Brad had written to his mother while she was a resident at Saint Lawrence Psychiatric Center. The other pile; was comprised of those written to Brad from his mother. Linda picked one out of the second pile examining it closely. Soon, she found herself tearing through the envelope in a hurried attempt to retrieve the contents. She unfolded the letter that was within and glared at it. Heart pounding, she frantically pulled each of the other letters from the second pile, opening them as she did so. Each time she found the same unbelievable occurrence.

Linda paused, reflecting on the situation. Each letter she opened that was written to Brad from his mother had different hand writing than what was on the corresponding envelope. She stared at the letters with confusion. "Why would the penmanship be different?" she thought aloud. Not grasping the reality of the situation, she quietly studied the letters. Soon reality came crashing upon her as she realized the truth.

Frantically she dove into the pile of letters Brad's mother had written to him. With the diligence of a forensic detective she opened each letter, pouring out the contents onto the bed comparing and examining each. The penmanship on the two letters was subtly different; but having lived her entire adult life with one man she had grown accustomed to his writing style. That same style rested on the letters in her hands. Brad! He had written the letters!

Linda's mind reeled at the mere thought of the proposition. Had he really been hiding the truth from her all these years? If so, why would he have done this? The questions came much faster than any answers. Her life had been a lie; his lie. With resolution, Linda calmly slowed her thoughts trying to take an analytical approach to the situation. She had lived her life in science. That was how she would get through this problem.

CHAPTER 81

Doctor Wright began to fidget in her chair as she awaited her client's response. She had gambled on a hunch and was impatiently waiting to see if she'd hit pay dirt. She found herself averting her eyes as Bradley pierced through her soul with his cold eyes. He sat motionless, his breathing calm and confident, staring at her with icy blue eyes. Minutes ticked by; Doctor Wright was usually confident and daring in her approach to Psychiatry but found herself sheepishly shying away from the man sitting so calmly in front of her. She was summoning the courage to barrage her patient with more direct questioning when she was abruptly cut off.

"Very good, Doctor. I must admit, you're very talented in your trade. I commend you". Bradley spoke without taking his eyes off his new found subject. Doctor Wright sensed she was the one being evaluated suddenly. The change was overwhelming to watch. In a blink of an eye she found herself sitting with an entirely different person; same clothes, same shoes, same features...different person. Having only dealt with a handful of patients with Multiple Personality Disorders, she carefully weighed her options. She had two choices; attempt to redirect the conversation so that Brad would reappear or be aggressive and attempt to pull out Bradley in his whole form.

The problem with the latter choice is the uncertainty of who or what Bradley may actually be.

Time stood still as Bradley sized up his new foe. Thinking to himself just how dangerous she was and how difficult it would be to stifle her growing curiosity. He longed for the taste of blood having been dormant for so long. Brad had been able to keep him in check, until now. Freedom bode well with Bradley, unleashing a rush of adrenaline as he was released from the constraints of his keepers mind. As he stared at Doctor Wright she noticed his pupils constrict. His breathing became noticeably shallower, as if tracking prey in the wild. An unsettling sneer crossed his lips as he bared his teeth. She knew she had pushed too far as she stood from her chair, crossing the room to her desk with haste. She spoke to Bradley as she moved to place her desk between them. Bradley stayed on the edge of the couch watching her every movement as though he was about to pounce her at any moment. Doctor Wright pushed the button hidden under the lip of the enormous desk. Within seconds her secretary appeared at the door as if on cue. Her appearance came as a shock to Bradley, snapping him out of his deep concentration. He glared at the secretary with disdain. The expedited manner in which she had arrived plus the defensive stance she took by not entering the room led Bradley to believe that this was a well-rehearsed act. Cutting his losses he stood, turning his eyes back to the doctor.

"I take it our session is over Doctor Wright?" His voice was steady and hushed; solidifying Doctor Wright's assessment that Brad had regressed into another personality. A transformation that was nearly seamless she thought.

"Yes Bradley. I think that is all for today. I need to see you again tomorrow however. Please make yourself free at the same time tomorrow morning. You did very well today." Without further discussion he stood and walked toward the door. He stopped and turned.

"Very well Doctor. Until tomorrow" he said nodding in the direction of the Psychiatrist. Bradley passed by the secretary as if she were not there. A cold feeling sent shivers through her. The two women said nothing until they heard the front door close. The secretary spoke first.

"Well, that was pleasant." Calista let out a deep sigh placing her two shaking hands on the edge of the desk. She stared at nothing as she spoke quietly.

"What in the hell was that?" she said to no one in particular. She continued, "Holy shit! I nearly pissed myself!" The two broke into an uncomfortable laugh. Calista knew she had witnessed an amazing transformation. She also knew that Brad's other self was a very dangerous person. She looked up at her secretary with a worn look about her face.

"Thank you, Jeanette".

CHAPTER 82

It was close to noon when the garage door opened, startling Linda. She hastily bound the letters with the same rubber band, breaking it with a resonating snap. She recklessly placed the small bundle in the same spot they were found. She managed to get to the top of the stairs before the door opened. Garnering her strength, Linda calmly descended the stairwell to meet her husband. Hiding her anger and fear as best she could she received Brad with a gentle smile and warm hug. Inside she silently shuddered at the thought of embracing him. Linda thought it best to tuck her feelings away for the moment, allowing her some much needed time to get a handle on things.

"How was your session honey?" She noticed something different about Brad's demeanor. He carried himself differently. The honest gentle look he exuded normally took on a hardened, predatory exterior. She knew something happened and she knew it couldn't be good. There was no way around the question. He would know she was up to something if she didn't ask; "What's wrong, Brad?" The response took her by surprise. She had never seen her husband like this.

"It's nothing. I just admitted to killing them." he stated with a distant, detached voice. One she'd never heard in all her years with the man. She was confused.

"Who?"

"*Them*. Every single one of them."

Like a truck slamming into a tree, Linda's world came to a screeching halt. There was no recovering from this. She knew better. Her husband admitted to murdering six people to his Psychiatrist. There was no way his doctor would be able to keep this to herself. There was no way any doctor would not contact the police. This crossed the line of patient-doctor privilege. And she knew there was no way of derailing the train that would soon crash into their lives. As Linda absorbed his reply, Bradley stood expressionless looking at his car keys as he twirled them on his index finger, like a gunslinger in an old spaghetti western move. She stood staring at her husband, waiting for some sign of remorse. She found none. His face remained expressionless.

The silence was broken with the arrival of Maggie from upstairs; her tail wagging excitedly with the arrival of her master. As she descended the stairs her playful tone changed to one of apprehension and soon, aggression. Her tail dropped in a defensive manner as the hair on her back stood up. Maggie growled at Bradley, barring her teeth. Linda had never seen her act this way toward anyone. Maggie sensed that there was someone else other than her master standing in the foyer. Linda's heart jumped at the sight, further proving her suspicions toward her husband. Bradley looked down at the dog.

"Shut that fucking dog up!" He stepped around the dog who refused to take her eyes off Bradley as he passed, walking to the kitchen. Linda didn't know what to do. Her mind was overwhelmed at what just transpired. She knelt down, patting Maggie on the head.

"It's all right Maggie Moo. It's all right". Maggie ceased her growling, but refused to take her suspicious eyes off the kitchen door. As Linda stood, the dog began patrolling the door. She was unsure what was happening, but her senses knew that this was *not* her master. Confused, she maintained a defensive posture to protect Linda. Linda had no idea what she should do next.

Linda decided not to approach her estranged husband, but rather quietly escaped upstairs closing the master bedroom door as she went. Maggie stayed in the foyer keeping her guard. It wasn't until she heard the click of the lock on the door that Linda took a full breath; releasing it slowly trying to calm her nerves. Finding her purse on the bedside table she hastily looked for the object which she sought. "There you are," she said quietly as she produced a business card bearing Doctor Wrights information. Linda once again sat uneasily on the edge of the king-size bed and dialed the doctor's office. Cautiously she listened to the phone ring, not taking her eyes off the bedroom door. She bit on her lower lip as she impatiently waited for the other end of the line to be answered. She felt a

pang of hope when the line stopped ringing but was
disheartened when she realized that the voice on the other end
was recorded. Linda bowed her head in defeat as she waited for
the beep. The voice on the line was that of the doctor's
secretary, she gave the usual instructions. When the beep finally
arrived Linda realized she hadn't thought the situation out this
far. What could she tell the doctor? That her husband was
acting strange? Not like himself? Or should she ask about his
confession? There were too many questions swirling throughout
Linda's pounding head. She wasn't sure which avenue to take.
What if Brad had lied to her, about confessing to Doctor
Wright? What would happen if Linda were to open that can of
worms? With uncertainty ruling the moment Linda decided to
hang up on the answering machine without saying a word. She
instead decided to remove the letters from their hiding place and
secure them in a different spot. If this situation turned bad
Linda needed to have an insurance policy. Someone had to be
here for the girls. Just as she placed the pillow over the bundle
of letters Linda heard the doorknob turn. After two
unsuccessful attempts to open the door Bradley began pounding
his fist on the wooden entry. With a start Linda leapt off the
edge of the bed, her heart racing as she stood alone in the room.
Beyond the door she heard Maggie barking from what must
have been the top of the stairs. The dogs barking grew louder,
ripe with anger and confusion. The pounding on the door

ceased seconds before Linda heard Maggie yelp with pain. Linda fumed at the thought of Brad hurting the family dog. She stormed to the door stopping just short of opening it when the pounding resumed; this time with more force. The wood visibly shuddered with each deafening blow; boom, boom, boom. The wind was taken out of Linda's sails as she stood helplessly staring at the white door. She shouted more out of fear than anger.

"What in the hell are you doing? What did you do to Maggie?" she demanded.

David Dumas

CHAPTER 83

Sharon Engleman entered the office building at fifteen minutes before one o'clock in the afternoon. She was always a little early to her appointments; she enjoyed her short chats with Jeanette. The Psychiatrists' office was located in a two story building that also housed a legal firm, a dentist's office, and a commercial cleaning service. The main doors led to a large foyer that held a sweeping stairwell and a central sitting area. Off to the left were the dentists' office and a central elevator. To the right was the commercial cleaning services' office. Neither had anyone sitting at their receptionists desks. The lunch hour was almost over and activity in the building was about to once again flourish.

Sharon made her way to the stairwell, opting for that rather than taking the elevator. The stairwell was crafted from Cherry and always gave Sharon the feeling that she was Scarlett O'Hare, ascending the beautifully crafted steps in a beautifully flowing evening gown. Gone with the Wind had always been one of Sharon's favorite films. Each time she had topped the stairwell a smile would cross her face. She would often turn to face Rhett Butler as she reached the summit, then quietly slip back into reality and continue down the hallway to Doctor Wright's office door.

The doctor's secretary, Jeanette Stevens, would rarely leave the building during her lunch hour. She enjoyed having some quiet time to herself, usually reading the latest fictional novel she'd chosen. Today she was not at her desk to greet Sharon, who found it odd, but not unheard of. Gently pushing the ornate French door open she found an empty waiting room. She took a seat on a leather loveseat to the left and picked up a Home and Garden magazine, oddly dated for the current month and year. She quietly flipped through the pages awaiting either the return of Jeanette or Doctor Wright who was surely in her office. Nonetheless, five minutes later Sharon found herself still seated in the empty room.

Like a deer feeling the approach of a hunter in the woods Sharon turned her head to ascertain the origin of a faint noise she thought she had heard; nothing. She returned her gaze to the magazine but left her head slightly cocked to the left. Sharon flipped through the pages thoughtlessly, bothered by the noise she thought she heard: Still nothing. She sat wondering if she'd heard anything in the first place, or if her imagination was in overdrive. Then, just above the crinkling of the paper as she turned the page she heard the same faint, muffled sound. This time Sharon clearly knew where the sound emanated. Standing, she replaced the magazine exactly where she'd found it and slowly, carefully, approached the doctor's private door. She could hear her heart beating loudly in her head. She softly knocked on the elegant mahogany doors, then Sharon heard it yet again, only this time a little louder. She firmly grasped the door handle turning it until the catch released. The door swung inward showering Sharon with a horrific sight.

The room was shaded with the heavy curtains drawn on the only two windows, though Sharon quickly made out the large desk opposite the double doors. Straining her eyes to make out anything else in the darkened room; she searched for a sign that the doctor was in her office when a bloody hand reached up, grabbing the unsuspecting woman by the ankle. Sharon screamed. To her surprise it was Jeannette, barely conscious and bleeding heavily from wounds to her head and neck. Her cries for help came in the form of gurgles as she slowly drowned in her own frothy blood. Jeanette's breathing was heavy and labored and increasingly loud; bubbling with every expiration.

Sharon's next reaction was to scream again, but was quickly stifled by the fear that the attacker remained in the room. With the curtains drawn it was close to impossible to detect if there was someone lurking in the shadows, ready to pounce her at any moment. Instinctively, she went down on one knee reducing the size of her silhouette against the lighted entryway. She reached out for Jeanette, only to find the dead stare of the woman looking back at her. Sharon gasped, fighting off an urge to vomit. As the seconds ticked away her eyes grew accustomed to the diminished light. She scanned the room from right to left not seeing anything or anyone out of the ordinary; still, no Doctor Wright. Sure she was now alone in the room stave Janette's lifeless body, still clutching her ankle, Sharon stood reaching for the light switch at the door. After fumbling for a few seconds her fingers made contact with the switch and she flipped it up, cascading the room in brilliant light. She gasped.

There was blood everywhere. Something Sharon was unable to discern in the poor light. Suddenly the harsh smell overwhelmed her senses causing a violent swelling in her belly culminating in projectile vomiting. Gasping to gain her breath she fought off a second wave resulting only in dry heaves. Fighting the weakness in her legs she stumbled forward finding the leading edge of the doctor's desk with the heel of her left hand with a resounding thud. She winced at the pain opening her eyes to the dreadful sight of Doctor Wright lying face down on the floor behind the enormous desk. Blood trailing from her head resulting in a large, semi-congealed pool under the expensive chair. There was no movement, no sign of life. Sharon raced to the doctor's side, unknowingly kneeling in the pool of blood. She shook the doctor, discovering yet another lifeless soul. Sharon turned her body over revealing the atrocity that occurred to her doctor, her *friend*. Dr. Calista Wright's once attractive face had been brutally severed from that which once held it firmly, fixed only by a thread of skin at the chin. Overwhelmed by her surroundings Sharon screamed as loud as she could muster. Her screams continued until the appearance of a young lawyer from the adjoining law firm drew her attention. Slowly, office workers trickled onto the scene; one finally dialing 911.

CHAPTER 84

The connection was made quickly as detectives read the caller ID on Jeanette's desk. The name that had appeared matched one that was in the scheduling book on the same desk. The detectives immediately dispatched a cruiser to investigate the origin of the call sending them to Linda and Brad's home. Camera crews arrived at the office building as quickly as the news of the double homicide spilled out over the airwaves on police scanners throughout the small city of New Haven.

White vans marked New Haven Crime Scene Investigation quickly arrived as officers attempted to cordon off the gruesome scene. Just as rapidly as the call was made, yellow police tape appeared everywhere. Black and White's blocked off the entire block allowing only official vehicles to pass.

The scene at Brad and Linda's house was less obvious. The street was quiet, nothing out of place. A dog barked but seemed muffled and distant. Neighbors' walked their dogs and pre-school children played in their yards as if nothing were out of the ordinary. Hardly anyone noticed the police cruiser glide down the residential street and pull into the large center hall colonial home. Everything was strangely serene to the policemen standing at the front door; except the muffled sound of a dog barking within. Suddenly a scream broke the placid air, then another from deep within the house. It was a woman's voice followed by a man's. Both officers instinctively drew their weapons, the older motioning his partner to cover the rear of the house. The officer tried to open the front door but was denied, finding the locks set. He then pounded on the door with a clenched fist sounding off.

"Police! Open the door!"

The man's screams faded allowing the terrified screams of the woman to echo throughout the quiet suburban street. The older officer kicked in the front door with some difficulty landing him in the foyer on one knee. As he fought to resume a standing position he felt the blow to the back of his head. It was the last thing the officer felt as the life poured out onto the ceramic tile of the foyer; the result of massive head trauma.

Sensing the presence of another officer Bradley slammed the front door shut placing his weight firmly against the wooden structure; however there was no immediate activity. Grasping the marble book end he'd taken from the hallway upstairs, Bradley peeked through the door at the cruiser sitting in the driveway. Nothing moved outside. He then turned his attention to the screams emanating from the master bedroom. Taking two steps at a time, he bound up the stairs toward Linda's shrieks. She lay on the bed bound to the four bedposts with a blue nylon rope; the type used by rock climbers. She fought at her restraints with ferocity causing her wrists to become raw. Brad

399

had not wanted to silence her, hoping he could reason with his wife after she awoke from the knock to the head she'd received. He'd clung to false hope wishing that not all would be lost at the end of the day. He approached her softly not wanting to cause more harm to his beloved wife. She continued to scream louder than before as he approached.

"You don't need to be scared Linda. I'm not going to hurt you." The crazed look that he showed earlier was replaced with the softer, milder one of the man she'd married. The transformation was incredibly smooth and made her wonder how often this transition occurred. He sat on the foot of the bed reaching out to stroke Linda's bare leg. As he did so he sat the book end on the mattress, smearing the comforter with fresh blood. Brad remained intent on calming his wife and failed to notice the stain. Her eyes bulged at the sight of the blood. She was unsure what had happened when Brad had left the room, but she had no doubt that Bradley had struck again; leaving more destruction in his path. She pulled at her restraints with more tenacity.

"What in the hell have you done?" she demanded. "You have to be stopped Brad. You have to stop!"

Brad stopped stroking his wife's leg, instead staring into her moist eyes. Unblinking, his eyes bored through her like a drill bit. She saw the change and froze. The ropes that bound her extremities went slack; then he spoke.

"I did it all for her you know: for my mother. She deserved so much more than life allowed her. The world is a cruel place Linda. I acted out of love for her. Someday I hope you'll understand." As he finished those lines he heard a scuffing in the hallway. Thinking that Maggie had escaped from the bathroom where he'd placed her he turned to see a young police officer aiming a gun at his chest.

"Get down on the floor asshole!" Officer Petty was twenty one years old and had never drawn his weapon on a suspect, but after seeing what Bradley had done to his partner, *and friend,* in the foyer he had no doubt he could end this man's life if provoked. The grizzly scene at the bottom of the stairs warranted the use of deadly force. Officer Petty leveled his 9mm Glock at the center of Bradley's chest with a steady hand. Seeing Bradley rise to his feet he pulled the trigger once. Brad's face contorted with the unbelieving knowledge that Bradley had been stopped. *At last.*

CHAPTER 85

"Lilly! Let your sister get the mail", Linda yelled from across the yard. She was planting bulbs in a garden when the mail man arrived. Lilly instinctively ran for the mailbox stopping only after hearing her mother's words.

"Okay Mom", she replied.

A beautiful young girl, all of two years of age ran past Lilly to retrieve the letters that had been deposited only seconds before. She gleefully stood on her tippy toes grabbing the envelopes before trotting off toward her mother.

"Patricia Alice! You forgot to shut the door!" Lilly yelled in exasperation. The youngest addition to the Fordam family ignored her older sister handing the mail over to her smiling mother.

"Mail's here Mommy". Linda's smile broadened.

"Thank you Patty."

"Is there a letter for me?" the little one asked hopefully.

"I don't know honey. Let me check".

Young Patricia Alice Fordam, named for her maternal Grandmother awaited Linda's answer with trepidation, rocking back and forth on the balls of her feet. She had long dark hair and piercing blue eyes. Linda often told her that she got them from her daddy, whom she'd yet to meet.

Bradley had recovered from the gunshot wound to his chest only to be convicted of three counts of Second Degree Murders and five counts of First Degree, premeditated murder. Ironically, he was sentenced to life in a mental institution much like the one his mother had been "sentenced" to. He regularly wrote letters to his beloved mother Patricia Alice Fordam that were always promptly returned. Linda had told her youngest daughter that when Daddy wrote to her he was playing a game, calling her mother. She also told young Alice that the letters they wrote back to her father was part of the game. Bradley believed that he was conversing with his mother.

THE END

Made in the USA
Charleston, SC
24 January 2013